Ethan Alexander was a marine engineer, spending 15 years tearing apart and rebuilding the guts of the engine room. He now spends his time at home, annoying his wife with crazy and funny jokes and noises.

He is an avid reader, with 1,000 books taking up space in every room in the house, which annoys his wife to no end.

He wrote this book as a way to de-stress and focus the mind after suffering mental health issues in the past.

He likes being home with his family, as he missed this before.

Dedicated to my loving wife, who puts up with me for some unknown reason.

Ethan Alexander

SET THE NIGHT ALIGHT

AUSTIN MACAULEY PUBLISHERS™

LONDON * CAMBRIDGE * NEW YORK * SHARJAH

A CIP catalogue record for this title is available from the British Library.

ISBN 9781035824908 (Paperback)
ISBN 9781035824915 (ePub e-book)

www.austinmacauley.com

First Published 2024
Austin Macauley Publishers Ltd®
1 Canada Square
Canary Wharf
London
E14 5AA

Chapter 1

The eyes. People always say the eyes are the windows to the soul. Doorways to the person inside. The true person hidden behind the veil of secrecy.

Who knows?

God?

Lucifer?

That answer was lost to all now.

Ah, but these eyes. These eyes are different.

It always amazed the figure how the eyes looked near the end. The greenish-grey eyes looked beautiful. They always did when the realisation of what was happening dawned on them. The figure stroked the face of the eyes with a black-gloved hand. The fabric of the glove soft to the touch. The figure looked at the woman. She was 34 and lived a life of, what, Love? Drink? Debauchery?

Ah, yes, that one. Debauchery. It surprised the figure how much they loved debauchery.

They said there were seven deadly sins. They were wrong. Very wrong. There were many, many more. Look upon the world and see. They stood as the pillars of this new world; they became the new norm. The new acceptance of a world abandoned.

Did she know she was part of the new world? It wondered about this thought.

Her eyes looked pleading. Asking for what the figure would not give. More time. The figure wiggled its finger in her face. A soft tut-tut coming from the figure's mouth. They always pleaded. Always.

How many times had it done this now? Too many to count, but each time was special. Exciting. Was it love? No. Maybe. Yes? Who knows. It was fun. It could remember this first time. The rush. The joy. How long ago was that? Long ago. Yesterday. Possibly. Time is what you make of it. And it wanted time to be fun.

The figure walked away from her and looked out of the window. For once, it wasn't raining. It looked out at its hunting ground. So much still to do. So much fun still to be had. It looked at her lying on the table. The dress she was wearing hung over the edges. So many had laid on the table. However, what did it matter, would more lay there? Would more have that privilege? It walked back to her, the footsteps quiet. As if in reference to the moment. A religious moment for it in a sense.

Her eyes moved more slowly, her pupils dilating. It was almost time. The figure sat, excitement rushing through its body, and watched as the end neared. Her eyes looked far off into the distance.

What would she be seeing? What regrets would be flashing in her mind? What memories of times past? A lost lover? An argument? The figure cared not. Why should it. It cared not for such trivial matters or thoughts.

Finally, the last lingering breath. The figure clapped happily. It was done. The figure leaned over and kissed the woman on the lips, like a lover kissing someone to sleep.

Saying goodbye one last time.

It was such a rush to see the end. Exhilarating.

The figure took up the tools and went to work on the body.

Nathan was woken up by the crash of an empty glass bottle. He looked down at his legs and realised he must have knocked them over during his sleep.

"Shite," he swore. He had fallen asleep on the sofa again.

He looked at the floor. He only drank one bottle of whisky this time. He coughed and got up. With wobbly legs, he walked to the bathroom to wash his face. He looked into the mirror facing him. He had not shaved in days, and the rough facial hair was filling out. His eyes were empty, with dark, tired rings around his eyes. He punched the mirror and broke it.

"Fucking arsehole," he said in general.

Nathan sat in the kitchen and drank a pint of beer. It was only 9:37 a.m., but it must be 5 p.m. somewhere, right? His kitchen was a mess. Dirty dishes littered the place, and partially empty food containers were scattered across the worktops. He drank his beer. '*Hair of the dog, it was called. More like drinking to just fucking drink,*' he thought.

He looked at his phone and swiped through his messages. About a dozen of them. Mostly from his friends, the few he had left. One from his local takeaway. And one from his work. He deleted that one.

'Fuck them,' he thought.

He walked to the living room, dodging the empty bottles strewn across the floor. He sat down and switched on the TV. The local news channel appeared.

"The prime minister is fighting two court battles against him. The first is related to a conflict of interest in his business dealings prior to him becoming prime minister. It is alleged he paid off several rivals so he could get lucrative contracts to corner the technology market in biomechanics. The second court case related to the deaths of 3,715 people during the Azure incident, in which the prime minister failed to heed the warnings of experts that the Uxbridge hydro dam was going to fail because of the government's withdrawal of maintenance funding and increased time between maintenance periods. It is alleged he threatened and bribed several members of his backbench during the hotly debated `Azure incident," said the female news reporter.

Nathan swore and flicked through the channels.

Another text message from his work. They never knew when to stop, did they? He looked at his phone. They were asking him to call in. Nope.

"Fuck that. Not today, dick heads," he said and deleted the message.

He caught a glimpse of the picture on the fireplace. He sighed and stared. "What do you think?" he said to the picture. "Should I reply or not reply? For that is the question," he said and raised his glass. No. He should not have said that. Not to her. "I'm sorry." He looked at her. She was beautiful. He was in pain. The pain of losing the woman he loved. He could still hear her voice sometimes when he was drunk. Strange. He never heard her voice when he was sober, but he couldn't remember the last time he was sober. "I miss you. Maybe I do not say that enough. I was happy once. You made that happen. Why did you love me? Why? I am not special. I am no movie star. No sports star. Why?"

'You make me laugh,' he remembered her saying once.

"Laugh. Surely, that is not the only thing you love. What about my wit or my singing voice?" he replied.

"Well, first off, you have no singing voice. I have heard you in the shower. I am surprised the neighbours have not complained. And you have zero wit," she replied.

"Ah, well, I'm sure they are warming up to me," he replied. "Besides, I can sing bat out of hell better than anyone."

"I will give you that. You know the words at least." She laughed. She stood beside the cooker and fried up her breakfast.

Nathan had offered to cook for her, but she liked cooking. "Smells good." Her long, fiery red hair flowed down past her shoulders. She wore her work dress, the silk green of it glinting in the morning light.

"You are getting none of it. You've already eaten."

"Pity. I could go for another breakfast."

She smiled. "You are going on a diet. You put on a few pounds."

"Muscle, I assure you."

"Fat muscle, more like." She flipped the pancake. "Besides, you are running late. David will be calling you soon to see where you are."

"I will say that I am questioning an important suspect."

"Oh, really. And what suspect would that be?" she replied, looking all innocent.

"Well, she is 5 feet 6. Fiery red hair. Currently, cooking a delicious breakfast and teasing the officer with her beautiful looks, sultry figure, and refusal to hand over pancakes."

"Oh my," she feigned and used the spatula to wave air in front of her face like women did in those old cowboy movies.

"If she isn't careful, I may demand a thorough strip search. And if the officer strips, then so be it. Can't be helped," he said, and he jumped up from his chair and wrapped his arms around her waist. "Well, do I need to strip search you?"

She laughed. "Maybe later. But now you must leave. You already used that one this week."

"Pity. Ah, well. Later then," he replied and grabbed some toast as he left the kitchen. "See you tonight, gorgeous."

She smiled. '*You make me laugh.*'

Nathan snapped back to reality. He looked at the picture again. '*I make you laugh,*' he thought.

He stood up and got another beer from the kitchen. He cracked it open and took a deep drink. "Never gets any fucking easier."

Nathan walked into the office looking; at least he tried to make an effort to give a shite. The duty officer buzzed him through. Nathan walked past other officers taking suspects and prisoners around the station. He came to his room. Chief Inspector of Homicide Nathan Andrews.

He opened the door and saw David sitting in his chair.

"That is my seat," he said and took his coat off. He threw it on the couch. "Up."

"You know I am your superior in this building," David replied, not moving.

"And?" Nathan replied, taking a drink from his coffee cup.

"I hope that's coffee in there?" David said, still not moving.

"Irish coffee."

David sighed and stood up. "We have been trying to get a hold of you for two days. I cannot keep covering for you. At some point, he will find out."

"Fuck him," Nathan said as he sat down. "He is a little jumped-up arsehole who owes his advancement to Mummy shagging the captain. Or the captain being shagged by her. Who the fuck knows."

David chuckled. "Don't think you could have said that any louder. Look. Are you OK?"

"I'm fine. Have my coffee," Nathan replied, holding up Exhibit A. "What's the problem? I am here now."

"You should have been here two days ago. That's the problem," David said and sat opposite Nathan. "There has been another. Same MO as the others."

"And this concerns me, how exactly?"

David turned around and looked at the sign on the door. He pointed. "That's why."

"I told all of you that this wasn't over. All of you. I told you that the killer was still out there. That the wrong man had been sent to jail. I told you all," he replied, leaning back on his chair. "None of you listened. I was removed from the case and replaced. And guess what? I was right. It kept happening."

"No one is disputing that. Now at least."

"I told you and told him I am not involving myself in the case. Not after the way I was treated. I was not listened to, and people died. So, my conscious is clean." He raised his coffee in salute and took a deep drink.

"You could be ordered to do so."

"Fuck orders. Who is going to tell me? Him. That jumped-up little fucker. Let him try. Knock him the fuck out, I will."

David leaned forward. "I am asking. Please. Look, the department is getting a roasting over this. This makes six. Six murders! Do you not understand? We are at a loss. We do not even have any leads. Nothing. Everything points to the same guy. It is not some copycat killer."

Nathan drank his coffee again. The whisky gave him a nice warmth. "Again, something I already told you."

"We are stuck. At a dead end. We need you back on the case. I need you back on the case."

"And what about him? What does he want?"

"He wants the killer."

"And the credit for catching him, I suppose."

"I don't care, and neither should you," David replied. "I won't make it an order, but he will. And knowing you, he will end up in the hospital and you in one of these cells."

Nathan looked at his friend. He sloshed the 'coffee' around his mouth and thought. "Fine. Let us go to the situation room. I take it everyone is there already."

"Possibly," David said with a cheeky grin.

"Wanker. Well, let's go."

Nathan and David walked into the situation room. Nathan looked around at the gathered team. Seven people. All good officers who, so far, could not find anything.

"You all know Nathan. You know what he said and what he found out during the previous investigations. Listen to him," David said and nodded for Nathan to take over.

Nathan walked over to the three whiteboards with all the information from the previous killings on them. Six women. All different ages. All different backgrounds. All different ethnicities. He threw the first whiteboard onto the ground. Then the next. Then the last one. He looked at the room. The officers looked at each other.

"Well, boys and girls, after what has it been, a few years, and you have a sum total of fuck all. I take it that is the stage you are at. I know cold cases are difficult to solve, but they are no longer cold. It's red hot. Like that itch, you caught from that special 30-second one-night stand. So, not only do we now have five cold cases, but one brand new one. So, what do you have to say?" he said and sat on a table. He sipped his coffee. "Well," he said and cupped his right ear.

A young woman offered an answer, "Sir, we have tracked down every lead. Spoken to every witness. We have tried everything possible, and yet we still have nothing."

"What's your name?"

"Constable Helena heart, sir."

"Well, first off, I'm not a sir. Unlike other inspectors here, I work for a fucking living. You will all call me Inspector or Nathan. Never liked this hierarchy shite," he replied, looking at David. "Secondly, from what I have seen of this investigation, all of you should be ashamed. You have nothing. You are trying to tell me that in this city, there is not one piece of CCTV footage or image showing the killer. My arse. Come on, people."

The room went deathly silent.

David coughed. "Well, we are off to a good start. Scare the hell out of your team. Awesome."

Nathan sniggered. "They need a good kick up the arse. You, what's your name?" He pointed to an older man with white hair.

"Inspector Alfonso Copco," he replied. His voice was deep and old.

"Well, inspector. Give your thoughts on the case so far."

"I think the killer is male. Middle aged. Possibly from the city centre."

"Oh, and why do you think that?"

"He would have to be young and fit to lift the bodies. He would also need to be close to the city centre. Plenty of places to hide. Good transport links. Easy to move around and be lost in the crowd."

Nathan sighed and pinched the bridge of his nose. "Honestly. You are all still going for this same old crap, which I told you all before was wrong. It does not need to be a man. Women are just as crazy as men when push comes to shove. Secondly, the killer does not need to be located in the city centre. Some of the killings have taken place outside the bloody city. Fucking lions hunt in a large area and don't always kill closest to them." He looked at David. "No wonder the case is at a standstill."

"And what would you do differently?" a voice shouted from the back.

Nathan looked around and saw the man who shouted, "What's your name?"

"Koper, inspector. Julius Koper," replied the young man.

"Well, Julius Koper, for a start, I would question every assumption that has been made so far." He stood up and walked towards the young man. "Then I would question them again. And again. I would then question every witness there until I nailed down their stories. I would cross-check every alibi and cross-check again. I would actually be doing the job I was paid to do."

"Like you have been doing?" Julius replied.

"Oh, I like him," Nathan replied with a cheeky smile on his face. "Guess what, Koper? I'm going to take you under my wing. Maybe you will learn something other than trying to be a hard-nosed bastard trying to show off in front of your buddies here."

"Ah, Nathan, take it easy. He didn't mean anything," David said as he walked forward towards the two men.

"He meant every word, David. Do not worry; I won't break him. He may walk away from this investigation with a few bruises, but nothing else. Maybe," Nathan replied and walked back towards the front of the room. "Right, we start from the beginning. You," he pointed towards Alfonso, "pick up the boards and take everything off them. I want all the evidence on this table."

Nathan sat at the table and looked at the evidence before him. His team sat on the other end of the table. David sat beside Nathan.

"OK. First victim. Miss Mia Nyhus. Recently divorced at the time of death. 55. Banker. Reported missing on 2 February 2003. Found dead two weeks later. Body in a well-preserved manner. The autopsy shows an injection of a high dose of morphine. Would have killed her in a few minutes. Eyes missing. Removed by an amateur. Damage done to the surrounding facial area. Found in a side street on Buchanan galleries."

"Second victim, Youna Kim. Single. 34. Nursery teacher. Reported missing 13 March 2003. Found one week later. Again, body well preserved. Eyes missing. Again, an amateur job of removing the eyes. Found near Glasgow Nautical College."

"Victim three, Abigail Rouland. Married. Two kids. 21. Reported missing 8 July 2003. Similar MO as the previous two victims. Found in the Calton area."

"Victim 4, Tanya Reilly. 53. Office worker. Report missing 5 December 2003. Found Christmas Eve. Again, similar MO as previous victims." He stood up and placed the four images of the victims on the first whiteboard. "Then for five years, nothing. No more killings that fit this description. The case goes cold. Then, on 13 April 2008, we find the body of Emily Millar. 19 years old. Found dead here," he said, pointing to a map on the wall, "outskirts of Cambuslang. Same MO as previous victims but with one difference. Autopsy shows that the eyes have been removed with more precision. Not like before. The eyes have

14

been removed with more care." He placed her image on the last board. "And two days ago, we found another body. 21 March. A gap of almost 13 years between Emily and this one. Miss Roxanne Lee. 27-year-old caretaker. Reported missing three months ago. Found near the river Clyde at Rutherglen." He placed the final image on the last board. "So, we have four killings in one year. A break of five years for one more, and then a break of almost 13 years for the other." He looked at the team. "Makes no sense."

"We asked the military for any records they had on people who joined around the time of the first killings. From what they gave us, we managed to rule them out. We thought it could have been a military doctor, but it was a dead end," said David. "We also checked the prisons and came up blank."

"It was after the fourth murder that Mr Derick Olden was arrested. 23 years old. Family man. Worked as a house builder. He knew the second victim and was supposedly having relations with her. He was seen on CCTV at the time of the other disappearances, close to where the third body was found. At the time, it was believed he was looking for places to dump the bodies. He was questioned about the murder of Youna Kim and gave an alibi that he was at home alone as his wife and kids were visiting her family up north. He could not prove that he was alone. The former head of the investigation pressed charges for the murder of Youna and the suspected murder of the other victims. Youna's DNA and fingerprints were found all over Mr Olden's house. No blood. Just bodily secretions, as you can imagine. Especially in the master bedroom."

He put the image of Derick on the middle board. "He was found guilty, and many believed we had caught the killer. All the evidence was circumstantial. A fuck up by the lead investigator at the time. So, halfway through Mr Olden's sentence, our real killer strikes again. The press gets wind of this, and an all-mighty uproar ensues that an innocent man is in jail for crimes he did not commit. So, it goes to retrial, and guess what? He is found innocent. He is released and sues the police force for millions. And then, for 13 years, fuck all happens. Not one thing. And then two days ago, BANG, another killing."

"I have managed to keep this away from the press. But it won't be long before they find out," David said. "And it better not come from here," he said, looking at everyone.

"I don't care," Nathan replied. "So, let's see what we have in the way of evidence, shall we?" He stood up and began placing the evidence before the victims. Once he was finished, he looked at what was there. "Not much. No

DNA. No strange fibres. Nothing. Not one victim gave up any secrets. Are we sure this was thorough?"

"Yes, Inspector," said a woman called Margaret. She was another constable assigned to the team. "Everything was processed and double-checked."

"OK. Witness statements?"

"Everyone who knew the victims was questioned. Nothing. A few names popped up, spurned lovers. Angry family members. Even the postmen were questioned. Nothing," replied Margaret.

"So, another dead end." Nathan looked at the boards. "What times did they supposedly go missing?"

David flicked throw his notes. "Victims 1, 3 and 5 were reported missing while out with friends. Out for drinks. Victim 2 went missing sometime around 11 a.m. while out jogging. Victims 4 and 6 reported missing after leaving work. Around 4 am."

"Wait. 1, 3, and 5 on a night out? Who reported them missing and where?"

"Work colleagues. Out for drinks after work."

"So, our killer has killed three victims while they were out drinking. Where?"

"Em, Sauchiehall Street. Near M8."

"It's a small lead. Time estimates for them going missing?"

"All said they were going to the bathroom and didn't return," Andrews said, looking through the notes. "Cameras at the clubs showed them going to the bathroom but never leaving. There are no emergency exits in the bathrooms. There are windows, but no one reported seeing anyone trying to leave out a window."

"OK," Nathan said and wrote on the board, 'Out drinking.'

"These three we focus on first. OK. Koper, you will come with me. We are going to look at the new crime scene. The rest of you, I want to look at these three murders under a microscope. I don't care how insignificant something looks; I want it reported. Check every piece of evidence again. Every statement. Every alibi. David is going to stay here and help you lost lambs," Nathan said and slapped David on the back. "OK, Koper, you look old enough to drive." He threw his car keys at the young man. "Let's go."

Chapter 2

Inspector Koper drove Nathan's Audi A6. The 2-LTR engine powered the car towards the crime scene.

Julius looked over at Nathan, who looked like he was asleep. "You sleeping?"

Nathan turned his head to look at the young man. "You can stop being a thorn in my arse anytime, you know."

"I asked a simple question."

"You are being annoyed," Nathan said and took out a flask from his coat. He took a swig. "Just drive."

"We will be there soon. Clyde Walkway at Vancouver Court."

"Fine. Once we are finished here, then we are going to the morgue." He put the flask back into his coat pocket. "According to forensics, the scene was found late in the morning. Found by a dog walker."

"Yes. A young student. Emma Guys."

"Her statement says that she took the dogs down this walkway daily. She is a dog walker," Julius replied as he concentrated on driving. "It was early, before 7 a.m."

Nathan nodded. "Body was put there probably sometime after midnight. They usually are. Never in the same location. Not even the same area."

"We will be there in a few moments. The police have sealed off the area. The story they are telling people is that they were doing a training exercise."

Nathan smirked. "No one believes that." He saw the police cars appear before him and shook his head. "If there is any evidence left over, it's probably contaminated by now. But bag anything and everything I tell you. Don't ask questions. Just do it." The car stopped, and Julius was about to leave the car when Nathan grabbed his arm. "If there is any press, you are to ignore them. I will deal with them. You just stand there and look tough. If you can."

Nathan opened the door and left the car.

Nathan and Julius walked towards the cordoned-off area and saw some locals standing there trying to see what was going on. Nathan pushed past them. A police officer saw him approaching and waved him through.

"Ah, Nathan. What rock did they find you under?" a voice shouted in the crowd.

Nathan turned and saw the man. "In your ex-wife's bed."

"Still with the funny comebacks?" the man replied.

"Still an arsehole who takes it for money, Robert."

"That is liable," Robert replied.

"Does it look like I give the smallest hint of a fuck?" Nathan said and continued past the police line. "Why don't you just stay there and piss off someone else?"

"Can I quote you on that?" Robert shouted to Nathan. The middle finger was Nathan's only reply.

"Who was that?" Julius asked.

"News reporter. Works for one of the daily rags. Lost track of who now. Never speak to him. Ever. He is the lowest form of scum. Worse than a fucking Westminster politician," Nathan grunted as he walked down the embankment. "If he ever asks you a question, never reply."

"OK."

"I mean it. The man is scum. He will twist your words beyond all recognition."

They both continued until they came to another officer standing not far from the fast-flowing river.

"Good morning, Inspector," the police officer said. "The body was found here." He pointed to an area of ground covered by a tent.

Nathan nodded and walked inside the tent. Julius followed.

A young woman looked up as both men entered the tent. "Nathan."

"Amanda. Been a while," Nathan replied and knelt down beside the woman.

"I'm nearly finished here. The body has been in the morgue for two days now. I'm just looking for anything that may have been left behind."

"Don't rush on my account, Amanda," Nathan said as he intently stared at the ground. "Time of death?"

"Between 10 and 11 p.m. From the way the plants have been flattened and the insects I have found, she was placed here sometime after 2 a.m. Maybe 3 a.m."

"Cause of death?"

"Same as the others. Massive morphine injection. Eyes removed post mortem."

Nathan put on latex gloves and poked around in the dirt, moving grass and broken wood around. "Julius, this is Amanda. She is the department's pathologist. She likes to work in the field."

"Good morning," Julius said to her as she turned to look at the young man.

"Since when did you take on a partner?" she asked Nathan.

"I'm not. He is my protege. I'm going to teach him all I know," Nathan replied, not taking his eyes off the crime scene.

"God help him then," she replied as she packed her stuff away. "I guess I would be wasting my breath by asking how you have been."

"I'm fine, Amanda," Nathan replied and lifted a broken branch. He smelled it. "Life is full of peaches and cream."

"And whisky? I can smell it."

"Irish cream then. This branch is strange." He lifted it up and smelled it. He could see it was not that old.

"In what way?" Julius asked.

"It is not from the tree above here. The tree above this tent has no broken branches," Nathan said as he stood up. "No. Not from here." He walked outside the tent and looked at the trees around him. He walked further along the embankment and stopped at an old tree. He held the stick up and tried to match it to one of the broken tree limbs. "There," he said, pointing to one broken branch. "Looks like a good fit." He turned back towards the tent. "Twenty yards, give or take." He looked at Julius. "She was taken through here first." He looked at his feet. "No drag marks. Carried. No footprint either, not with this overgrown embankment. Clever. He brought it with him. When he walked through here, it must have caught on a piece of clothing, and he dragged it to her final place." He looked around him. He felt something in the air. Felt like ice on the back of his neck. He casually looked around him and across the river. Nothing. Was he being watched? "Bag what I point to. Don't argue." Nathan pointed to several items: an old beer can, a dead flower, one broken branch, and a magazine. He handed Julius the broken branch. "Bag it and follow me."

Nathan walked up the embankment and stopped on the footpath. He looked up and down in both directions.

"Bagged it, sir," Julius said as he stood beside Nathan.

"Not, sir, remember," Nathan replied, not paying any attention to the man. "Come with me." Nathan walked away from the crime scene and looked to the flats on his left. He stopped suddenly and walked towards one of the flats' main entrances. He looked at the flat to his right and pressed the buzzer.

A moment later, the reply came, "Hello," came a woman's voice.

"Police. I have a few questions for you," Nathan replied. The door buzzed, and he opened it.

Both men walked to the first-floor door, and Nathan tapped. The door opened slightly. "Inspector Nathan Andrews and this is Inspector Koper. May we come in?" Nathan said and flashed his badge.

"Yes. Officer. Please come in." The door opened to show a woman in her late 40s.

Nathan walked into the flat and followed the woman to the living room.

"My name is Susan. Is this to do with the police exercise that is happening outside?" she asked.

"Yes and no, Susan. Last night, a woman was attacked out on that path. We are seeking witnesses to the crime. Did you see anything?"

"No. Nothing. I was home all day, but I never heard or saw anything."

"And what about the CCTV camera on your balcony?"

She turned towards the balcony and then said, "How did you know?"

Nathan walked towards the door that led to the balcony and pushed the curtain aside. "You put the sunflower in the corner of the balcony that gets no sun."

"I got it for home security. Just for peace of mind. That's all. No crime in that," she replied quickly.

"No, there is not. How long have you had it?" Nathan said as he turned back to the woman.

"Three days ago. Why?"

Nathan turned to Julius. "Maybe someone scouted the area and thought they were not being filmed."

Julius smiled. "It is hard to see. I missed it. How did you know?"

"Like I said. No sun in that corner of the balcony. Plus, it is not the growing season. So, why would there be a fully grown and fully bloomed sunflower now? There wouldn't be." He turned back to Susan. "I need all recordings from that camera. All of them, please."

She nodded and went to the other room. She came back quickly with a USB data stick. "That's everything since it has been activated. I hope it helps."

It watched as two men walked across the embankment. It saw the older one pointing to items to pick up and put into bags. Who was this man giving the orders? Something about this man screamed danger. He watched them both walk up the embankment and across the pathway. He saw them stop and look around. They walked towards the flats. Maybe they saw something or someone. It did not care. It was careful. It left no tracks. It was perfect. But this man was different. It could sense it. Could feel it. The figure shivered in pleasure. Finally, someone to play with. A new toy to break. This was going to be fun.

Nathan banged open the door and scared the morgue doctor. "Did I scare you?" Nathan joked.

"I wish you would stop doing that. I am holding a scalpel, you know," the old man shouted.

"Keeps you on your toes, doc," Nathan said and took the flask from his coat then took a drink. He offered it to the doctor.

"Bit early for me, Nathan."

Nathan shrugged and returned the flask to his coat. "So, what can you tell me about this one?" He said, pointing to the naked women laying on the table.

"Injection point is into the neck. Artery. No signs of struggle. Death would have taken several hours as the morphine was administered over a period of time. She has the IV line injection here on her elbow. Most likely, she was fully dressed as all her clothes were on her when found and didn't show the tell-tale signs of someone else putting on her clothes."

"And her eyes?"

"Surgically removed. This was precise. It was done with surgical instruments and by a professional."

Nathan leaned forward and looked into the empty eye sockets. He turned and saw Julius stand away from the body. "Come here and learn something." Julius walked forward and stood beside Nathan. Nathan noticed he couldn't look down at the body. "What is wrong with you?"

"Nothing."

"My arse. Have you ever seen a dead body before?"

"Not like this."

"Well, congratulations; you just lost your virginity. Look at the body and tell me what you see."

Julius looked down and tried not to vomit. A maggot crawled out of her left eye socket. He vomited on the floor.

"Here, wash your mouth out with this," Nathan said, handing him his flask.

"Sink is over there, young man," said the doctor. Julius ran over and vomited again.

"Don't make them like they used to, eh, doc."

The doctor shook his head. "They can't all be as tough and heartless as you, now, can they?"

"Ouch, doc. You still upset about me slamming the door," Nathan replied as he used tweezers to remove the maggot. He lifted it up and said, "Or did you upset him, maggot? Bad maggot."

The doc rolled his eyes. "You need help."

"I'm beyond help, doc," he replied and tossed the maggot into the biological waste bin. "OK, Julius. I'm sure you are feeling better now. Why don't you get your arse over here and do some police work?"

Julies walked back over and handed the flask back. "I hope you cleaned that." Nathan said as he put it back into his coat pocket. "OK, young pup. What do you see?"

Julius looked at the naked, eyeless woman before him.

"According to the driving licence recovered with her body, she is Roxanne Lee. 27 years old. Lives in the Calton area. She was reported missing three months ago. She lives with her elderly mother," he said quickly, trying not to be sick again. "Boyfriend lives in Cambuslang. His alibi is rock-solid. He is currently working down south, as he is a power generation engineer. He has been away for two weeks."

"So, he isn't our killer then. Anything else?"

"She wasn't out with friends at the time. She was coming home from work."

"Which is?"

"She works in a strip club. Seventh Heaven. Barmaid."

"Another Sauchiehall Street location. Do we know what her route home was?"

"Down Sauchiehall Street, then down Buchanan Street. Turn left and past Queen Street Station. Down High Street and along the Gallow Gate to her home. Her mother said she never deviated from that route."

"Something or someone changed her route. There are plenty of dark alleys along that route. Plenty of hiding places. A good hunting ground. I think she got spooked and changed her route. Did she mention at any time to her mother if she felt she was being followed?"

Julius read through his notes quickly. "Nothing. But I wasn't the one who questioned her."

"We will go to her address and ask." Nathan leaned forward and sniffed the woman's mouth. "No alcohol in her system?" he asked the doc.

"Blood says no," he replied. "But the full blood works will be known tomorrow."

Nathan moved her head from side to side. "No strangulation marks. No marks on her wrists or ankles to show she was restrained. No scratches or self-defence marks on her body. It has always been like this."

Julius looked at the woman and saw that she had no marks on her body other than post-mortem cuts. "So, do you think that these women knew their attacker, and that's why they never struggled?"

"No. They didn't know him. We have checked all the friends of every victim, and there is no common denominator in any of their friendships. No. This person is a predator. They know how to hunt and hunt well." He straightened up and took off the latex gloves. "Why return now? If he had stayed hidden, we would never have found him. Why come back? Something has changed. This killing is different, I am sure of it."

"What makes you say that?" the doc asked.

Nathan grunted, "This arsehole has been hiding for over a decade and then suddenly reappears out of thin air. Plus, as you said yourself, the eyes were removed with precision. It started out looking like they had been torn out, and by the fifth, he had gotten good enough not to make much of a mess of the face. But this. It looks like a plastic surgeon did this."

"It does look like a medical professional did do this, I will grant you, but you have ruled that out, have you not?" the doc said.

Nathan nodded his head. "We have hit a lot of dead ends during these cases. But this one is different. Did you find anything out of the ordinary?"

"Nothing. She wasn't pregnant. None of the usual rape marks. She has been taking vitamins and supplements. Her stomach contents showed she had eaten, none of it toxic. No alcohol, from what I can tell. No needle marks to show she was taking drugs. Her heart was fine. Liver, kidneys, and brain all fine."

Nathan closed his eyes and thought. "It's too perfect. I'm starting to think the others were test runs. Like he was trying to achieve something."

"Possible," agreed the doc. The door opened into the room, and another doctor handed a folder to the old man. He read the contents and nodded. "Blood results back early. Nothing in her system bar the morphine."

"Shite," Nathan swore. "What the fuck am I missing?"

Julius looked at him and swore that, for the briefest of moments, he saw a black haze around Nathan.

"That's strange," said the doc as he flipped the page.

"Care to share?" Nathan asked.

The doc flipped to another page. "Her clothes have a white chalk residue on them. Very small. Smaller than a pinhead. It was only noticed because of her black trousers."

"Could be contamination. She was outside for a few hours," said Julius.

"But this is on the inside. Left trouser leg. Seam," the doc said as he looked at the evidence bag. "Composition is Calcium Sulphate Hemihydrate."

Nathan straightened up. "That's Plaster of Paris."

"How do you know that?" Julius asked.

"I read a lot," Nathan answered and took the folder. "Could be contamination when the teams were using it to take moulds of footprints and anything else. But being found on the inside of her trousers makes that less likely." He closed the folder and placed it on the table. "Did he make a mistake? Did he leave a mark on her?"

"It was only spotted because of the darkness of her clothes," the doc said. "It wouldn't have been seen otherwise."

Nathan took out a notebook from his coat and flipped through the pages quickly. After a few moments, he slammed it shut. "Every other victim wore bright-coloured trousers or a dress. We need to check their clothes again for any plaster residue or marks."

"I can have it all brought here. It's all still in storage," the doc said as he walked to the phone. "I will test the clothes myself and call you as soon as I have the results."

"Do it. Julius, give him your number also, in case I can't be reached. This animal left us a clue, and I'm going to use it to hunt him down." Nathan smiled towards the doc. "When I find this monster, I will try and leave you enough to autopsy."

Nathan and Julius pulled up outside Roxanne's home.

Nathan walked up to the front door and chapped. The door opened to reveal a young man. "Yes," the man said.

"Inspector Andrews and Inspector Koper. We have questions regarding Miss Lee," he showed his badge. "May we come in?"

The young man nodded, and the two policemen followed him into the home. Nathan saw in the living room a crying old lady and a younger lady sitting together and talking quietly.

"I am sorry to disturb you. Mrs Lee. May I offer my condolences on your loss?" Nathan said as he stood in front of the old lady.

She looked up with bloodyshot eyes and nodded. "Thank you," she whispered.

He knelt in front of her and took her frail hand. "I must ask you some questions if you are able." She nodded. Nathan nodded to Julius, and the young man took out his notebook. "Did your daughter have any enemies? Anyone who disliked her." The old lady shook her head.

"OK. Did she mention at any time if she felt she was being followed?" Again no.

"Did she say if she was being sent any mail that was out of the ordinary?"

"No. Because she worked late, she would sleep until late in the afternoon. I would open her mail, and I saw nothing like that," Roxanne's mother replied.

"I worked with her," said the younger lady.

"Your name?" Nathan asked.

"Bridget. Bridget Hammersmith. I dance at the club."

Nathan could believe that. The woman had a figure that would make status weep in joy.

"All the customers loved her. No one had a bad word to say about her. Even all the girls loved her. She was like a mother figure to us. She kept us safe. If a customer was getting a bit handsy, she would deal with it. She made sure we were treated right," Bridget said and cleaned the tears from her cheek. "Not once did she ever mention to any of the girls if she felt scared or threatened."

Nathan nodded. "Thank you for that info."

He turned back to the victim's mother. "With your permission, I would like to check her room. Just in case she was hiding anything."

The old lady nodded. "Albert can show you. He is…was her boyfriend." She started crying again.

Nathan stood up and looked at the man. "Please take me to the room." All three men entered the room, and Nathan looked around. It was like any other lady's bedroom. Make-up littered all over the table. Messy bed. Clothes lying on the floor. "She got ready for work and didn't have time to clean up," Nathan said to Albert. The man nodded. "So Albert, did your girlfriend tell you anything she wouldn't have told her mother?" Nathan said as he looked through the chest of drawers.

"No. I have thought about every conversation we had lately, and not once did she ever mention anything out of the ordinary," the man replied. He leaned against the wall and rubbed his eyes. "When I'm not working away, I pick her up from work. I never cared what time it was. I would pick her up. But I had a call from my boss the day before. A power plant in Newcastle was experiencing an issue with its generators, so I had to rush down."

"I want the contact details of your management and also the address of the power plant you are working in," Nathan said as he looked through some letters.

"You don't believe me?" Albert responded in anger.

"Whether I believe you or not is not relevant. I want to remove you as a suspect. Now, please give the details to my assistant here," Nathan replied and put the letters back into the drawer. He moved to her wardrobe and looked through her clothes. "How long was Roxanne working in the strip club?"

"Ten years. She loved her job," Albert replied as he looked through his mobile for phone numbers.

"Was she always a barmaid?"

"No. For the first few years, she was a stripper. But then we got together, and she stopped. I told her I didn't mind what she did, but she said to me that she wanted a change. They made her a barmaid, as they didn't want to lose her. The girls loved her."

Nathan nodded. "And not once did she ever mention to you that she felt in danger?"

"No."

"Was she cheating on you?"

"NO!" Albert shouted.

"You are sure?"

"I loved her, and she loved me."

Nathan moved in a blur, grabbed Albert by the throat, and slammed him against the wall. Julius stood there, dumbfounded.

"Are you lying to me? Were you cheating on her? Maybe you thought she found out and hired someone to get rid of your problem, so you could move on."

Albert struggled against the iron grip now holding his throat. "I fucking loved her, you bastard," he choked as tears ran down his face.

Nathan looked deep into Albert's eyes. "I know you did." He let him go, and Albert slid down the wall. "I had to get you angry. For that, I apologise. When people get angry, you can see better if they are lying. You did love her; I can see that. I found no letters from a lover, and an investigation of her mobile and call records shows she made no strange calls to other people. She wasn't cheating on you, either. Don't worry; I had your call records checked also. But I had to make sure."

Albert rubbed his neck. "That's police brutality."

"No, it wasn't. It's called investigating. My investigation methods are more to the point than other inspectors. Like I said, get people angry, and you can see if they are lying. How to achieve that anger is different from person to person." Nathan sat on her bed and looked at Albert. "Your girlfriend was killed by a serial killer. The same one that has been terrorising this city for over 20 years."

"The Keeper of Eyes killer?" Albert said as he leaned against the wall.

"I shouldn't be telling you this, but I think you deserve to hear it. We have no fucking idea who this person is." Nathan held up a hand as Julius was about to speak. "You better learn quickly, Julius, that from now on, we need to play outside the rules. This cunt isn't playing within the rules, so neither will we. Albert, you are going to help me out?"

"In what way?"

"Have you ever been on TV before?"

"The police are out of their depth. They have no witnesses. They have no clues other than dead bodies. Are we even sure they know what they are doing? Six women have been slaughtered, including my beautiful Roxanne," Albert said on the TV. The whole investigation team watched in the room, Nathan sat with his feet up on the desk and smiled. "When will the police catch this animal? Are they too busy to find a serial killer? How long must this city live in fear? I demand answers. What is the station captain doing? The families of the six victims demand answers."

"That statement was from the boyfriend of Roxanne Lee, the latest victim of the keeper of the eyes killer," said the news reporter. David turned the TV off.

"This is not good. We need the public on our side," David said to Nathan. "What did you say to that man?"

"Not a thing, David," Nathan replied as he took a drink of coffee. "Can you blame him? He is angry."

"Going on the news and saying that we are useless is not good for us. We didn't need this publicity. You know he is pissed," David replied as he sat down beside Nathan.

"And, how exactly is that my problem? He is always pissed about something," Nathan said as he looked at the clock. "You want to place a bet?"

"For what?"

"Before he comes storming in."

"No."

"Oh, come on. Where is your sense of fun? OK. I say three minutes."

David shook his head. "Five."

"Done. OK, ladies and gentlemen, you all better sit down and look busy. Soon, an almighty arsehole is going to come flying in and make a shite storm for us all," Nathan said and looked at the clock.

Tick.

Tock.

Tick.

Tock.

Two Minutes and 25 seconds later, Nathan could hear the thunderous footsteps of someone who was very angry.

"You owe me," Nathan said, still sitting back relaxed on the chair.

"Damn. Fine. The usual?" David replied as he straightened up his uniform.

"Agreed. Oh, and don't interfere between him and myself."

"I wouldn't dream of it."

The door slammed open.

"What was that I just saw on the news?" the man shouted.

"Christopher, what brings you down to the deep, dark dungeon?" Nathan asked, sipping his coffee. "Shouldn't you be upstairs with the rest of the inbred elite?"

"That's Captain to you, Nathan," replied Christopher. The captain stood around 6 feet tall with a slim frame. His black hair was beginning to thin out and would be bald in a few years. "What did I just see? We are being called incompetent."

"Sounds about right," Nathan replied, still relaxing in his chair.

"You are supposed to stand to attention when a superior officer enters the room," Christopher demanded.

"When one comes in, I will," he replied, and someone in the room sniggered.

Christopher looked around the room furiously, trying to find the culprit. When he couldn't, he focused on Nathan again and asked, "Why was that man allowed to speak to the press? Why didn't we stop it? That interview makes us all look bad. Worse than bad."

"We couldn't be doing any worse now to be fare. Fuck all leads. Fuck all the evidence. Fuck all on everything, really," replied Nathan. He took a deep drink of his coffee and watched as Christopher's face went red. "The only way it could get worse is if you took charge. Oh, wait, you are, aren't you? The buck stops at the top, boyo."

Christopher marched over to the table and placed his knuckles on the desk. He leaned close to Nathan. "Don't talk to me like that. I will have you fired."

"No, you won't, you jumped-up little shite. I know it, and so do you. You couldn't find your arse with a map, GPS, and a fucking Sherpa," Nathan replied. He didn't flinch at the man now trying to intimidate him. "I was brought in to fix the mess you made. Yes, you. I told you all those years ago that it wasn't finished. He would be back. And what did you do? Hmm. You told me that I was wrong. After the third body, you removed me from the case. Didn't like someone telling you something different from your own stupid, narrow ideas."

"Listen to me, you fu…"

Nathan was up in a flash and grabbed the captain's tie. He pulled him across the desk and a few centimetres from his face. "No, you listen to me. I'm going to find this killer. I'm going to do it my way. The way that gets results. Now, listen to me very carefully, dickhead; I don't give a shite about your rank or who your daddy is. Come in here again, trying to act all tough, and I will break you. Do you hear me? This has gone on long enough, and half of it has been during your watch. You didn't listen to me before, but you will listen to me now."

Nathan grabbed Christopher's fist as the man tried to punch him. Nathan squeezed and made the man whimper in pain. "Tut tut. A captain losing his temper in front of his subordinates. Not a good example you are setting. You know who I used to be. You have seen the files that you were allowed to see. I guarantee you, it's worse than you read."

"You just assaulted a superior officer," Christopher shouted into his face. "I have witnesses."

"Point to one." Nathan looked around, and everyone was busy doing their work and looking at their own desks. Even David was staring at the ceiling. "See. What witnesses?" Nathan pulled him closer and spoke softly into his ear. "I know about your thing on the side. I wonder what your wife would say. Especially when I send her the pictures. You know what ones I am talking about. The one in the club with you in a compromising position. Wonder what would happen to your career if it suddenly appeared in the press? Or even better, on every billboard in the city." Before the captain could reply, Nathan let go of his fist, grabbed his ear, and twisted.

"I am losing my patience with you. You think you can shout and threaten me. Mother fucker. I've killed animals that had more courage than you. Now, this is what is going to happen. I'm going to let you go. You are going to straighten yourself up. Then you are going to tell my team that they must do their best to find this killer. You will tell them to do whatever it takes to get the job done, and you will turn a blind eye if that means being a bit more aggressive in getting those answers. Then you will walk out of this room and not return unless I fucking ask you to. Nod now." Christopher nodded. "Excellent. It seems you can be trained."

Nathan let go. He sat back down and drank his coffee again. He nudged David.

David turned around and acted like he had just seen the captain for the first time.

"Good evening, Captain," David said, standing to attention. The other people in the room stood to attention. Except for Nathan.

Christopher coughed. "Thank you, David. OK, people. Do whatever it takes to bring this killer to justice. I don't care how you do it; just do it. That's all." He turned quickly around and hurried out of the room.

Everyone looked at Nathan. They were all stunned.

"Well, you heard our glorious Capitan. We must do what it takes," said Nathan as he put his feet back up on the table.

"Jesus, Nathan. You went a bit too far there," David said as he slumped down on the chair.

"No idea what you are talking about. The captain came in, gave a speech, and left."

David laughed. "I'm sure everyone else in the room will have seen and heard the exact same thing?" They all nodded, still stunned at what they had heard and seen. "Good. So, what's our next move?"

"The doc is checking all the clothes again to see if anything else was missed," Nathan replied and walked to the three whiteboards. Something was standing out to him. In fact, it was screaming at him. It was the dates. It was the months, years, and days. The numbers. They screamed at him. Several numbers kept appearing. Almost every victim had the same numbers. Nathan stepped back and looked at the three boards. It was there. The clue was there. "Mother fucking piece of shite. The killer left a clue. He fucking left a clue staring at us with its fucking pants down. How did we miss this?"

David stood beside him. "What do you mean?"

"What? Can you not see it? It's right fucking there," Nathan said, pointing frantically at the boards. David shook his head. "Look at the dates the victims were found. Seeing them put up on the board like that, something is screaming out to me; it should be screaming at you also."

David looked. "What do you see?"

"2 February 2003. 13 March 2003. 8 August 2003. 5 December 2003. 13 April 2008. 21 March 2021." Nathan wrote the number on the side of the board. "How did I miss this? Nathan, you complete arsehole."

"Miss what?" David replied as he watched Nathan write down the dates in numbers.

"2, 3, 5, 8, 13, 21. It's the Fibonacci sequence."

"OK, you lost me now."

"Someone tell me the age of the victims now!" Nathan demanded as he stared at the board.

Julius looked at the files. "55, 34, 21, 53, 19, and 27."

"21, 34, 55. Part of the sequence also."

"What are you on about?" Julius asked.

"The Fibonacci sequence. What the fuck do they teach you in school these days? This sequence is believed to prove the existence of God. The sequence can be found everywhere. In nature. Mathematics. The universe. Fuck, even your ear shows it. You take 1 add 1 to give you 2. 2 add 1 is 3. You take your new answer and add it to the previous one. It is found in flowers. How they grow. The galaxy follows the exact same sequence." He drew a spiral, then, starting from the same point, another spiral but slightly bigger. He then drew lines between each spiral.

He wrote the numbers in the spiral, staring from one into the first Box and so forth. "OK, people. Look. As you can see from my drawing, the numbers and sequence. The first box is 1. The next is two. Three, five, and so on. This spiral is found in nature. Flowers, trees, and even animals. The galaxy is spiralled the exact same way."

"And people believe this proves the existence of God?" David asked.

"Yes. Some say this is the God equation. The perfect number sequence. Others say it is just a universal law that all living beings must follow. Me, I think it is just a coincidence," replied Nathan, writing lines between the dates on the board.

"So, our killer is some sort of genius and kills according to this sequence?" Helena asked.

"Not sure. Some of the dates only follow the sequence of months, not days. Others include days, months and years. Even some of the ages of the ladies are in the sequence. Roxanne was missing for three months. Again the sequence," Nathan replied as he looked at her. "I can't believe we missed this. I only noticed because we have more dates up on the board." He looked at the birth year of each woman. "Fucking hell. Even the dates of their births when taken away from each other, match the sequence. Victims 1 and 2 have a 21-year difference between them. Victims 2 and 3 have a 13-year difference between them. Victims 5 and 6 have a 5-year difference."

"So, we have a clue," said David. "This is good. We can surely use this."

"Helena. Call the mortuary and tell them I want everything they have sent over. Tell the doc to bring it all himself. Alfonso, I want you to go through every file here and double-check the dates they went missing and the dates they were found. See if this sequence pops up again." Nathan's phone chimed for a message. "Julius, you are coming with me," he said as he put the phone back into his shirt pocket.

"David, when the doc comes, I want everything split up between each victim. I want dolls brought in and placed exactly the way each victim was found."

"OK," David said as he went for the desk phone. "And where are you going?"

"To meet an old acquaintance," Nathan said and walked out of the room.

Chapter 3

"You are very quiet, Julius," Nathan stated as he sat in the passenger seat of his car.

Julius drove towards his given destination. He shrugged his shoulders. "Nothing to say, Inspector."

Nathan drank from his flask. "Bull shite. Spit it out."

Julius sighed. "How could you do that to a senior officer? I mean, I thought you were going to hit him."

"I have hit him before. Punched him the fuck out. Flat onto his back." Nathan smiled.

"How do you still have a job?"

"Politics. I am needed more than him. I have connections to certain people and organisations that owe me big time," Nathan replied. He looked through his phone and opened up a picture. He showed it to the young driver. "See."

Julius looked and saw Nathan shaking hands with the first minister of Scotland. Nathan then flicked to another, and he was with the president of the USA. Another pick showed him with several well-known billionaires. "Who are you?"

"I ask myself that every day. Everyday. Trust me, you really don't want to know. All you need to know is that I am in charge, and you will do what I say," Nathan told him with a cheeky grin.

"Christ, seriously. Who the hell are you?"

"Hope you never find out," Nathan replied. He looked out of the window. "Pull up here." Julius pulled over. "OK. This place is full of bad people. They will be doing bad things. Don't say anything and don't do anything."

Julius looked out of the window. "It is a dry cleaner."

"Oh, very dangerous places dry cleaners are," Nathan said and exited the car. Julius followed. "Stick with me, young pup."

Julius followed Nathan into the shop.

"Where is he?" Nathan said the dry cleaner behind the desk. The Chinese woman looked at him. "You know who I am talking about."

"I don't know," she replied, waving her hands at him in frustration.

"Don't mess me about. Not today," Nathan said and walked behind the counter. The woman started shouting at him in Chinese. "Stop being annoying," he hurled back.

Nathan marched into the back room and saw clothes hanging up, waiting to be cleaned. "Julius, stay close and don't look anyone in the eyes." Nathan walked quickly to the back of the room. He opened the door and looked down a flight of dark stairs. He walked down.

After a minute of walking down, Nathan came upon a well-built Asian man sitting outside another door. This door was metal and had no locks on the outside. Just a visor slit about three-quarters of the way up.

"Open it," Nathan said as he approached the man. The man stood up and blocked the door.

"You have to leave," the man replied and crossed his very muscular arms.

Julius never actually saw Nathan move, but when Nathan was near the man, the Asian's head slammed into the door with a bang. He slid down it unconscious.

The slit opened. Nathan stood there, tapping his watch. "Tick fucking tock, buttercup."

The door opened, and Nathan went inside.

Julius saw dozens of men from different ethnic backgrounds around multiple tables. They all drank and smoked while naked ladies danced on their tables. The men played cards and dominoes. They laughed and slapped the ladies on their backsides. Julius saw various drugs lying across the tables.

Some of the men were eating food off the naked bodies of lying women and men.

Some men were getting oral sex; others had naked women grinding on their laps. Most of the men were older than he was by the looks of it. He could hear the moaning and groaning of the women and men. It turned his stomach.

Nathan walked past them all and straight for a table at the very far end of the room, almost surrounded in complete darkness.

Nathan sat down and grabbed a whisky from a passing naked waitress. "It is so very hard to get in here these days, Jian."

An old Chinese man leaned forward into the light. "It has been a long time, Nathan."

Nathan lifted his glass towards the man. "It has, old friend. It saddens me to see the place in such a state. I mean, seriously, you will catch food poisoning from those ladies."

"I must change with the times. I am old, and my nephew runs this place now," Jian replied. He sipped from a glass of water. "It is his business now."

Nathan shook his head. "Still plenty of life in you."

"It does not feel like that. I feel death's hands near me."

"Fuck death. Let him wait," Nathan replied and downed the whisky in one gulp. "You know he owes me a few favours anyway."

"I take it you are not here to catch up and talk about old times?" Jian said as he leaned back into the shadows.

"No, old friend, I am not. I need to find your old friend, Hanz."

"Now, that is a name I have not heard for a long time," the voice came from the shadows.

"I need to find him. Any ideas where to start?"

"The last time I spoke to Hanz was over a decade ago. Ever since that little incident, we had with the Lorenzo family."

"I fixed that issue, as you well know. Hanz was lucky I didn't kill him. But that was part of the deal. My next stop will be the Lorenzo's to see if they know anything about his whereabouts," Nathan said and looked out of the corner of his eye. He saw three men approaching the table. The angriest of them was very well dressed and around 5 feet 10" slim built. His suit was expensive, and his waistcoat looked to have gold buttons on it. "I take it the angry-looking arsehole approaching us is your nephew?"

"Yes. Try and be gentle with him. He is young and thinks much of himself. He is quick to anger and will cause you problems in the future if not handled with care," the voice replied.

"Is this the mother fucker who knocked out my door security?" a very angry young Asian man said.

"Mother fucker, no. Knocked out that cunt at the door, yes," Nathan replied, not looking at the man. He grabbed another drink from another naked waitress.

"Who are you, mother fucker?" the man shouted at Nathan.

"This is my friend, Nathan. You will show respect to him, Sheng. He is here at my request," Jian said from his shadow.

"Listen, old man. I decide who comes in here, not you. You handed this business to me. I will do whatever I want. Let in whoever I want," Sheng replied smugly.

"I can't believe you handed the business to this prick, Jian. What were you thinking?" Nathan said to the shadow.

Sheng took a knife out of his waistcoat. Nathan moved quicker than Julius could believe. Sheng screamed as his hand was slammed onto the table and his own knife was driven through it. The hand was pinned to the table, and blood was streaming out. The two bodyguards moved to attack Nathan and the inspector. Nathan punched one so hard that he flew a few feet backwards across another table, scattering people across the floor. Nobody in the place seemed to be paying any attention to the fight going on before them. The second bodyguard was kicked in the groin just as swiftly, and he fell holding his now ruined testicles. Nathan brought his knee up and smashed the man's teeth out of his mouth.

Nathan sat down and grabbed Sheng by his hair. "You really need to learn respect, Sheng. It could have saved you so much embarrassment just now." Nathan grabbed the knife and twisted it slowly. Sheng screamed. "Oh, that must have hurt, princess. I mean, seriously, Jian, I thought your family bred hardy folk. This little shite must be the runt of the litter."

Julius looked around and noticed that still, no one was paying the scene any attention. They all seemed focused on their own tables, unaware of what was happening around them. Was it the drink and drugs? Even the women seemed not to notice. This unsettled Julius.

"Do you know who this man is, Sheng? This is Nathan. The same Nathan who saved my life all those years ago," Jian said.

"Not possible," Sheng grunted. "The man you speak of would be the same age as you. You must be losing it, old man."

Nathan slammed Jian's heading into the table three times. "You better be nice to your uncle. I am the man who saved your uncle's life."

Sheng spat blood across the floor. "You can't be."

"Sorry there, sweetheart, but I am," Nathan replied and pulled the knife out of Sheng's ruined hand. The man fell to the floor, holding his bloody hand. "Your uncle has told me that I can come back here anytime I wish. I will take him up on that offer. As will my friend here." Nathan pointed to Julius. "He is almost as tough as me. So, if you see me or him, I would be very, very nice. And if I ever hear you speak to your uncle like that again, I am going to make your last moments on this earth as painful as possible. Jian is a very good friend of mine."

Nathan stood up and put the knife into his coat pocket. "Jian, my friend, look after yourself. I will see you soon, and we will drink together like old times."

Jian leaned out of the shadow and smiled. "Ah, that would be good, Nathan."

Nathan turned and started to walk out of the room.

Sheng stood up and said, "Nathan. Yeah, I heard about you. Also heard your wife died. Pity. She had an arse you could fuck all day. What a waste."

Nathan stopped and turned around slowly. "What the fuck you say?"

Sheng laughed. "You heard me, white boy. I would have destroyed that pert arse of hers. She would be begging for more. Like the whore she was."

Nathan kicked Sheng on his kneecap. Julius heard the crack and saw a wet stain begin to appear on the man's trousers, no doubt blood from a bone sticking out of the skin. As Sheng began to fall, Nathan brought his right elbow up into Sheng's jaw. Teeth flew out of my mouth. Nathan then punched Sheng right in Adam's apple; the crunch of cartilage was painful to hear. Julius watched as Sheng fell forward and crashed face-first onto the floor, gurgling. Nathan stood above him and brought his right foot crashing down onto the small of his back. Julius heard bones break. Sheng's legs went limp, and the man was barely able to breathe.

Nathan grabbed Sheng up by his hair. The man was barely conscious. "As you spend the rest of your fucking pitiful life in a wheelchair, pissing and shitting into bags, unable to get your small dick hard, I want you to remember something. I am a fucking monster. Ask your uncle. He will tell you. He will tell you about Xiaowan Bay, and you will know the monster you are dealing with. They still talk about me there. I'm the monster parents tell their children about. Oh, you might think you will get revenge for what I have done, but it will never happen. I crushed your throat. You will never talk again. You will never eat solid food again, as your jaw is nothing but a jigsaw puzzle now," Nathan pulled the man closer and whispered into his ear. Julius watched, and the broken man pissed and soiled himself.

Nathan threw the man to the floor. He looked into the shadow at Jian.

"He deserved to die for what he said," Jian said. "You should have killed him. You may regret not doing so."

"This punishment is worse than death. I made sure of that," Nathan replied.

"Agreed. I will make sure all know what happened here. They will side with you in this matter."

Nathan nodded and left the room.

Julius closed the door to the car and started the engine. He looked across at Nathan and saw that he was looking straight ahead.

"What happened in there?" the young man asked.

"Nothing. Nothing happened. We asked a respectable business owner a few questions to help us in our investigations," Nathan replied and put on his seat belt.

"Seriously. That place should be shut down. What in the hell are we letting it stay operational? And what you did to those men, including Sheng, was way out of our remit."

"Oh, shut the fuck up," replied Nathan and turned to face Julius. "Do you honestly think the world is all sweet people and smells of roses? Grow the fuck up. The sooner you learn the truth, the better. Glasgow is like any other shithole city on this miserable planet. Full of very nasty people who do very awful things. Did you think you would join the police and make the city better? No chance. This city will fuck you up, choir boy. This city is Glasgow. You think New York or Tokyo are bad? They are Disney fucking land compared to this city. Glasgow is a city full of evil. The fucking gates of hell reside in this city. So, you better toughen up, Julius. I am going to show you the real Glasgow. The Glasgow that even hell itself is afraid of." Nathan smiled and grabbed the boy's neck. "You better learn quickly, boy. I don't have time for wasters." He let go.

Julius rubbed his neck. "Who the fuck are you?"

"Told you before, you wouldn't believe me." He took out his phone and sent an address to the young man. "Drive here."

Julius recognised the street. "Fine." He slammed the car into gear and drove off.

Fifteen minutes later, they arrived outside a restaurant called La Benevento, near the central station.

"Let me guess. Another respectable business owner to aid us in our investigations," Julius said sarcastically.

"Yes, and stop being an arsehole," Nathan said. He leaned over and honked the horn. He got out of the car. A young Italian man came out of the restaurant and shook Nathan's hand. Nathan leaned down and told Julius to get out of the car.

"Nathan, my friend, it has been too long. I heard what happened. You have my deepest condolences. Did you get the flowers I sent?" the man asked.

"I did, Matteo. Thank you for the kind gesture," Nathan replied.

"I only wish I was there to help you. But my attention was needed elsewhere. But I should have helped you. I am sorry," Matteo said and placed his hand on Nathan's shoulder.

"No. Trust me, it was good you weren't there. Better that way," Nathan replied, patting his arm. "Now, to business. I need to speak to Mother Bear."

Matteo laughed. "You know you are the only one she allows to call her that."

"That's because I am her favourite. You're her son, and I think she prefers me over you."

"I think she does too." Matteo laughed. "Come, I will take you to her."

All three men entered the restaurant. Matteo took them through the kitchen and upstairs to a flat. They stopped at the front door, and Matteo knocked and entered.

"Mother, I have brought guests to see you," Matteo said.

A woman in her late 50s came out of the kitchen, wiping her hands on a towel. She had short black hair that was starting to grey. Her face was still young-looking, and she had ice-blue eyes.

"Nathan. I pray to God every day to keep you safe," said the woman and held her arms out towards Nathan.

"Mother Bear," Nathan said as he walked forward into her arms. She hugged him tightly and kissed him on his cheek.

She let go and grabbed his face. "Let me look at you. My god, you look bad. Are you eating properly? Come into the kitchen. I will make you something to eat. No arguments. Come." She walked back into the kitchen and then said, "Matteo. Go get some wine. Red. The 67. Take that young man with you. Then both of you come and eat."

Nathan sat down at the large kitchen table. He watched the woman stir a pot of red tomato sauce. "That smell, it is as good as I remember."

"I haven't changed the recipe in all these years. Same ingredients as always." She smiled. "Why didn't you come and see me before?"

Nathan sighed and took his flask out. "It was my problem. Not yours."

"Bullshit. God forgive me for swearing," she said and blessed herself. "You know you can always come to me. Always."

"I know. But I wanted to deal with it myself. It was my burden to bear," he offered the flask to her. She took it and drank. "Plus, you are needed here. Your sons need you."

"They are old enough to look after themselves. They are big boys. They are all married now. Good women. I made sure of that," she replied and gave the flask back. "I was at the funeral. I cried so much. I have never cried like that. Never."

"I saw you."

She nodded. She walked away from the pot and kissed his forehead. "It is so good to see you. I have three boys that I gave birth to. You are my son also even though you didn't come from me. Never forget that. I'm your mother. You are my son."

Nathan nodded and hugged her. "You're too young to be my mother."

She laughed. "I don't care. You're my boy. From now until the end."

Matteo and Julius walked into the kitchen with two bottles of wine each.

"You don't hug me like that, Mother," said Matteo as he placed the wine onto the table.

"I see you every day. I haven't seen Nathan in a long time," she replied. She looked at Julius. "I am Alessia Lorenzo. And you are?"

"Julius Koper. Inspector," Julius replied, holding out his hand.

Alessia shook the young man's hand. "I hope you are keeping my Nathan safe."

"From what I have seen, he can look after himself," Julius replied.

"You are right there. Sit and open a bottle of wine. Lunch is almost ready."

"I am on duty," Julius replied.

"Ah, a choir boy," Alessia replied. "On duty, off duty. I don't care. Drink the wine."

A few minutes later, four plates sat on the table, almost overflowing with spaghetti bolognese.

Nathan took a large portion onto his fork and shoved it into his mouth. "Mother Bear. It's as good as I remember. Better even."

Alessia patted his hand. "Thank you."

Nathan ate fast and emptied his plate before the rest. Alessia smiled wide as Nathan got up and took another helping.

"Only you could eat two helpings of my food, Nathan," she said. "My boys can barely eat one."

"Ah, they are still babies. They don't appreciate your cooking like I do," Nathan grinned.

"Stop trying to get me into trouble, please," Matteo joked. "I love your cooking, Mother. You're even a better cook than my wife."

"I bet you never said that to her." Laughed Nathan between mouthfuls.

"I'm not that crazy. I would never be allowed back into the same bed as her," Matteo replied.

Julius had to admit that the food was very good. "It is very good, Mrs Lorenzo."

"You are very welcome," she replied. "So what brings you here, Nathan?"

"I need a location on Hanz," he said as he swallowed another mouthful.

"Ah! Him," she replied. "He was moved on by me after I found out what he was doing. Though I know who to ask. When do you need to know?"

"Now, if possible. I have questions, and he had better have answers."

She nodded and left the kitchen. Julius heard her speak on the phone in Italian. A few moments later, she returned and handed Nathan a piece of paper.

"He is here. You go to this address and give them my name. They will take you to him." She sat down again and held Nathan's hand. "I was also told you visited Jian and that soon after his nephew was taken out by an ambulance. The doctors I have on pay are saying he is on life support. Back broken. Jaw ruined. They could barely intubate him, as his throat had been crushed. Care to explain what happened?"

"He called her a whore," Nathan replied and took another mouthful of food.

Julius knew when someone was swearing, didn't matter the language. Right now, Alessia was swearing so hard in Italian, it would make a sailor blush.

"You should have killed him," Matteo said. He slammed his knife into the table. "Give me the nod, and I will do it. It would be a fucking pleasure."

"Language, Matteo. God can hear you," Alessia shouted. "But my son is right. He should have died."

"He will live a life of constant pain. Killing him would have let him off. Don't worry. Jian is backing me up," Nathan replied as if he didn't care.

Alessia stroked his hair. "My brave boy. In the old days, you would have killed him. I see she made you a better man. I miss her." She lifted his head so she could look into his eyes. "I see the pain is still there. My boy, my sweet boy. She would not want you to suffer like this."

Nathan kissed her hand. "My choice, Mother Bear."

Someone banged hard repeatedly on the flat door.

Matteo walked quickly to the door and answered. There was a rushed conversation. The door closed.

"He did it again. God damn, fucking animal!" shouted the man.

"Language. Do not take the Lord's name in vain," his mother shouted. "What happened?"

"Viktor did it again. He raped her," came the reply.

Nathan saw the anger on Alessia's face. "Who is Viktor?" he asked.

"An animal. A Bastardo," she growled. "A Russian. Lives a few streets up. Married my waitress, Lucia. She is a good girl but picks bad men. And he treats her like dirt." She spat on the floor.

Nathan stood up and looked at Matteo. "You know where to find him?" The man nodded. "Find him. Bring him here. Is the old warehouse still standing?" Again, a nod. "Good. You and your brothers get him. Take him there. Wait for me. Make sure he is unharmed."

"It will be done," Matteo replied as the door behind him opened.

Nathan saw a young girl walk in. Her clothes had been ripped off; a few strands of top covered her shoulders. Her bra was torn badly and had blood stains on the fabric. Her underwear was ripped but covered her private area. Nathan saw her body covered in bruises and cuts. Her lip was bleeding and beginning to swell. She wrapped her arms around herself like a blanket. Nathan walked over to her and saw the black eyes caused by fists. He took her hand gently and lifted her head slightly so he could look at her. "Lucia. I am a police officer. Do you wish to press charges against your husband?"

The girl looked frightened and looked for guidance. She saw Alessia. "Please no police. It was my fault. I made him angry," she stammered. She tried to back away from Nathan but couldn't. He seemed to hold her in place with his demeanour. She looked at the floor.

"You did nothing wrong, Lucia. Nothing," Nathan said. "Look at me." The scared woman looked up at him. She saw his eyes. She flinched. "Do not be scared of me. Never be scared of me, young one." He smiled, and she felt loved. "One of two things is going to happen. Either I arrest him and charge him, or he goes away. I leave the choice up to you."

She started crying. Nathan hugged the girl to his chest. "I love him," she mumbled.

"This is not love. This is you being held prisoner." He looked at Alessia. "How many times has this happened?" She held up four fingers. Nathan swore. "Lucia, you are better than this. You deserve better than this. Alessia looks after you, doesn't she? She would never hurt you. Look to her for guidance."

Lucia turned her head so she could see Alessia. "I love him. I love him."

"My, sweet girl. This is not love. You have been forced to believe that this is love." She walked over and took her hand. "He isn't a man. Men do not treat women like this. He is an animal."

The girl nodded. She looked up at Nathan. "I'm sorry for being weak. I'm so sorry."

Nathan leaned over and whispered into her ear. Julius watched as the girl's face came to a realisation. The girl cried, and tears streamed down her face.

She began to punch his chest. "Let it out. Hit me as much as you want. Give me your rage; let it out. He made you like this. He treated you like shite. You are beautiful. You are brave. But now it has gone too far, and you have now come to the understanding. My dear girl, love is not a weapon. It is not used to beat. It is not used for rape. It is not used to hurt. Listen to me and understand, there are people who love you right here and right now, and they will do everything they can to protect you. Let me protect you. Please," he said as she hammered his chest. "Tell me what you want?"

"I don't want this anymore. I don't want the pain. He let his friends watch," she screamed. "They laughed as he raped me." Nathan held her tight as her legs began to give way.

"Was it Jürgen and Isaac?" Matteo asked.

She nodded.

Nathan lifted her head. "Tell me now, tell me what you want!"

"I want them out of my life. I don't want this anymore. Please. Please help," she begged.

"If I arrest them, they will only get a few years, and they will be out again," Nathan told her. "If you nod, I will make sure that does not happen."

"Hold on a minute," Julius said.

Nathan turned his head towards the young man. Julius took a step back. He was sure Nathan's eyes were nothing but black holes. In that instance, Julius knew true fear; he thought he could feel the room shake a little. "Shut up." He turned back to the girl. "Do you want to live in fear or be free?"

She nodded.

"Find the three of them. Alive and unharmed. I want the poker, the adrenaline, and the chairs. Also some Viagra; they want a good time, and I will make sure they get it. And, Matteo, I mean unharmed. You can have your fun afterwards," Nathan said to Matteo.

"Alessia, look after this girl. Julius, come with me."

Nathan left the flat and marched to the car. "Get the fuck in," he said to Julius as the young man chased after him.

"I'm not going anywhere. You seriously think I am going to allow you to kill three men? Are you fucking kidding?" Julius stated.

Nathan grabbed the young man and slammed him against the car. The car actually moved with the force. "You will do what I fucking say. You have any complaints, walk back to the station and speak to whomever the fuck you want."

Julius was stunned into silence.

"I fucking told you; this is how the city works. Learn quicker. Learn better. Now, get in the fucking car. We are going to see Hanz. Then we will deal with the rapist and his friends. You don't want to come, then the station is that fucking way. But if you get in the car, then you do what I say when I say it. You don't fucking complain. You don't fucking bitch. You little prick. It's time you drop your fucking morals and actually act like a policeman." Nathan let him go. "Now, fucking choose. I don't have time to waste."

"I will come. But understand this. I will note everything you do and report it when I get back to the station. I will make sure you face justice," Julius said, pointing at him. "You're fucking insane, you know that."

"Probably," Nathan agreed. "Now, shut up and take me here."

Julius looked at the paper. "Are you fucking kidding?"

The car stopped, and Nathan got out. Julius opened the door and walked onto the street. He looked up at the sign.

"Well, here we are. The Barras. Closed. You know this place is open on weekends only," Julius said.

"Yes. But not everything shuts," Nathan said and took a drink from his flask. "You can find anything in the Barras. Even people."

"And pray tell me, is this where we will find this man, Hanz?"

"Yes," came the definite reply. "Come on. Let's get this over with." Nathan walked into the empty street. Julius followed closely. Nathan walked towards one of the shutters and banged hard.

"We are shut!" someone shouted.

"Alessia sent me," Nathan shouted back.

"Nathan?"

"Bingo."

Julius heard someone swear. The shutter opened, and three men stood in front of them with guns. Assault rifles, SCARS.

"Seriously. Guns," Nathan scoffed.

"Alessia called, and we were told to let you in. But she doesn't pay us. Our boss doesn't want you here. When he found out it was you, we were told not to let you in. He told us to make sure you get the message," said a large, muscular man.

"Boys, this is not your day. First mistake: you brought guns. The second mistake is that you are going against Mother Bear's orders. Third mistake." Nathan's hands moved in a flash, and he pointed a gun at the central man. "You have just pissed me off."

"What the fuck are you doing?" Julius whispered.

"Teaching you a lesson," Nathan replied, not taking his eyes off the big man. "Now, boys. I know you are just doing what you are paid to do. Now, if you knew who I was, then you wouldn't have been this stupid. So a lesson must be taught. So, I want you all to remember this lesson. You." He nodded towards the man who was doing all the talking. "Hands up."

The man slowly held his hands up. "Perfect. Now is everyone paying attention? Good." Two bangs erupted, and all three men fell to the ground.

Julius saw the two men behind the first man collapse to the ground, holding their shoulders, blood weeping out between their fingers. The first man screamed as a bullet had been shot through each hand. He rolled about on the ground in agony.

"Jesus Christ. You fucking shot them," Julius said as he watched the men cry in pain. "Where the fuck did you get that gun?"

"A gift from an old friend a very long time ago," Nathan replied and put the gun back into his coat. "Now, I believe the lesson has been learned. Hmm. Yes. Good." Nathan walked to the first man and kicked him in the ribs to get his attention. "So, where is your boss?"

"Bastard. He is downstairs," came the painful reply.

"Are there more people who require lessons between me and your boss?" Nathan asked as he looked in the direction of the stairs.

"No!" the man shouted.

"Good. Now, boys, I am sure I won't see any of you when I come back. I'm sure you will be somewhere else. Somewhere that is maybe a few hundred miles away?" They all nodded. "Good. Then here ends the lesson," Nathan said. He grabbed Julius and dragged him away from the injured men.

"What just happened?" Julius asked, still in shock.

"A lesson. What's so hard to understand?" Nathan replied.

"You are fucking insane," Julius said and ran in front of Nathan to stop him from walking forward. "This stops now. I'm taking you in."

Nathan laughed. "Seriously."

"Yes, I'm fucking serious. Put your hands behind your head and lay down on the floor," Julius replied and took his baton out. He flicked it, and it extended. "Get down now."

Nathan laughed. He folded his arms. Julius's baton was in Nathan's hand.

Julius looked down at his hand, his now empty hand. "How the fuck?"

Nathan Tutted. "You really need training." He slammed the baton into the young man's stomach. Julius folded over, the wind taken out of him. "I guess you can put me down now for assaulting an officer."

Julius limped over to a wall and tried to catch his breath. "Arsehole!"

"Yes. Let's get this over with now. I am not a very nice being. I am the person who gets things done. Think of me as a judge, jury, and executioner. I decide the punishment. I deal out that punishment," he said and slammed the baton down on the table. The force of it made it retract. "You think I am actually an inspector. I'm not. I'm someone the police bring in when they need things done that can't be on the books. When the law must be ignored, broken, beaten, and buried. A lot of people bring me in when things have to be done in a certain way. You want to know something? I have killed a lot of people. I stopped counting after 3,000." He saw the look Julius gave him. "I'm not lying. You can tell, can't you? So, listen to what I say next very carefully. I am above the law. I am so far above the law that I cannot see it. If you had even managed to bring me in, not a fucking thing would have happened. Not one fucking thing." He held the baton out to the young man. "Now, pick yourself up and fucking follow me. No more of this macho police shite." Julius looked at the baton and grabbed it.

46

"I'm done with you," he said through gritted teeth. "I'm leaving."

Nathan laughed. "No, you are not. I wounded your pride. Stop being a little bitch. Have you forgotten that we are trying to find a serial killer? The man we are about to talk to may have the evidence we need. So, it is time to put your big boy pants on and do your job." Nathan walked away.

Julius swore. Nathan was right. He still had a killer to find. "This still doesn't make it right, you know."

"Don't give a fuck," Nathan shouted back.

Nathan walked down the stairs and smiled when he heard Julius wheezing behind him.

Nathan kept going and pushed past a pair of doors. He walked into a room full of drug-making equipment. Ecstasy, cocaine, Meth. You name it, it was there. Julius looked around, stunned.

"Oh, Hanz. My, Hanz. Come out, come out wherever you are," Nathan sang.

"Nathan," said a voice through a speaker. "I see my help failed to give you the message."

"They did," Nathan replied very sarcastically. "They are now seeing the error of their ways. You know me; I am a very good teacher," Nathan replied and looked at a camera on the wall. "I am in no mood to play hide and seek."

"And I am in no mood to be found," replied Hanz. "What do you want?"

"Morphine. I know you are the biggest dealer in Glasgow. So, who have you sold to recently?" Nathan said walking slowly around the room.

"I have sold to many people. I provide a valuable service to the community, you know."

"It would have been roughly three months ago. It would have been a lot," Nathan said as he pushed a beaker off the table. It smashed onto the floor.

"It's so hard to remember," giggled Hanz. "Three months ago. I can't seem to remember."

"Ah. So, you want to play that game? So be it." Nathan flipped a table, the drugs scattering all over the place.

"You have anger issues, my dear Nathan." Laughed Hanz.

"You remember me when I am angry, don't you, Hanz? So, don't push me." Another table was flipped. "Remember quickly, Hanz."

"I sold much three months ago. Many drugs. You can't expect me to remember every little detail," Hanz shouted as another table was destroyed. "You can break everything in this room. I can always make more."

Nathan flipped another table. "Oh, I know that. But what you need to ask yourself is, will I let you?" Another table was destroyed. "You better tell me what I want to know, Hanz."

"I don't remember. Maybe I sold morphine to someone. Maybe it was more than they would require," shouted Hanz. "Stop destroying my business."

Nathan flipped another table, and cocaine scattered across a wall. "Oh, Hanz. My dear, old Hanz. I want that information by the time I count to 10. If I don't have it, then I will have to take it."

"You can't expect me to remember!" Hanz screamed as Nathan began to count.

Nathan walked slowly around the room, counting. "STOP COUNTING," Hanz shouted afraid.

"8, 9, 9 and a half, 9 and three quarters. 10. Oh, Hanz. Ready or fucking not, I'm coming," Nathan said and punched his hand through the wall. He tore the hole wider and saw an electronic control panel. "Seriously, Hanz. A safe room. How cliche."

Hanz laughed. "You won't get in, Nathan. I'm safe here. There is two feet worth of steel between me and you. Not even you can get to me."

"A simple 10-digit lock. Seriously, Hanz. You cheap Nazi bastard," Nathan said as he leaned against the safe room door. "So, Julius, there are a few thousand possible combinations for this lock."

"Millions," Hanz said triumphantly.

"Shut up, Hanz. Like I was saying, there are lots of possible combinations. But you see, I know, Hanz," Nathan said to the young man. "But before I open this door, I will tell you a bit about Hanz. He is a drug-dealing, Nazi-loving paedophile. He likes very young boys and very young girls. That bad ecstasy that was flooding into Manchester. All from Hanz. The LSD that caused several people to go insane and slit their own throats. From Hanz. The only reason he has been allowed to get away with it is because of the people backing him. Certain politicians use him. Politicians from a certain blue cunt of a party. He has dirt on some of their most senior members, both here in Scotland and in Westminster. Let's just say that a few cabinet members get their medicine from this man behind the door. So he was considered untouchable. But now I am going to put that right." Nathan punched in a number on the pad. "You see, Hanz keeps a record of important people who come to him and buy their poison of choice. He keeps records of everyone who comes and buys his products." He punched in another number. "So, Julius. Tell me what I should do when I open this door?" Another number was punched in.

Julius stood there and didn't know what to say. He watched as Nathan punched in another few numbers. His index finger then hovered above the keypad.

"Well, Julius. Tell me what you want me to do. Behind this door is a prize. This prize is the worst possible scum you can imagine. But if you take him in, he will be out for free in less than an hour. You will see that the police can actually do fuck all when push comes to shove. It will be a hard lesson for you to learn through those rose-tinted glasses you seem to wear. Or when this door opens, I get the answers I want, and then I put an end to his rotten empire."

Julius stared at the man. "I can't make that choice."

"Well, you will when this door opens," Nathan said as he pressed the last number. The panel beeped, and the door swung open. "Oh, Hanz. Seriously. Fucking Goering's and Himmler's birthdays. You never change," said Nathan as he entered the safe room.

Julius followed and gagged at the smell. The stench of sweat and piss filled the room. Julius looked around and saw several monitors on one wall. He had to look away at the images and videos being played. He saw a fat old man sitting on a swivel chair with his trousers around his ankles.

"You sick fucker, Hanz," Nathan said as he strolled towards Hanz. "OK, Hanz. Before my young friend decides what I am to do to with you, you had better tell me what I want."

Hanz looked terrified. "I...I...I..." he spluttered.

Nathan punched him square in the nose. Blood exploded from the man's nose. He screamed in pain. "Oh, Hanz. Hanz. Hanz. HANZ. That felt good," Nathan said and wiped the blood onto Hanz's shirt.

Hanz pointed to a cupboard on another wall. "In there," he cried.

Nathan walked to the cupboard and opened the door. Hundreds of hard drives filled the shelves inside. They were all dated. Nathan grabbed the drive that had December printed on it. He plugged it into a computer. "Give me a date."

"Third, I think," Hanz replied as blood poured down his face.

Nathan clicked on the video. He scrolled through the video. He then stopped and played the video. He saw someone walk into the room. They wore dark clothes, the figure's head covered by a jumper hood. He couldn't see the face, as it was always looking away from the cameras. He was over 6 feet tall at least.

Shoulders hunched over a bit. "He knew where all the cameras were. He is clever. Who is this?" Nathan pointed to the figure.

"I don't know!"

Nathan grabbed the fat man and pulled him over with such ease. He smashed the man's face into the screen. "Tell me, Hanz."

"I really don't know," the man protested. "He came in, placed an order, and I gave it to him."

Nathan threw the fat paedophile to the floor. "You don't mind if I take this, do you?" He unplugged the hard drive and tossed it to Julius. "OK, Julius. Time to decide. Are you going to do it by the book or actually do the right thing?"

Julius looked at Hanz and then at the screens of the other computers. "Are you sure if I take him in, he will get off?"

"Guaranteed. Probably at this moment, there is a lawyer getting into a car heading towards the home station as we speak," Nathan replied and heard Hanz give a small giggle. He looked down at Hanz, who smiled weakly. Nathan grunted and kicked the man in the head. Han'z head snapped back violently. He coughed teeth onto the floor with lots of blood.

Julius believed him. "I don't know."

Nathan took the gun from his coat and then shot Hanz in both kneecaps. The man screamed. "Shut up, Hanz." He looked at one of the cameras next to a monitor, and by its angle, it was aimed at the chair Hanz was sitting on. It was aimed at about groin height. "OK, you sick fucking bastards. I know you have been watching all of this. You see here, Hanz is not going to be on your sick little dark net again. But he is going to leave in style. Isn't that right, Hanz?" Nathan said and kicked the man in the ribs; he felt two breaks from his kick. Nathan walked to a screen and took pictures of the users who were watching this all happen. One he knew and smiled. Government minister. "I now have all your user names and low and behold all your IP addresses. Tut tut. You, silly fuckers, did you not know that Hanz was using some very illegal but sophisticated software to track all your locations? And one address, oh, one address, is right now shitting themselves because I know who they are. Isn't that right, minister? Once I am done with Hanz, I may pay you all a visit. Hmm. How would you like that? But don't go just yet. You're going to miss the grand finale."

Nathan turned to the young inspector and said, "I tell you what, Julius. Why don't we let fate decide?" He turned back to the camera. "Why don't we let fate decide, boys and paedophiles?" Nathan shouted towards the camera and walked out of the safe room and picked up a glass beaker. He sniffed it. It was ethanol. "If Hanz can get out of here before the fire gets him, then you can take him in. What do you say?"

"That would be murder," Julius stated.

"No. It wouldn't be. Trust me on this. I let him live once before to keep the peace in Glasgow during a particular bad turf war. In order to stop the war from spilling into the streets, I had to compromise. He lived, and I have regretted it ever since. He had certain people at his back, people who wanted him alive. But now, I don't give a fuck about him or them. I will deal with his friends when they come for me. Don't you worry about him. Trust me, you will be doing the world a favour. You see what he was watching in there. You tell me if he deserves to live."

"I can't," Julius replied in exhaustion. It had been a long day, and it was beginning to take its toll on his body and mind.

"Good. Oh, did you hear that, Hanz? That's the deal. If you can crawl out of here before the fire gets you, you will be taken to the police station, where, I have no doubt, your friendly lawyer will be waiting for you," Nathan said and put a rag into the beaker. He pushed Julius towards the stairs and lit the rag. He threw it into the ruined tables.

"NATHAN, YOU BASTARD. YOU WON'T SURVIVE THIS. MY FRIENDS WILL MAKE SURE OF THAT. YOU WAIT AND SEE. THEY WILL BE COMING SOON ENOUGH," Hanz screamed from the safe room. "YOU, FUCKING BASTARD."

"Language, Hanz. There is no need for that language," Nathan said and walked up the stairs.

It watched the flames fly high into the midday sky. This was getting interesting. Thrilling. This man had tracked down its supplier. How did he do it? Did he have evidence of its dealings? No. Its tracks were covered. Maybe it was just a coincidence. But it didn't believe in that. No, it didn't.

It watched intently but saw that no one left the building but the two policemen. Hanz must be dead and was burning to ash now. The fire brigade was fighting the fire, but it was still raging angrily. It would be expected that the amount of flammable chemicals and substances would keep the fire fed for a long time.

This police officer had piqued its interest. This man was getting very interesting indeed. It would find out what it could about this new puzzle piece.

Very interesting.

Chapter 4

Nathan walked into the police station and saw a suited man sitting at the duty officer's desk. The man screamed lawyer.

"Your client isn't here," Nathan said to him. The man looked at him. "Last I saw of your client; he was getting a sun tan. One that only cremation can provide. If I were you, I would look for a dustpan with some ashes in it and ask if your client would like to press charges." Nathan leaned in close to the man and pulled out the hard drive. He whispered, "You might want to pass on this message to your other clients. I have them by the balls now. If I want, I can knock them all down one by one. Be a good rent boy and tell them that." He put the hard drive back into his pocket and walked away. Just before he left the waiting area, he turned around and saw the man looking very worried. "Toilets are over there if you feel like shitting yourself."

Nathan walked into the incident room and saw his team working away.

"Did the doc bring the evidence?" he asked the room.

"Yes, I did," replied the doc as he stood up from behind a desk. "I am just setting it all out now."

"Good. How long before everything is ready?"

"Give me another 30 minutes," replied the old doctor.

"OK. I'm hungry. I'm going to get something to eat," Nathan said and left the room.

Julius looked for David and went over to him. "Can I talk to you, Sir?"

David nodded and took Julius to his office.

Julius sat down and explained everything that happened. David sat there and listened.

"What am I supposed to do? I joined the police to stop people like Nathan," Julius protested.

David sighed and took a large file out of his desk. He threw it towards the young man. "Open it."

Julius opened the file and saw a piece of paper with all the words blacked out. He turned over to another page. Again, all words blacked out.

"They are all the same. Every piece of paper. There are another 10 files like this one. Nathan's entire record is there. Everything the world knows about him. I have known him for over twenty years, and I know practically nothing about his past," David said and took another file out of his desk. "In this file are two bits of paper." He opened the folder. "This bit of paper is from someone I know in American Intelligence. It has a list of organisations on it. These organisations are all military. SAS. SBS. Navy Seals. Commandos. Green berets. French Special Forces. Spetsnaz. There are even some I have never heard of and 12 that are blacked out because they officially do not exist. On this bit of paper is a report of everything American Intelligence has on Nathan. Everything says unknown. DOB, age, everything. Before I met Nathan, he never existed. As far as the entire world is concerned, he appeared out of thin air fully grown." David leaned back in his chair. "Nathan has contacts across multiple governments worldwide. You name the country, and he is well in with them. Christ, even organised crime is terrified of him. Mafia, triads, yakuza, fuck, even the Albanians are scared of him."

"Why, is he a policeman then? You make him sound like the godfather or something like that," said Julius.

"He isn't on the police force. We bring him in when we can't do the job. Shite, so do governments," David replied. "Look. I will tell you this because I want you to understand who he is and what he is capable of."

"I've seen what he is capable of. He shot three men. Burned another alive, and more than likely, tonight will kill one or maybe three more. Seriously, what the fuck! You can't stand by and watch. Surely not," pleaded Julius.

"Shut up and listen," David replied. "You know his wife died. It was an accident. Two years ago, the police caught wind of a terror cell in Glasgow. We found out where they were hiding. It went to shite quickly when we tried to assault the building. Two of the cells managed to shoot their way out of the warehouse. They managed to get away in a car. We chased them. They were driving all over the place. Shite. We should have been better prepared, but we didn't know when they were planning the attack. We moved too fast. We chased them down the M74. They were driving too fast. They lost control shortly after the Polmadie cut-off. It caused a multi-car pileup. Seven people died. Sadly, one of them was Nathan's wife. She was driving to work. She didn't even need to work, but she liked her independence."

David stood up, walked to the door, and closed it. "I was the one who had to tell Nathan that she was one of the victims. I could not even tell you the odds of that happening, that she was in the wrong place at the wrong time. It was his day off from his special duties. He stood there without any emotion whatsoever. He simply put on his coat and went to the morgue to identify her. I still remember it clearly as day as he stood over her body lying on the table. He stroked her hair for over an hour. He whispered to her over and over again. It broke my heart to see her like that. He loved her more than anything in the world. Like I said, after an hour, he then took out his phone and made a call. It was over in five minutes. He then asked me to take him to the airport. I asked him why, but he didn't say a word. Not a thing. When we got to the airport, he directed me to the private entrance. He flashed something from his wallet to the guard, and we were let through. I then drove him to one of the hangars. Waiting inside were one man and one woman. Behind them was a private jet. He got out of the car and walked onto the plane. The man and woman followed him. The plane took off."

David opened his desk drawer and placed a glass in front of the young man. He then took out a bottle of 21-year-old Johnnie Walker and poured it into his glass. He then poured one for himself. "I called a friend in the British Secret Service and asked if they could keep an eye on the plane and tell me where it was going. The next day, I got a call that it had landed in Egypt. One person got off the plane and hired a jeep at the airport. The man and the woman must have been the pilots. So, I used one of my favours to make sure he was followed. The tail lost him the next day. Two days after that, I was sent a report by my spy friend. The terror cell that was in Glasgow had been sent from a camp in the Sinai Peninsula. Some sort of headquarters for that group. That camp had been attacked. Satellite surveillance had witnessed it happen. From what I saw in the video, it was one attacker. Just one. The camp had been observed to have around 20 terror members in the camp at the time. Being trained for the holy war to come. So, the Americans sent a special recon team in to find out what happened." David drained his glass in one gulp.

"Nineteen terrorist dead. One was found alive. If you can call it alive. The 19 dead were found in various states of, well, torture. Some had been crucified. Others were ripped open; their own intestines were used to strangle them. Some had their hearts torn out. They all died in agony. Real wrath of God stuff. The recon team then went into the headquarters of the camp. They found the leader. He had been skinned alive and nailed to the wall. The man was still alive when he was found. His voice cords had ripped because of the amount of screaming he had done. The only sound he made was like a screaming, breathing sound. Also, his genitals had been cut off, and he was made to eat them. He had vomited them out on the floor."

Julius closed his eyes and tried not to think about that image of a skinned man nailed to the wall.

"Three special forces members quit not long after that. The leader of the camp was taken to the hospital but died a few days later, I was told. My contact said that of the powers that he knew, it was Nathan who had attacked the camp. They were shocked at what happened but would do nothing about it. A terror cell had been removed. It would be used to make others think in their ways. I lost track of Nathan after that. But I heard that another terror camp had been hit. Same MO as the last one. Everyone dead. Same way too, but this time, it was around 30 terrorists dead. Both sites were burned clean. One week later, Nathan returned to Glasgow. I met him at the airport. He had changed. I could feel the rage and anger he was barely holding in check. It was like watching a volcano getting ready to erupt. That week, we buried his wife. I watched people drop roses onto the coffin as it was lowered down. Then Nathan dropped something. I managed to catch a glimpse of what it was before they began to put the dirt on top."

"Do you know what it was? It was a box. I then remembered that from the reports on both camps, every person killed had one of their fingers ripped off. But then again, all of them had body parts torn off. Now, do I think he put the fingers in the box? I don't know." David refilled his glass. "That's Nathan. I have no idea who he is. In truth, I don't care. They killed his wife, and they deserved worse. If it was really him that hit both camps, then what does that make him? One man slaughtering over 50 well-armed maniacs. And not even getting a scratch on him. It would take dozens of men to do what he did. Trust me when I say this, Julius, Nathan is a weapon. A weapon of mass destruction. Governments use him to topple other governments. Christ, he may have trained every special force on the fucking planet."

Julius drank the whisky. "Who the fuck is he really?"

"I don't care. He is my best friend. He is a man who gets the job done. I know his methods are extreme, but he gets results. He has saved my life on four occasions and the lives of many others. Do you know how untouchable Nathan is? Remember a few years ago, the prime minister was taken to the hospital. They said he had tripped and fallen down the stairs. He didn't. Nathan punched him and broke his eye socket. Don't ask why; you don't want to know. But Nathan walked out of Downing Street, and not one single security officer tried to stop him," David replied and filled the young man's glass again. "If Nathan is going to kill those three men tonight, then I guarantee you that they deserve to die, and there is fucking nothing you can do about it."

Nathan looked at the six dummies lying on the floor. Each had been placed exactly the same way as each victim had been found. He looked at the photographs to make sure each was right.

"Each victim was placed on their back and laid out like they would be in a coffin," Nathan said as he walked around the dummies. "Each one. Two had their hands clasped together. The rest of their arms are at their sides. Each victim's hair was patted down and away from their faces. This took time. Our killer took his time to get this right." Nathan knelt before victim 3. "Did he do this out of honour?"

"Maybe regret?" the doctor said.

"Regret. No, doc. If he had any regret, he would have stopped after the first victim. No. He laid them out in a respectful manner," Nathan replied. He stood up and looked at another set of images. "There is a clue here. I know it." He squinted really hard at one image. "Helena, bring image 46 up on the big screen." The woman pressed a few buttons on her computer, and the image was projected on the canvas screen. Nathan moved as close as he possibly could and squinted at a small section of the wall. "Victim 1 was found in an alley just off Buchanan Galleries. I want this area here enhanced," he said and pointed to a wall. Everyone saw some sort of marking on the wall. It looked like graffiti.

"Give me a second," Helena said as she tried to enhance the image. "Coming up now."

Nathan kept his head close to the canvas and watched as the image resolution improved. "Is that an O with a horizontal I inside?" he asked in general. Everyone nodded. "Use pattern recognition to see if this appears in any other images."

Helena started up the software and began the process. "It will take 30 minutes for it to scan all the images."

Nathan looked at the photo in his hand. The strange symbol was at her head. Something tugged at his thoughts. "Show me the images to her right and left. Also at her feet." Helena brought all of those images up on the screen. Nathan moved his hands across the canvas. Looking. Searching. Hunting. "There," he said, "according to this picture, i-dent this is her right side. And here. Her left side. And guess what? At her feet." Everyone saw something resembling the same symbol on each image. One on a bin. Another on a drainpipe. And one on a poster.

"What is this symbol?" Julius asked.

Nathan turned to face them all. "It's an old Christian symbol. It represents God."

"God?" David said.

"Yep. And look how it is placed. Head. Left and right. Feet," Nathan said and then began to bless himself. "Father, son, holy ghost, and amen."

"Bloody hell," said the doc.

"Our killer is into his religion," Nathan said and took the photos of another victim. "Fuck. I found an X on this one. It looks like normal graffiti. Shite. He gave us clues all the fucking time."

"And X stands for?" Alfonso asked.

"Christ. X stands for Christ," said Nathan. He wrote down symbols on a piece of paper and handed it to Helena. "Scan these into the system and get it to look for these images."

She looked at them. "OK."

"So, I have asked Helena to look for more symbols. I, Y, E and a fish," Nathan said and drew the symbols on the whiteboard. "I represent Jesus. In early Latin, Jesus actually starts with an I. Y is for son. E is for a saviour. The fish symbol represents the Eucharist and is considered part of the holy trinity. It is known as the Ichthys symbol. This is some very old religious shite. I am beginning to think our killer is not only insane but also believes he is doing God's work. Crazy fucker," Nathan said to them. "I'm going to ask you a very strange question, doc. What was the last meal for victims 1, 3, and 6?"

The doc grabbed his notes and read quickly, "Em, Victim 1 was some sort of cake. Possibly something sweet. Eh, victim 3 was bread. And victim 6 was similar to victim 1, some sort of cake. Possibly a bun."

"Shite." Nathan laughed. He used his hands to cover his eyes, and then he kicked a table, making it topple over.

"What's wrong?" David asked.

"13th December, Catholics eat St. Lucia buns. 5th February, they eat buns called St. Agatha's breasts. And on the fucking 1st of August, they eat bread called Lamas Loaf," Nathan replied.

"Those dates are the same numbers on that sequence," said Julius. "This is crazy."

Nathan pinched his nose. "I'm absolutely sure that we will find the remaining symbols on the other images. All placed head, arms, and legs."

The room went silent. Nathan went to his desk and took out the report on the plaster that was found on the victims 6 trousers. "Plaster of Paris is used to make statues. Religious status. It is called chalk ware." He handed the report to David. "The reason we couldn't find anything on the bodies, fibres, anything is because he washed the bodies. He washed them because he made fucking moulds from them."

"And you know this how?" the doc asked.

"Because the bodies were too clean. No scent of deodorant or perfume," Nathan replied.

"But the clothes showed no signs of being put on incorrectly. Everything was neat," the doc said.

"That's because he had help. We are not looking for one killer. We are looking for two. Two people can dress anyone and make it look like they dressed themselves. Ask anyone in the funeral business."

"This keeps getting worse," said David. "We have more than one serial killer."

"I would presume that one gets the victims and the other then kills them," Nathan said and walked over to Helena. "So, Helena, when you are out clubbing and have had a few drinks, who do you trust more when walking home late at night? Male or female?"

"Female. They are less threatening," she replied and sat down.

"Female. What female would think that another female would harm them or cause harm to them?" Nathan said to the room. "One of our killers has to be female. They set a trap and lured their victims in."

"In all the CCTV footage, we have been looking for men, not women," said Julius.

"Fucking bastard. Helena, bring up the data drive I got from the last victim's location," Nathan said. The video appeared, and Nathan watched the video. "Four times speed." Helena sped up the video. Nathan watched. "Stop. Here.

This woman has walked up and down this path four times. She did it in a 30-minute interval two days before the body was found. Play again, but skip to the next day. Stop. Here she is again. Same fucking time. Before noon. I want her image enhanced as much as possible."

"Quality isn't good at that distance. It will be difficult," Helena replied.

"Try!" Nathan demanded.

"How do you know it's the same woman? The image isn't the best," said David.

"Build, height. Hell, even the way she bloody walks. She walks slowly and keeps looking at the bank. She is looking at the bank as a predator would look at prey. It is what I would do. Nathan told him. He looked at Helena. "Play the night the victim's body was found. Same speed." Nathan watched intensely. He jumped up after a few minutes. "Got you, 'ya fucker."

"Where!" said Julius.

"Rewind and zoom in on the fence here," Nathan said. "See the shadow move through the tree line here. If I am guessing right, if this was a man, he would have to be over 7 feet tall to be seen like this from the CCTV angle. But he isn't that tall. He is carrying a body."

Everyone watched the playback.

"It's just a shadow. We can't get anything from the video. Not a chance," said David. "But at least we have something."

"David. Contact the archbishop and tell him I want a meeting with him tomorrow morning. First thing," Nathan said and took his jacket from the chair as his phone rang. He looked at the message on the screen. "Forgot about that for a moment. OK. I have to be somewhere else. OK, team, I want this video checked and re-checked for any clues. See if this woman appears again. Also, check every picture we have to see if more of these symbols appear. Alfonso, I want you to find any company in Glasgow that supplies Plaster of Paris to anyone in large quantities. It won't be bought via a person, but maybe a company, probably a few weeks before the killing took place. They may have bought some three months ago. Helena, do your best with the computer enhancements of this bitch in the video. The rest of you go through all the evidence again. Find anything of any religious significance. Baptism, communions. Anything. Find out their religion and what places of worship they attended."

Nathan put on his jacket.

"I take it you are going to visit Alessia?" David said to him.

"Someone has a big mouth," Nathan replied and looked towards Julius.

"Call it a lucky guess," David replied.

"Dickhead. OK, Julius. Are you coming with me or going to stay here and do some work?" Nathan asked him.

Julius looked at David. The man gave a slight shake of the head. "I will stay here and help the team. I don't think I would be any help to you tonight."

Nathan nodded. "That's OK. Trust me, you are probably better off staying here. OK, David, remember and call the archbishop. I want that meeting."

Alessia opened the warehouse door for Nathan.

"You are late," she said to him.

"I'm trying to catch a serial killer. I lost track of time. I was eating dinner. The traffic was bad. Take your pick," Nathan replied to her as he stepped inside the building.

She slapped the back of his head. "You're not that big; I won't hit you."

"You love me too much for that, Mother Bear." Nathan smiled. "I take it the three stooges are in there." He nodded towards another door.

"Yes. Unharmed like you asked," she said and closed the door behind them.

Nathan walked towards the other door and slammed it open. He saw three men tied to chairs that had been bolted to the ground. Matteo and his two brothers stood behind the seated men. Matteo was holding a poker in a gas-fired BBQ, the tip of the poker white hot.

"It is good to see you again, Alberto and Little Pippino," Nathan said to the other two men.

"Nathan. Mother said you were coming," Alberto said and walked over to hug him. "You lost weight."

"And you gained it, my friend," Nathan said, jiggling Alberto's stomach.

"Nathan, my big brother," Pippino said and looked down at the man. He stood a head taller than Nathan.

"Pippino. I heard you got married. I am sorry I couldn't come. Work kept me away," Nathan said, hugging the man.

"Chiara missed you. You know she loves you like a brother; she left an empty chair for you. But she understands. Your work takes you to faraway places. She told me to tell you that you are to come over for dinner anytime you want. She loves cooking. Mother is teaching her."

"I promise I will." Nathan looked at the three men tied to the chairs. "I take it the very angry-looking bastard is the rapist. The other two, who have pissed themselves, are his friends?"

"Yes," said Alessia.

Nathan walked over and leaned over to Viktor. "Viktor, today I was having a bad day. And then it got even worse when I saw your wife. That lovely girl you raped and beat up. So, I went from a bad day to a fucking bad day. But you. You started with a day you thought was good, but I can tell you, it will end really fucking bad. And you two cunts," Nathan said and rounded on the other two men, the force of his voice making the warehouse vibrate. "I have been told that you like to sit and watch. Tut tut." Nathan wiggled his finger in front of their faces.

All three men tried to shout, but their mouths were gagged. They all tried to break free of their bonds but to no success.

"Now, Viktor, you know this family. You know the reputation they have. Well, I can tell you that they are living saints compared to me; you should trust me on that. Also, you should know that Lucia is like a daughter to Mother Bear over there." Nathan pointed towards Alessia.

"So, if you think about it, you raped her daughter. And because of that, you in effect raped these three men's sister. But what you should really know is that woman behind me; she is a mother to me." Nathan shuffled over to Viktor and leaned forward. He spoke quietly, "She loves me like her own son. Probably a bit more. So, you raped my sister, and that I won't stand for. No. No. No." Nathan took his jacket off and handed it to Pippino. "Now you must face justice. Fuck. Not justice. Judgement. That sounds better, doesn't it?"

Nathan took a knife from his trouser pocket, the same knife he used on Jian's nephew. He flipped it open. "Now, if I left you to my three brothers here, they would beat you. Break a few bones. That would be all. But I want you to really, really understand this, Viktor, so please pay attention. Once I am finished with you, they will give you one hell of a fucking kicking. That I guarantee, and you will have wished that all you got was the beating. Oh, Viktor. You really have no fucking idea how bad it is for you. On a scale of 1 to 10, you are hovering at around 500."

Nathan began to cut off the man's trousers. Viktor struggled and tried to shout, but his legs were tied to the chair legs. "Now, about an hour ago, my brother Alberto injected you all with Viagra. Yes, the dick medicine. So, soon you will all be standing to attention." Nathan cut away the last of Viktor's trousers and underwear. He started on the next man. "Don't be shy in front of Mother there; she has seen all this before. She did bring up three boys, after all. She may be shocked at how small you are," Nathan joked. "Now, you two naughty men watched him rape and beat his wife. Lucia told me that you just sat there and laughed. Did it make you feel tough watching a woman get raped? Hmm. Well, speak up!"

Both men screamed and thrashed in their bonds.

"Can't hear you. You have to speak up," said Alessia as she slapped the back of one man's head very roughly. Nathan noticed that Alessia had turned her rings round backwards, so when she slapped the man on the head, the jewellery would hurt more and cut the skin.

"I'm sure they are agreeing with me. These big, tough, brave men have no fear. They don't even know what fear is." Nathan smiled at both men. They saw his eyes. They screamed.

A few moments later, all the men were standing to attention. Nathan put on latex gloves. "Fucking pathetic." He grabbed a chair and sat in front of Viktor. "I want you to understand here and now, Viktor. I asked Lucia what she wanted. I gave her the option. I could arrest you and make sure you spend a few years in jail, where I would guarantee that every day you would be gang raped. Every fucking day. Can you imagine that? You being forced to do something you don't want? I guess not. Oh, and don't worry. I know you are supposed to be some big, scary Russian with friends in jail, etc., etc. But you see those same people are shite scared of me. When I say jump, they jump. So, you would have no protection at all. In fact, I would make sure that they would be the ones to rape you. Every day."

Nathan patted the man's leg. "But I told Lucia that you would be out in a few years and that, more than likely, she would live in fear. So, the other option I gave her was for me to deal with you. She cried. Said she loved you, blah blah blah, so I told her why she should live in fear. She can be free of you. So she begged me to help her. And as a good brother, I am going to help her." Nathan grabbed the man's penis and squeezed. "So I am going to disarm you, Viktor." Nathan twisted, and the cracking sound bounced around the room. Viktor screamed. "I just snapped your weapon, Viktor. It's completely broken. So broken, in fact, that no doctor on the planet can fix it. You will never have a hard-on again. And just to make sure you understand that."

Nathan grabbed the man's testicles and sliced them off. He threw the bloody ball sack to the ground. He held out his hand, and Matteo gave him a red-hot poker. Nathan stuck it between Viktor's legs to cauterise the wound. Viktor thrashed so much that Nathan thought the man might break a few bones. "Viktor, Viktor, calm down. This happens to animals all the time." Nathan slapped the man's face a few times. "You know, when they no longer need their reproductive organs." The other two men were screaming. One shite himself. "Did you think I forgot about you two? I am shocked you could think so little of me. Here, you hold this for me." Nathan placed the still red-hot poker on one of the man's thighs, which caused him to scream in pain. "And you hold this." Nathan then stuck his knife into the other man's leg. Both men thrashed around.

Nathan took a syringe from Matteo and stuck it into Viktor's neck. "Pure adrenaline. Don't want you passing out on me now, do we? You have to witness what will happen to your friends here. You know, cocksucker and cunty face." Nathan moved his chair to the next man, the one who was trying to get the searing poker off his thigh. "And you must be Jürgen? You look like a Jürgen. So, what shall I do with you? Let me take that off your thigh. Silly of me to put that there wasn't it, you fucker? Why didn't you tell me it was burning you?" He slapped the man hard across the face. "Now, where was I? Oh, yes. Your punishment. You like to watch, don't you? Should I cut out your eyes? Well, I won't do that as I am trying to catch a serial killer who actually does that. So, no. You tell me what your punishment should be?" the man screamed.

Nathan leaned back. "Oh, I know you are sorry. But it is too late for that. I tell you what. How about I just cut off a few fingers? Maybe leave you your thumb and pinky." Nathan grabbed the man's right hand and placed it down against the arm of the chair. He leaned over and pulled the knife from the other man's leg. "Need to borrow this." He chopped off the man's fingers. He then grabbed the left hand and cut off the same fingers. He pressed the poker against the wounds. The hissing and smell of burning flesh filled the room. The man kept screaming until the poker was removed. "Now, like Viktor here, you are going to get a fucking kicking. Enjoy the rest of your day."

Nathan moved to the next man, the one who had shite himself. "And that leaves Isaac. Oh, Isaac, you have made quite a mess here." He tapped the man on the forehead. "Not very nice of you, is it? So, Isaac. You have seen what I have done to your two friends here. What do you think I should do to you? What punishment fits the crime?" Isaac shouted.

"You love jogging; did you say? Ah, well. That's what I will do then." Nathan leaned over and twisted Isaac's ankle with such force that man's foot was pointed in the opposite direction. He then did the exact same thing to the other foot. "You will walk using crutches for the rest of your life. I think you will agree that this was just, don't you?" Nathan said to the crying man. "Yes. Good. OK, you bastards, I would like to thank you for your attention this evening. You have been a wonderful audience. If you like to leave a review, then please make it 5 stars. It's a pension thing. You know, bosses always looking for the gold star. So I bid you a good night and stay safe. You hear me?" He winked at the men.

Nathan stood up and walked over to Alessia.

"Thank you," she said and handed him his jacket.

"I am sorry you had to see this," Nathan said and put his jacket on.

"I have seen worse. You are going soft. The old Nathan would have skinned them alive," she said as she looked at the three men.

"Maybe I am getting soft in my old age," Nathan replied. He looked over to Pippino. "They are all yours now. Beat them up good but leave them alive. A few broken bones will be forgiven. Dump them outside Viktor's flat. Then call an ambulance for them. Oh, and Viktor, just so you know, don't go near Lucia ever again. If you do, if you even think of contacting her, I'm telling you now, I will kill you. You have seen what I am capable of, but I will do much worse to you. Do you understand?" Viktor nodded groggily. He looked at the brothers. "Make sure Lucia does not see this."

"She is safe. I made sure of that. A friend is looking after her," Matteo replied and cracked his knuckles.

Nathan nodded. "Do you think you could make me something to eat, Mother Bear? I'm hungry."

Alessia stroked his face like only a mother could. "Nathan, I am really worried about you. Is everything OK?" She took his arm and walked him out of the room. When she reached the door, she turned to her sons and said, "Make it hurt. Make them understand."

Her three sons nodded and began the beating.

Alessia closed the door behind her and looked at Nathan. She took him inside the restaurant and guided him to a table. "Sit. I will bring you something nice."

She went to the kitchen and grabbed some food. Soon, she returned with some cooked rabbit, potatoes, mushrooms, and a bottle of whisky. She sat in front of Nathan and watched him eat.

"What's wrong?" she asked him.

"It's nothing. It's just the case. It's getting to me," Nathan replied as he cut into the tender meat.

"No. It's more than that. Even when I was a girl, I could tell when something was bothering you," she said and poured the whisky into a glass. She handed him the glass. "Please, let me know."

Nathan sipped the whisky. He dropped his head. "I miss her."

"Oh, my sweet child. I know. Oh, I know. She made you smile. She made you laugh. The two of you were so happy," she said. She took his hand. "I am always here to talk. You know that?"

"I know, Mother Bear. I know. I just have to work through it," Nathan said as he shoved food into his mouth.

"You come to me at any time. Day or night. My door is always open," she said. She poured herself and him a glass of whisky. "I miss her also. When you brought her to me that first time, I was so happy. You finally managed to find someone. The boys loved her right there and then. She was their sister, and she was my daughter. Even though you were at the time not married, I knew. I knew. A mother knows these things." She drank some whisky.

He sighed. "I'm just struggling. I wake up every morning hoping that this is all a bad dream. Or that I am about to wake up from a coma and she is alive and beside my bed." He looked at Alessia. "I'm lost without her."

Alessia nodded. "I know, my son. But she wouldn't want you to be like this. You know that. She would want you to move on and be happy."

"I was happy with her. But that's gone," Nathan replied.

"It will take time. Hell, I've known for more years than I can remember. I have seen you happy. But when you were with her, you were truly happy. In time, you will be again," Alessia replied.

Nathan shrugged. "I don't know."

"You will be. Trust your mother." She smiled. She looked out of the window and saw the restaurant's van drive away. "They are taking them home now."

Nathan continued eating. "I didn't kill them because she wouldn't want me to."

"I guessed that. Have you been to her grave?" Nathan shook his head. "Please go. Speak to her. Or just stand there. But please go."

Nathan nodded. He gave her a cheeky grin. "You are such a pushy mother."

Chapter 5

Nathan woke up on his couch. He looked at his watch. 6 am. He only managed to get a few hours of sleep. At least this time he didn't drink himself to sleep. He looked at his mobile through sleep-encrusted eyes. There were two messages. One was from David. He managed to get an appointment with the archbishop for 8 a.m. The second was from Helena. She had managed to find more images in the evidence pictures.

He sat up and turned on the laptop sitting on the small coffee table in front of him. Her image appeared on the user's screen. He smiled. She was beautiful.

He sighed and entered the password. Her image disappeared.

He looked at the email from Helena.

"The programme found the images you wrote down on various pictures. All were located at the head, arms, and feet," he read. "There was an image in which all symbols were together. This image was located with the first victim but not at the points of the others. It was found around five feet away. It was drawn with chalk on a single brick." He opened the image and saw. She was right. The five symbols within the sixth.

"Shite!" he said out loud and leaned back on the couch. He thought back and remembered what the symbol was once used for. Entire countries had burned because of it. "I am too old for this shite again." He picked up his mobile and ran through the contacts. He opened up the one he was looking for and sent a message. It was a very explicit message that got across his emotions quite well.

He then turned his attention back to the laptop.

"I ran the programme again and found no symbols on any other images. As for our mysterious woman, I am unable to improve the image by any degree to get an ID on her. I have called Glasgow University and told them I will be arriving around 9 a.m. to use their more sophisticated imagine-enhancing software. I am hoping that by early afternoon, I will have a clear image of the women."

Nathan was impressed. Finally, someone on the team actually working on their own initiative. Maybe he was rubbing off on them. He went to the bathroom and gave his face a quick wash. He had to look as if he at least tried to be presentable for the archbishop. He then went back to the living room. He walked to the window and opened the blinds. It wouldn't be long until the sun rose. Spring was right around the corner.

He looked out and felt something. That same feeling when he was at the river bank with victim No. 6. Someone was watching him. He looked around outside as if he was just seeing what was happening, but he was studying. He couldn't see anything out of the ordinary, but he definitely felt like he was being watched. The old skills were kicking back in. He could feel the eyes on him. He smiled. He was being watched. He walked back to the coffee table and wrote something down on a piece of paper. He grabbed his coat and stuck the paper next to the living room door.

It watched him from a distance. This was his home. It had tracked him to here. It sat and watched for many hours. It watched as the man opened the blinds. He looked tired. He looked old. He looked dangerous.

It froze.

The man's demeanour changed. He tried to hide it, but it was noticed. Did the man know he was being watched?

How could that be possible? It was well hidden. Many people had walked past and never noticed its presence. No. The man was just looking around now. Yes, it was safe. It watched him write something down. The man was getting ready to go somewhere.

It watched as the man placed a piece of paper on the door and left. It watched the man get into the black car and drive away. It waited for a while, then moved closer to where he lived. It looked at the paper.

"It's not polite to stare," was written on it.

The man knew he was being watched. He knew.

This man was very interesting indeed. This was going to be fun.

Nathan arrived at the archbishop's home. He took a drink from his flask. This would be interesting.

He rang the bell and waited. Soon, an old housekeeper opened the door.

"Nathan Andrews. The archbishop is expecting me," he said to the woman and showed his ID.

"Ah, yes. You are expected. Please follow me."

She took him to the drawing room. The archbishop was sitting behind a large wooden desk. A PC screen sat in front of him, and paperwork was neatly piled as well.

"Your reverence, Mr Andrews, is here to see you," she said to the bishop.

The man looked up and smiled. "Good morning. I am Archbishop Frost." He held out his hand.

The archbishop was in his early 70s and had thinning white hair.

Nathan shook his hand. "Thank you for seeing me at such short notice."

"Not at all. I am happy to help the police in any way I can."

Nathan took a seat on the other side of the desk. "You may not be saying that soon."

"Oh, and why do you say that?" Bishop Frost asked. He sat back down.

Nathan handed over a piece of paper with the symbols drawn on it. The bishop looked.

"Religious symbols. Old. Still used, but not very often," the man replied looking at them.

"Found with six dead women," Nathan said and leaned forward. "Each symbol found at the head, arms, and feet. Like a blessing." He then handed another piece of paper with the symbols within the fish. "First victim had four symbols plus this."

The archbishop looked at the two pieces of paper. "This is awful. Truly awful."

"It gets better. All the women were found with dates corresponding to the Fibonacci sequence. Even some of their ages correspond to it. Three of the victims have food in their stomachs, which also coincides with holy bread and buns, which again fall in with the sequence. Even their dates of birth fall into the sequence. I think you can see a picture forming. The sequence is also known by some to prove the existence of God."

The archbishop leaned back in his chair. "This is very disturbing. Very disturbing indeed."

"The police have asked before for all your records pertaining to the priest or other people who work for the church. You have been very forthcoming. But I need it all. I mean everything. All those secret files and folders that you don't want people to see," Nathan said to the man.

"Do you think a priest did this?" the archbishop protested.

"Truly, I don't know. I don't. But I need to know. All these dates fall under the auspices of the Christian faith. The Catholic Church looks upon the sequence with great intrigue," Nathan replied. "I need to see everything you have. I need to find anyone who was here at the beginning of the killings and then maybe was moved for a few years, came back, and then left again."

The archbishop stared at Nathan for a while. "There is no one that springs to mind."

"That's why I want the files. To double-check. To triple-check," Nathan replied quickly.

"But it has been. By the police and the church," Archbishop Frost replied. "I have checked myself."

"Archbishop, this is serious. I have a serial killer who has killed six women. He may kill again. I need leads, and so far everything is pointing me here. To this faith," Nathan said and took out his flask. He took a drink. "You know I must be getting soft. I haven't sworn once yet."

The archbishop smiled. "I am surprised also. I have been told about you, Mr Andrews. How was it put? Ah yes, a hurricane in human form." The archbishop leaned back in his leather chair, staring at Nathan. Studying him. "You are being very restrained, I must admit."

"Fucking tell me about it," Nathan replied and took another drink. "It must be too early for me. The brain not woken up yet."

"The reason I am saying that no one springs to mind is because I checked the records personally myself. Last night, in fact. I haven't slept, and I have a busy day today," the archbishop said and took out a gin bottle from his desk. "When I was told that it was you who asked for this appointment, I knew I had to check again. I remember the last time we were asked for the files. Even back then, I was astonished to think that any priest could be involved in this horrible crime."

"There is definitely a religious link to these killings, and they all point to this religion."

"Maybe they do, but they could have nothing to do with my religion. Maybe they are linked to another, but my religion is being used to cover it up."

"All religion is the same, Bishop."

"And what is that exactly?"

"You want my truthful answer or diplomatic?"

"Let's try the first one."

"It's all a crock of shite. The biggest money-making scheme in history. It's up there with gambling and prostitution in its money-making capability," Nathan replied, leaning back.

The archbishop smiled. "Dare I ask for your diplomatic answer."

"It's all a lie. People think they need to believe in something better than themselves. So, in ages past, people thought they could make something of it. They said that mysterious things lived in the sky and below the ground that required worship. If you did that, then when you died, you would be rewarded."

"Not very diplomatic of you, but I was told that you would not coat things in sugar to make them easier to swallow. There is a divinity that some people can feel. I truly believe in God. I believe that he loves us all," the man replied.

"Whatever gets you to sleep at night, Bishop?" Nathan said to him. "Philosophy aside, I still have a killer to catch. I need those records."

"And you shall have them. They will be delivered to you this afternoon. I pray to God that you find nothing, as I do not want anyone under me to be responsible for such a crime."

The archbishop watched Nathan drive away.

"I am surprised that you are here," the archbishop said.

"I am," a woman's voice replied.

The archbishop turned to face her. "It would seem that there is much I must still learn about you and the others."

"Yes," she said and walked into the room. "What did you make of him?"

"You can feel the rage. It is like pressure against the body," he said to her. "I felt fear. That man scares me."

"He hasn't changed much then," she said.

"Are you sure that he will complete the task?"

"No. But he will try," she replied. "No one has ever made him do anything he didn't want to do. Not even the bosses."

"That does surprise me."

"As it should. That man is what everyone fears. All sides. There is a reason for that. The last time something like this happened, many people died. Too many to count."

"And this is all we have? Surely, there must be a better option."

"No. He is it. The only one."

"Then may God help us if he fails." He turned to look at the women. "God help us."

Nathan stood at her grave. He looked at the headstone. He should have come earlier.

"I am sorry I haven't been here for a while," he said. "It's too painful. Just standing here hurts."

He knelt down and pulled out the weeds around the headstone. He put his forehead against the cold stone.

"You are mental"

"Well, are you coming in or not?" He said to her.

She stood at the bottom of the bed, fully clothed, ready for work. "You are mental; you know that."

"Call in sick. Say you have a 24-hour bug or something," Nathan replied from the bed. He had the covers up around his chest. "I haven't seen you in a week."

"I have work. I need to go," she replied, fixing her earrings.

"Well, someone may have sent a message to your work saying you are not well. And also sent a sick note." Nathan smiled cheekily.

"You didn't!" She replied, horrified.

"Wasn't me. You have no evidence."

"You just said."

"Anyone could have sent the message plus proof of a sick note. Just because I know doesn't make me guilty."

Her phone chimed. She went and read the message, "Hope you feel better tomorrow. Seriously." She looked at him and shook her head.

"Are you sick? You should have said. Come, lie down, and I will look after you," Nathan said and throw the bed covers back. "Come. Lie down."

"You have issues, you know that?" she said as she undressed. "So, doctor, what do I have?"

Nathan put his head on the pillow and started to speak, "From your symptoms, I would say missing Nathanitise. Not serious, but recovery time is 24 hours." He laid his left arm out across the bed. "Medicine is lots of hugs."

She slipped into bed and into his outstretched arm. She shuffled across and put her head on his chest. "Oh my. I hope it's not contagious."

"Not to worry, I am immune." He laughed. He hugged her tightly. "This feels good. Been a while."

She nodded. He stroked her beautiful red hair. "It does feel good," she said.

"Sorry, my work is keeping me away. So much to do, not enough hours in the day," he said.

"I know. This new job is taking your time, but it is worth it. You don't miss the old one, do you?"

"No, I don't. Don't miss it at all. I'm happy. This is the happiest I have been in a long time. A very long time. I don't have to work, but this makes me feel like a human being."

"Good. I know this is a big change, but it will be worth it."

"I know. It's not as if I need the money. I put plenty away. This is just to keep me occupied. I don't mind. I like it," he replied. He rubbed his eyes and yawned. "Just these long days are taking their toll."

"I know. Look. Why don't you ask for a transfer? They would do it for you. They wouldn't want to lose you. In the short time you have been there, you have been a big bonus to them. Hell, David keeps singing you praises," she giggled. "Think you have a boyfriend there."

Nathan smirked. "He wishes. You're the only one for me." He hugged her tightly. "I will ask."

"Good. So now, doctor, what medicine do you prescribe to aid me in getting over this terrible 24-hour bug I have? Hmmm?" she said. "Well?" She lifted her head and looked at Nathan. He was asleep.

She smiled and put her head back down on his chest.

Mental.

"I am sorry I fell asleep," he said with his head still against the headstone. "After all the effort I put in, I should have stayed awake."

"Talking to the dead, are we now?" a woman's voice said behind him. "Is that a new skill you have acquired?"

Nathan growled and stood up slowly. "I told you to stay the fuck away from me. I told your lot and theirs to fuck off."

"I think your exact words were, 'Stay the fuck away until the last atom in the universe stops spinning, and even then don't come fucking near me'." She replied.

"You haven't changed one fucking bit, have you?" Nathan stared at her. She stood about 10 feet away from him. Her long brown coat was tied shut. Her blond hair was down to her shoulders and fluttered in the afternoon breeze.

"And neither have you, no matter how much you try to hide it. You are still the same," she replied and walked slowly around him. "How have you been?"

"Like you don't fucking know. I'm sure one of you is still keeping tabs on me," he replied and crossed his arms. "Why are you here? You were told never to contact me again. Tell me, why I shouldn't smash you through one of these headstone? And it better be a good reason."

She smiled. "Straight to the point as always. I can see why you were his chosen. You know that the others were always jealous. I must admit that I was also. But he made his choice, and I supported it."

"I am losing my patience here."

"Well, I wouldn't want that. The last time you lost your patience, a certain conflict erupted and cost a few million lives, did it not?" she replied as a matter of fact. "Not good publicity for us."

"Stop messing about and fucking talk. After the warning I gave all of you, you must be fucking desperate to be here now. Aren't you scared that I will end your life? You know I will. That I can. Not even he could stop me," Nathan said and pointed to her. "Tell me now or fuck off."

She smiled. "Very well. You are needed."

"No."

"No! That's your answer. No."

"Not interested. Don't care. Fuck off. Take your pick."

"You can't be serious," she said in astonishment. "You are saying no to us. To us."

"I'm saying no to you all. Both cunts. No to you. No to him. And no to them," Nathan said and turned his attention back to the headstone. "I got out for a reason."

"And that reason is no longer here," she rebutted.

"Be very very fucking careful what you say, cunt," Nathan shouted. "You have no right, no right at all to talk about her."

"I have every right, as you well know," she replied. She stood on the other side of the headstone. "You know these things happen. There is no grand plan. That is what he wants. 'Well, wanted the last time I heard.' Things happen, whether for good or bad."

"I don't care. The one thing I truly cared for in this fucking miserable world is gone. Gone. So, let the fucking world burn for all I care. Let them fight each other for the few remaining ashes. I don't care. As long as you all leave me alone, then do whatever the fuck you want," he replied. He turned to walk away.

"It's to do with your case," she shouted. She looked at her fingernails. "Damn. I need to get these re-done."

Nathan turned around slowly. "You had better be winding me up."

"Nope," she replied and put gloves over her hands. "We have been tracking a few strange sightings across the spectrum. So upon further investigation, we found them gone. Six of them."

"You are kidding. They are protected. Sealed away. Can never be touched or seen," Nathan replied. He pinched his nose. "I take it your friends know nothing about this?"

"Well, they would say no. You know what they are like. Can't be trusted."

"And neither can you or your lot. Remember, you are all cut from the same fucking cloth."

"That's not very nice. Look. The six have been taken. You have six dead women. It happened roughly at the same time. Do the math," she said and walked towards him. "I have friends out looking for the reason why."

"Then you don't need me," Nathan replied and pointed to her. "This is your fucking mess. Not mine."

"This will soon be everyone's mess. The last time this happened…"

"The fucking last time this happened, I stood alone. No help from you or your fucking friends."

"Yes, I remember. We couldn't get involved."

"Couldn't or wouldn't? Fucking bastards, the lot of you. I stood alone for weeks. While you watched, I fought. I fought alone! Do you know how many I killed? How many did I send fleeing? You couldn't dig a pit big enough to fit them all in."

"You were the only one that could. We were not ready. Even now, we still are not ready. If it happens again, we cannot stand against it."

Nathan held his arms out in despair. "You're not kidding, are you?"

"No, I am not."

Nathan grabbed her by the collar and pulled her close, her feet off the ground. "Tell me, why should I fucking care?"

"Because she would."

Nathan roared into her face, and thunder followed.

Chapter 6

Nathan stood at the information desk at the university.

"Can I help you?" an old man asked.

"I'm looking for your image processing lab," he replied and showed the man his ID.

"Ah. Your college is still there, I believe," the man replied and began to print the directions. "Please follow this, and it will take you there. Have a nice day."

Nathan took the paper and took a drink from his flask. "There are no more nice days left."

Nathan walked through the university and watched as the students wandered around. He had been at the university a long time ago. He didn't really remember much, but he never enjoyed it. Full of lecturers who thought they knew the world better than anyone else. He had shown them. They didn't know everything. No one did.

He arrived at the lab and walked in. He saw Helena sitting at a desk. She looked tired.

"I got the message from David. What's the problem?" he asked her.

"It is taking longer to process the image. The lab leader is reluctant to let us use the lab's full potential. They are currently using all their processing power to analyse images of a distant galaxy," she replied and pointed to a young man hunched over a computer.

"Did you tell him that this is a criminal investigation? Did you say that's important?"

"He told me that this isn't a priority at the moment as they are halfway through this task. If they stop now, then someone in NASA will be pissed. Don't ask me."

Nathan wanted to shout but managed to hold his anger in check. "OK. I will deal with this."

"Should I stand outside?" she joked.

"Not yet," he replied. Nathan walked over and tapped the young man on the shoulder. He looked at him. "What's the problem?"

"As I told your colleague, we are at a critical phase of the processing of the images we received from NASA. All our computer runtime is being used in the analysis. I can only allow your image some run time," he replied.

"You do know that this image may lead us to a serial killer. You know, actual important tasks."

"This is important. Very important. It will help us understand the universe better."

"The universe does not give a shite if we understand it or not. Trust me on this," Nathan replied and took a drink.

"No food or drink allowed in this lab," the man said to him and pointed to a sign.

"Fucking arrest me then. Look, I know for a fact that you are not in charge here. So, go to that phone and call the person that is. Do it now or I swear you will become a fucking missing person case," Nathan said and sat down at a desk. He put his feet up and took another drink. "Do it now before I lose my temper."

The man looked flustered and rang someone. Soon after, a woman entered the room.

"I take it that you are the police officer who just threatened my lab assistant here?" she said as she marched to the desk.

"The one and the same," Nathan replied. "And who might you be?"

"Doctor Tracey Logan. I run this department. Look, I do not appreciate my staff being threatened. Not in any way. Tell me why I shouldn't have you removed?"

"Well, let's do this right then. 1, I am currently looking for a serial killer. This image may lead us to that person. 2, You cannot have me removed. I know the higher-ups, and they won't touch me. Trust me there. 3, Anyone who tries to remove me from this lab will end up in the hospital on life support, and when they are released from the hospital, I will have them arrested and thrown into the deepest, darkest cell on earth. 4, Look at 1, 2 and fucking 3."

"I don't believe you."

He pushed the phone towards her. "Call the chancellor and find out."

She picked up the phone and dialled a number. "Hello. It's Professor Logan. Can you please put me through to the chancellor?" She waited a moment. "Yes, hello, Chancellor. I have a police officer here. They are asking my department to process an image. They have been informed that we are currently using the system to process images for NASA. One of the officers threatened one of my staff." She listened on the phone. "Yes." She looked at Nathan. He raised his flask. "Yes, he looks like that. OK, I will ask. I have been told to ask you a question. What is the Alpha Ladder?"

Nathan laughed. "Fucking hell. That's easy. Alpha Ladder, also known as the triple-alpha process. It is a nuclear process by which massive stars convert helium into heavier elements. It stops at Nickel 56, as that process absorbs energy. Energy is released in the form of gamma rays."

The woman looked truly shocked. "How did you know that?"

Nathan grabbed his crotch. "My brains aren't here, sweetheart. Now, tell the chancellor to ask me a really difficult question."

She listened on the phone. "Yes, Chancellor. I understand. Thank you for your time." She hung up the phone. "The chancellor has told me to give you all assistance the that you require." She looked at her colleague. "We are to stop the image processing for NASA and finish the image for the police. Run it through all computers and filters." She looked at Nathan. "I hope this meets with your approval."

Nathan kicked the chair next to him so the professor could sit next to him. "Take a seat, doc." She sat down, and Nathan offered her his flask. "Drink?"

"No, thank you," she replied. "How did you know the answer to the question?"

"Simple. I helped formulate it," Nathan replied.

"Not possible. It was theorised in 1952," she replied in a mocking tone.

"I am older than I look. OK, you think this is some kind of trick. Ask me a really difficult question, then."

She looked at him. "OK. What were the dark ages?"

Nathan smiled. "I said a difficult question. OK. Dark ages. Period between 379,000 to 400 million years after the big bang. Two sources of protons: one due to recombination when neutral hydrogen atoms formed, and photons emitted when the electron flips itself to make it spin antiparallel to that of a proton."

Her jaw dropped. "How did you know that? How did you know I wasn't talking about the dark ages during mid-evil times?"

"In a university, near the physics lab. Do the math," Nathan replied, taking a victory drink. "Look, professor, I am intelligent. Very intelligent. I sat the Mensa exam and got 100%, and nobody gets 100%. They made me for sit six different tests, and I aced everyone. They believe my IQ to be well over 300. I have 27 degrees and five doctorates. But then again, I did them all in three years. I could have done more but got bored of them. I have more letters after my name than numbers in Pi. I have helped some of the most important scientists in the world with their work. Hell, I even helped Korea with its plasma reactor. I helped NASA reach Pluto. I even helped Mensa with the creation of new tests. When I say I am smart, I am not lying. I stay in the shadows. I take no credit for anything I help with. I prefer it to stay that way."

She looked at him in wonder. "You could help humanity in more ways than possible. You could lead a new golden age in science, engineering, and everything."

"Ha, why should I? Look at humanity. Do you honestly believe they deserve to survive? They look out into space, hoping to claim new worlds but destroy the only one they inhabit. They slaughter one another at a whim. They embrace greed and hate the poor. No, doc, humanity doesn't deserve to live. Humanity is slowly dying, and it deserves to. The sooner humanity is gone from the universe, the better."

"You can't honestly believe that? Humanity has done great good for the world."

"Only for profit and the benefit of a few. Look at America: someone with diabetes has to buy the medicine that can save them, and yet huge companies pay fuck all tax and give the top cunts tens of millions for sitting at a desk while getting a blow job from their secretaries. Russia has had a tyrant at its head for decades, and when the people tried to stand up, the rich, who benefited from the tyrant, they shot them. France, Germany, Poland, China, fucking every country shites on the poor and feeds the rich. Humanity kills every living thing in sight. Humanity fears what it does not know. Humanity fears each other. How many species are now extinct because of humanity? In the last 100 years, hundreds? Thousands? Humanity pillages and rapes the planet at a whim. Look me in the eyes and tell me humanity deserves redemption. No, doc, humanity is a fucking cancer that deserves to die."

"That is a very bleak but powerful statement. I don't believe it, of course. I have to believe that we are better than that. God has a plan for us," she replied.

"Fuck god. And you can trust me on this. He does not fucking care one bit about you or anyone else."

"I can't believe that."

"Up to you. But if you want one thing in your life to be 100% guaranteed, then believe me, it is this. God doesn't give a flying fuck at all about you or humanity."

She looked at him with questioning eyes and then grabbed the flask from him. "I don't know why, but I believe you." She took a drink.

"That's good, professor. Humanity is a waste of matter and energy. I can guarantee you that the world would be better if humanity had never existed," he replied and leaned back. He closed his eyes and snuggled into the chair. "Shouldn't be long until the image is processed. Think I will take a power nap."

The professor placed the flask on the table and stood up. "I will come back when the image is finished. I will go over the results with you." Nathan nodded. She walked out of the room. By the time she got to the door, Nathan was snoring.

"Inspector, inspector," Helena said as she shook the man awake. "Wake up; they have finished."

Nathan opened his eyes and looked at his watch. It had been just over an hour. "OK, Helena. You can stop shaking me now. I'm awake." He stood up and stretched.

"Your snoring was rattling the windows," Helena joked.

"Why, do you think I have no neighbours? Now, let's have a look at this photo," he replied and walked to the professor. "So, professor, what do we have?"

"The image is appearing now," she replied and watched as the image began to appear on the screen. "Due to the poor quality of the original, the image won't be crystal clear but should be enough to do the job. The programme sort of tries to fill in the blanks, AI intelligence, you could say. It is taught what should be in the gaps and process it. It's not 100% accurate, but close enough."

Nathan watched as the woman began to come into focus. She had short brown hair, by the looks of it. She had a pronounced nose, thin and long. She had a thin face. "So, who the fuck are you then?" Nathan asked as the image fully appeared.

"This is the best image we could process. After looking at the video, this was the only one that gave us a clear picture of her face," the professor said. "The computers filled in the blanks the best they could with all the information you provided. Times, dates, etc. to place the sun and shadows in the correct lighting effect."

"She looks European. Eastern. Not Russian. More from Ukraine or Romania. Late 20s, I would say. No, wait. Late 30s. Her eyes look older than someone in their 20s," Nathan said and printed off the picture. "So, this is our lead. This was the only person who was seen multiple times at the site where the body was found. We can use this image to see if she was near the last victim."

"That will be a lot of video and images," said Helena.

"And I don't think NASA will wait for us to process all that. They're already annoyed, and I've had a few calls from them already," replied the professor.

"Your lab won't be needed. Now, I know who to look for. I'm sure we can do this at the station," Nathan said to her. "I will show this image to a few bar and club owners and see if I get a hit. Helena, go and get some sleep. But before you do, swing by the station and give the picture to the team. Have them look for her in the CCTV archives. We may get a hit."

It was around 3 p.m., and Nathan was sitting at a bar. He had been to several bars so far, and no one knew the woman in the picture.

"Double Johnnie Walker blue. No ice," Nathan said to the woman behind the bar.

"Coming right up, sir," she replied.

"Not, sir. Fucking hate that shite. Nathan," he said to her and took out the picture.

"OK, Nathan. Someone having a bad day?"

"Bad fucking life more like."

"That bad, huh?" she said as she brought him his drink.

"Yip," he said and down the glass in one shot. "Another."

"Hell, it must be bad. That was £10 you just drank in under a second." She laughed.

Nathan put down £50. "Get yourself one while you're at it, if you are allowed, and even then, fuck it."

"My bar, I do what I want." She brought two glasses of whisky. "Thanks." She raised her glass. "So, what's the problem that is bringing you here and drinking?"

"Shitty life."

"The usual then. So, Nathan, what's this paper on the table?"

"Looking for a woman."

"Aren't all men?" She looked at the picture. "What did she do to deserve your attention?"

"Classified," Nathan replied. He downed the whisky.

"Interesting. She must be special." She took a drink. "Haven't seen her if that is going to be your question."

"You and a hundred other fucking people."

"I work days, not nights. Heh, Dean, come here a minute," she shouted to someone in another room. A man walked out. "You seen this girl?"

Dean looked at the picture. "Not sure. She looks familiar."

Nathan stared at the man. "Where and when?"

"Em, two nights ago. I remember her because she ordered a £100 bottle of wine. Drank it alone. That table over there. Was on her phone most of the time. Didn't talk to anyone that was here." He pointed. "She spoke with an accent. Thought it was Russian, maybe."

Nathan took his phone out and sent a message. "Dean, you are a fucking legend. Let me buy you a drink." He looked at the owner of the bar. "If you have CCTV, I need all the video from when she was here."

She looked at him and gave a cheeky smile. "I guess asking for a warrant is out of the question."

Nathan patted his pockets in mockery. "Seems to have been misplaced."

"OK, I get it. I will give you the tape. Dean, be a sweetheart and get the nice policeman his tape, please." She watched the young man disappear into the back of the bar. "Level with me now; who is she?"

Nathan downed the whisky. "More than likely a cunt."

She laughed. "You really don't mince your words, do you?"

"Life is too short. Give me another, please."

She took his glass and refilled it. Dean reappeared and gave her the tape. She turned and handed both to Nathan. "I hope that this will help you find her."

"I hope so too," he replied and drank the whisky. "Thank you." He put more money on the bar and got up.

"Well, you know where to find me if you have any more questions," the owner replied. "I guess if I want to contact you, I just dial 999?"

Nathan smiled and took out his wallet. He gave her a card with his details on it. "I can be contacted 24/7." He left the bar.

He arrived at the station and went straight to the incident room. He tossed the tape from the bar towards Julius, who caught it quickly.

"Two nights ago she was at this bar; find her," he said to the young man. He looked at Helena. "Did you find her in any other CCTV videos or images around the time our victims were taken?"

"I have our computer running her image, and so far, nothing. I don't think we will find anything about the first four victims. Too far back; she would be too young then. But for the last two, I think we may get hits," she replied. "It is a slow process."

Nathan nodded and then looked at David. "Did the archbishop deliver the files?"

"Yes, he did. Hundreds of them. I'm going through them now. I've split it into two piles. Who was around Glasgow at the time of the killing, and who was left in one pile? The other pile is those who came to Glasgow only around the time of the killings," he said pointing to the floor where the files were piled up. "So far, I am getting nowhere. None of them match the profile."

"Keep going. If you need more manpower, then get it," Nathan replied. He looked at the doc. "OK, doc, what good news do you have for me?"

The old man walked towards him and gave him several files. "Well, you were right about the food. All religious. After several further inspections of their clothing, I have found the same plaster that was found on our last victim. Small and was missed the first time." Nathan patted the man on the shoulder and smiled. "On a hunch, I have ordered their medical records. Don't know why I did but just had a gut feeling."

"Always trust your gut, doc," Nathan said and turned to his team. "For the first time since this bastard has been killing, we have leads. people. Fucking proper leads. Hunt them down. Let's find this prick before he kills again. The best clue we have is this cunt," he said, pointing to the woman's picture on the whiteboard. "I want her found. I want her brought to me. I don't care how you do it, but do it. Get me a location on her today. Someone knows who she is. Find her on the CCTV and trace her steps. Am I clear?" A yes sir rang out across the room. "Not fucking, sir. Told you all before. Good, then get to it."

He walked into his office and threw his coat onto the couch.

"That wasn't very nice of you," a woman's voice said.

Nathan ignored her and sat at his desk. "I threw the coat at you so you could take the hint. Get the fuck out."

"Can't do that; I am afraid," she replied and carefully placed his coat on the arm of the couch. "Orders. I am to stay with you."

"I told you at the cemetery to fuck off."

"Yes, I know, but what can I say? Here I am." She smiled back. She stood up and walked to his desk. She pulled back the chair and sat opposite Nathan. "So, what do we do now?"

Nathan growled under his breath. "Can you just not fuck off?"

"Nope," she replied and smiled.

"I have enough issues to deal with without you adding to them," he replied and took the whisky bottle out of his drawer. He unscrewed the cap and drank a big gulp.

"Does that actually help?" she said and pointed to the glass bottle.

"Are you a pain in the arse? Both answers are yes," he replied and placed the bottle on the desk.

She shook her head. "Never understood why they drink it."

"Water of life it is. Yesterday's rain is tomorrow's whisky."

"They are a strange bunch."

"You would never understand," he said and put the bottle cap back on. "Can't you really just fuck off? It's not like I am going to tell you that you weren't here."

"Doesn't work like that, and you know it," she replied and leaned back in the chair. "You're stuck with me." She watched as Nathan sat back and thought. She had absolutely no idea what was going through his head. He could kill her, and she would not be able to stop it. He was the most powerful being she had ever seen. She wasn't scared of him; how could you be scared of something like him? She was in awe of him. She had seen before what he could do. What he could do scared her. The last time she witnessed what he could do, she stood and watched as he turned the tide single-handedly. That scared her. Terrified her. She knew exactly what he could do; she had witnessed it. But she knew he wouldn't do anything to her. He couldn't. He wasn't like that. No matter what had happened to him while being here, he was still honourable. Maybe?

Nathan took out a coin from his drawer and flicked it up into the air. He caught it just above the table, snake-like. "Heads, you fuck off; tails, you can stay. I think that is agreeable, don't you?" She nodded. He opened his hand and looked at the coin. "Fuck me. Tails. Don't think I have enough alcohol to cope with this."

She took the coin from his hand and looked at it. "Luck was on my side."

"Not for me; it fucking wasn't," he replied. "Fine. You can stay. Just don't get in the way, or I will make you disappear. Are we in agreement?"

"Yes. You are in charge," she replied and placed the coin back on the table. "So what do we do first?"

"Come with me," he said and walked out of the room.

She followed him to another room and saw several people working with files and folder. A woman was sitting in front of a computer, analysing some images and videos.

"OK, ladies and gentlemen, this is Mary Aqua. She is an old friend who I have worked with before on several other cases. She will be working with us on these cases. Bring her up to speed on what we have and where we are at. She is here to help," Nathan said to the team. David looked at him, and Nathan just waved his hand in a way that suggested he didn't have a choice. "Does anyone have anything for me?"

Nathan listened as people gave him some new information.

Helena was about to speak when her phone rang. "Hello."

Nathan listened and asked questions when Helena waved at him, "What's wrong?"

"You have to take this call," she replied and clicked her fingers towards Julius. "I need a trace on my line now. He says we are looking for him."

Nathan grabbed the phone and nodded towards Julius to put it on speaker. "Who is this?"

A deep, inhuman voice came from the line, "You may call me Duke. Yes, that would be appropriate. Is this the police officer who has been hunting me?"

"This is Inspector Nathan Andrews, and I am hunting lots of arseholes. You need to be more specific," Nathan replied and looked at Mary.

"I watched you this morning. You were not that hard to track down. You should be more careful; there are very dangerous people out there. Wouldn't want anything to happen to you now, would we? The note you left me was very funny. You sensed me but could not see me. That was very interesting. No one has ever been able to do that before. You are special. I also watched you when you visited your old friend Hanz. Poor poor, Hanz. I'm sure the fire cleared his gift from this world, but I'm sure your police officer friends would like to know what really happened, hmm. Or should that remain our secret? I also saw you at my last gift site. You looked very professional."

"Well, it is not nice to look into other people's houses, but then again, pricks like you don't really care now, do you? As for Hanz, he had it coming, just like you do."

A deep, booming laugh filled the room. "You are strange. I haven't come across someone like you before. You have piqued my interest. You should be honoured. Honoured like the women who I took. The six gifts I left. The six beautiful gifts. You should have seen them. I made them beautiful. I made them worthy. And in return, they blessed me. They blessed me in my work."

"Don't flatter yourself, prick. You're just another psycho cunt who deserves the shite kicked out of him. Just wait till I find you. You won't be so happy then."

"I can feel your rage and your anger from here. It is so sweet. The ladies I took, they had no anger. Just fear. Fear of what they knew was going to happen to them. It was so invigorating. So beautiful. I have been doing this for such a very long time that it has become second nature to me. I hunt. I take what I want for reasons you could never understand."

"I don't want to fucking understand, you sick bastard. You honestly think you can justify anything you have done. You, fucking sick psycho. Oh, look at me; I'm killing women because they would never look at me because I'm a dick-less nobody. You, fucking bastard."

The caller laughed hard. "You are not very good at this, are you? Your anger is getting the better of you. I can feel it. It is very powerful. I wonder who you are? Who you really are? You're not a policeman; I know that now. You are special. Do they know who you are, I wonder? I suspect not."

"You really don't want to know how special I am, you daft prick. Anger, you have no idea," Nathan replied and looked at Julius. He was struggling to get a trace on the line. "I found the clues you left at the crime scenes. The symbols. Religious symbols."

Again, the laughter. "You, poor fool. You think they are clues. You really don't know what you are getting yourself into now, do you? What you call a symbol, I call freedom."

"Try me."

"I could, but would you understand? I think not. No."

"Then why the call? You just stroking your own little nob, trying to get yourself off? I bet you are having a wank right now, you sick bastard. The tweezers must be chaffing something terrible. Or are you desperate to be caught? Try me." There was a silence in the line, only breathing. "Oh, I am sorry, buttercup, did I touch a nerve? Well, guess what? I don't fucking care. You think this call changes anything? It doesn't. In fact, you have just pissed me off. The last time I got this pissed off was in 60, and it wasn't pretty. So, I want you to listen very fucking carefully. I will catch you, and I will fucking break you. There won't be enough left of you to fill a thimble. You want to play games; fine, I will play. Congratulations, cunt, you're a dead man walking."

The voice laughed hard. "Good. Finally, a challenge worthy of my skills. This is going to be fun. Your rage is so powerful. You must be extraordinary to keep it in check. I look forward to our meeting, but it will have to wait, for you see." Nathan stood rock still when he heard the groaning of a woman's voice over the line. "I have things I must attend to. You see, it is all coming together, and I have people who I must help. You know the deal: so much to do, never enough time. This young woman will help me with this given task. You should see her; she is so very beautiful. Yes, you are, aren't you? She would be considered a queen in many cultures just because of her beauty. But I must be going now. I shall see you soon."

The line went dead. "Hello, hello. Fucking bastard." Nathan roared and tore the phone off the desk and smashed it against it. He turned to Julius. "Did you get a trace?"

The young man shook his head. "He was using some sort of jammer."

Nathan roared and punched the concrete column in front of him. The column buckled under his punch and split in half, the metal rods snapping.

"That's enough, Nathan," said Mary and placed her hand on his shoulder. "Not now and not here."

Nathan looked around the room and saw the expression of shock and fear on his team's face at what he had just done with the steel-reinforced concrete column. He looked at his right hand. "The column was weak. Was probably about to break anyway." He turned to face his team, "That prick not only insulted me, but he also insulted you. All of you. And he now has something else. Someone who he is going to kill. I want the latest reports of missing women. Look for dates that fit the sequence. I want this animal found, and we can do that by finding her. Fucking find me here today. I don't give a fuck how you do it, just do it. This bastard is not killing another woman. Do you all bloody hear me?" They all nodded. He turned and looked at the column he just broke. "Weak piece of shite. Remind me to tell that idiot Christopher that we really need to renovate this place." He then walked out of the room.

Mary looked at the team. "You heard him. Back to work."

David watched as this new woman began giving out orders. He didn't care. He ran out of the room after his friend. "Nathan!" he shouted as he caught up with him in the hallway. "What was that in there? Let me see your hand."

"I am fine, just lost my temper a little," he replied as David took his hand.

"Not a scratch on it. What the hell?" David said in surprise. "You know I have never asked you about your past, but this may change things, Nathan."

"Look, I am fine, and that column was asking for it. Don't worry about it," Nathan said as he tried to make what happened look insignificant.

"That was a steel-reinforced column 30 cm thick, and you snapped it like a small twig."

"I am just stronger than I look."

"That's not funny. I am worried about you. And this friend of yours, Mary, who is she?"

"Like I said, an old friend. She can be helpful when she isn't being a total pain in my arse. Look, I'm going to get something to eat. I will be at Mother Bear's. Call me when you have something."

David watched as his friend left. "You know, Nathan, that I am your friend; you can bloody talk to me."

"I know, and that's why I'm not going to tell you. Better you don't know."

Chapter 7

Nathan drove from the station and headed towards the restaurant.

He thought about the phone call and what was said. In his mind, he tried to disseminate what the caller had said. Looking for any clues. Anything that gave away.

He shouldn't have gotten angry with the caller. He knew he shouldn't have, but ever since he lost her, he was losing control of it.

"I know who you are."

"What?" Nathan asked her.

"I think I know who you are," she replied. She sat across from him at the restaurant. She took a sip of wine. "I'm going to say the retired military."

"Close, but I have many jobs to my name," he replied.

"You have to give me a clue. We are going to be married, and I think I should know who the man was before I met him."

"I was a different man back then. Very very different. You changed me and for the better. Leave that man in the past." He looked around the place and saw that they were the only people in the place. It was still early, and the lunch rush would be soon.

"I will find out, you know. I'm not one to just let this go. You know that."

Nathan smiled and placed his hand on top of hers. "I know, and one day I will tell you, but not today. I love you, and for now, that should be enough."

Before she could reply, Alessia came to their table and clasped her hands together.

"Pippino told me that you were here. You should have told me. I would have prepared a special meal for you two. Shame on you, Nathan, for not telling me," she said to them.

Nathan stood up and hugged her. "I didn't want to put you out. You know I don't like the special treatment."

"It doesn't bother me. And you," she said, looking at his bride-to-be, "it makes my day to see you. My future daughter. I hope he is treating you right. If he isn't you, tell me, I will sort him out."

She stood up and hugged Alessia. "I will. I think he knows better than to mess with us two. He knows he wouldn't stand a chance."

"Yes, he does. You look beautiful." She stroked her face. "So beautiful. I am so happy Nathan has you. He actually smiles now. It has been so long since I saw him smile like he does when you are around. You have made my boy so happy. Not just him, but all of us. My boys love you. They can't wait until you become their sister."

"Thank you, Mrs Lorenzo."

"You call me mother. None of this Mrs nonsense. You are my daughter. I don't need to wait for the wedding to know that. How are the preparations for the big day?"

"Good. I am actually looking at dresses next week. I want you to come if you would like."

Alessia started to tear up. "I would be honoured. I only have boys, so I have never been out looking at dresses with a daughter."

"Then it's a date. I will pick you up on Tuesday, say at 10 a.m. I'm visiting several shops; so will it be a long day."

"I will be waiting with bated breath." She looked at Nathan. "You are very lucky; I hope you know that?"

"Yes, Mother Bear, I do. Every day," he replied, smiling.

Alessia hugged her and went back into the kitchen, shouting orders to her sons to get back to work.

Nathan looked at the front door and saw four men walk in. Right away, he knew something was wrong. The four men waited at the reception, waiting for the greeter. A young man approached them and took four menus from the holder.

"A table for four, gentlemen?" he asked.

The man closest to the door turned around and flipped the open sign to closed.

"Whatever happens, just keep close to me," Nathan said to her. She gave him a puzzled look, but he grabbed her hand and squeezed a little. "Stay close to me."

One of the men said, "We have been sent to give a message to one Alessia Lorenzo. Please get her." His accent was very thick and Eastern European.

'Shite,' thought Nathan. 'Albanians.'

"I'm Mrs Lorenzo. What do you men want?" Alessia shouted at them as she left the back room.

"We are here to make sure you understand that our boss is taking over. Your family no longer has the business. It is his now," said the lead man. He took a machete out of his trousers. "He said I am to make sure you get the message." The other three men took out their machetes.

"Do you think you scare me with them? Please. I have seen bigger. And tell your boss that this is still my business. He will have to go somewhere else. Maybe the middle of the ocean, with no water wings," Alessia replied and crossed her arms.

One of the men approached her and put the blade on her shoulder. "You should really listen." He turned and saw Nathan sitting at the table. He crossed over and placed his hand on her shoulder. "You wouldn't want anything to happen to your customers now, would you?"

"Get your hand off me!" she shouted and shrugged her shoulders until his hand fell off.

The other three men laughed. "You are losing your touch with women." One laughed.

The man turned and slapped her.

The other three stopped laughing as Nathan suddenly appeared behind their friend holding his machete, blood dripping from its edge. They watched as their friend's right arm lay on the floor, cut cleanly from his body.

Nathan spun around and plunged the blade down the man's left shoulder, splitting his heart in two. The other three men stood there at the speed of the attack. One of them regained some semblance of mind and ran at Nathan.

Nathan grabbed the man's falling arm and punched him in the throat. He then grabbed the choking man's face, lifting him up. He then brought the man down hard onto the ground, smashing his skull open. The other two men charged him. Nathan kicked out and smashed the knee of the man on the right, sending him crashing into the table. The second man swung desperately at him, and Nathan dodged the swings easily. He punched out and cracked the man's eye socket, making him scream out in pain. Nathan grabbed him by the wrist, twisted the machete back, and plunged it into the man's stomach. The man looked at him in terror. Nathan smiled and pushed the blade up in a flash and spilt the man in two. He turned slowly and saw the last man crawling across the floor. The man's leg was bent the wrong way. Nathan walked towards the man and leaned down to pick him up. Lifting him easily, he pulled his arm back to punch him. He felt someone grab his arm. He turned, ready to attack, but stopped when he saw her face.

"Please stop," she pleaded. Her cheek was very red, and blood covered her lips.

"They hurt you. They caused you pain," he replied with barely-controlled rage.

"Yes, they did, but I don't want this," she replied, not letting go of his arm. "Please." She caught a glimpse of his eyes and felt scared, but just for a fleeting instance. She stood firm and held his arm, not wanting to let go. She now understood him. She now knew why he kept it from her. She now knew him.

"This is who I am. This is the real me," he said, turning back to the man he was holding up in the air. "This is what I do. He must die for what he did to you. He must suffer." He looked at the man in the eyes and saw the sheer terror held within them. He squeezed his hand ever so slightly and could hear the facial bones begin to crack. "Look away. You do not want to see this. This is who I am. I am this man you see before you once again."

"I don't love you for what you think you are; I love you for I know who you are," she said with tears streaming down her face.

Nathan turned back to her, and the rage fled his body. She was crying. He made her cry. He felt awful. Her face was not meant for tears. He let the man drop heavily to the floor. He hugged her. "I am so sorry you saw this."

She hugged him back. "I don't care who you were before I met you. I know who you are, and that wasn't you."

Nathan fell to his knees before her. "I have lost you, haven't I?"

She knelt with him. "No, you haven't. I love the man you became, not the man you once were." She lifted his face so she could look him in the eyes. "I know who you are."

"I know who you are."

"Who am I really?" he said as he looked at himself in the mirror. "Even when you saw what I was, you still stayed with me. I didn't deserve you."

Nathan came back to the station with bags full of food. Alessia came with him to help.

"Alessia has been kind enough to cook all this for us. Eat up. Trust me, you won't get a better meal in your life," Nathan said as he placed the bags on the table and began to empty them. "OK, people, help yourself."

Alessia began handing out knives and forks, along with napkins. "Eat up. You all need your strength. Nathan has explained what has been happening, and if I can help by cooking, then I will cook. While you are here working on this, you call me, and I will make sure you are all fed three times a day. No matter the time you call. You all understand?" She saw them nod as they tucked into her meals. She smiled as she saw them all enjoy the freshly cooked lunches. "Good. Now, does anyone need a drink? Julius, you look like a man who needs a drink." She walked over to him and placed a bottle of Irn-Bru on his desk. "Now, who else needs a drink?"

Nathan watched Alessia walk around the room, giving his team whatever they needed. He tucked into his lasagne. It was delicious. Alessia really knew how to cook. He saw his team eat the meals, and they too were enjoying them.

But the doc and Helena were missing.

"Where are the doc and Helena?" he asked David.

David swallowed what he was eating. "They went to check something. Said they would be back soon." He waved at Alessia. "Alessia, this is amazing. Marry me," he joked.

"You are already married, David, but I accept the compliment," she replied, throwing him a can of juice.

"I will call Helena and see where they are." He took his phone out and began to dial her number. "Voice mail. Helena, it's Nathan; call me please." He hung up.

"Must be important if the phone is turned off," said Julius.

"Nah, must be somewhere there is no signal," Nathan said and ate another piece of lasagne. "Does anyone have anything new? It's OK. You can speak in front of Alessia."

Mary stood up and walked to the middle white board. "We have three missing women who have dates corresponding to the sequence. I have asked for the files to be sent down from missing persons."

Alessia turned when she heard Mary's voice. "You! It has been a while, hasn't it?"

"Yes, it has," she replied. "You have gotten older."

"And you're still a bitch, it seems." She turned to Nathan. "You didn't mention her."

"It was more fun this way." Nathan smiled cheekily.

"I am here to help, I assure you," Mary said to Alessia.

"You said that the last time, and I remember what happened then also. Be warned: I am not that girl you knew before. It was I who picked up the pieces last time. You hurt my boy here, and I will hurt you back."

"Yes, I can see you have changed. Nathan sure knows how to pick his friends."

"I am family; he is my son. This is the only warning you get." She approached Nathan and whispered, "You can't trust her; you know that."

Nathan shrugged. "Maybe, but I can't do anything about it now. Coin toss, and she won."

"You serious?"

"Yip."

"You are an idiot; you know that, right?"

"Maybe, but right now, I will take all the help I can get. But I will keep an eye on her. Plus, our old friend is on his way."

"You don't mean…"

"Yes. He will be here tomorrow evening. It has all been arranged. I need Matteo to pick him up and bring him here." He handed her a slip of paper.

She opened it and read its contents. "OK. I will make sure it's done. This is a big list. I will struggle to get this by tomorrow."

"Just do what you can. If it's not all there, then it's fine. He will have to make do," he replied between mouthfuls of food.

"I can't believe he is coming here. Wait, if he is coming, then does that mean…?"

"I don't know, but with Mary here then maybe. I'm not taking chances. Plus, if anything happens to me, he will make sure you are looked after."

"Nothing will happen to you. If you think he is needed, then surely it must be them then. I thought this was all finished with."

"Apparently not. Seems it never ends."

She nodded. "OK, I will go back now and do what I can before he arrives." She picked up her bag, and before she left, she turned to Mary. "I will be watching you."

"That's you been warned then, eh?" he said to Mary and turned to his computer. "Looks like missing persons sent the files. OK, let's see what we have."

He opened the first file. "We have 21-year-old Samantha Lily. Went missing five weeks ago. She was on her way to the university. Born 17 January 2000. No2 is one Ruth Upton. Date of birth is 8 May 63. Went missing five weeks ago while coming back from the gym. And last is Jessica Richards. 21. Born 1 March 2000. Reported missing after a night out with friends one week ago." Nathan leaned back in his chair. "They all have numbers in the sequence. Jessica fits the profile more than the other two. She was reported after a night out. Three of our victims follow the same pattern."

"We should check all three just to be on the safe side," said Alfonso.

"Yes, and we will. But No3 is who he has. I'm sure of it," Nathan replied. "She fits the profile. Let's get a hold of everything we have on her. Get a list of everyone she was out with. I want them questioned. Get the CCTV from every bar and venue she was at. Don't bother asking nicely; just get them."

The door burst open, and Helena ran in. "I think we have him."

Nathan stood up and walked towards her. "What do you mean?" He turned as the doc entered the room, out of breath.

"We have him, I am sure," the doctor wheezed.

"OK, calm down. Get your breath back and explain slowly, please," Nathan said, giving the old man a chair to collapse on.

"It was the medical records. It was staring me right in the face," the doc said between gulps of air. "Bacterial Vaginosis and Mycoplasma. It was right there."

"Doc, you need to explain to everyone here that hasn't gone to medical school. What the fuck you talking about?" Nathan said, giving the man a drink.

The doc took a big drink. "Each victim was treated for these infections. These infections are most commonly associated with women who have had abortions." The doc smiled. "Each woman had an abortion at some point in her life."

"When the doc showed me, I checked where the women had been treated. Three clinics treated the women, two women at each," Helena said as she sat down at her desk. She began to use her computer and brought the information up on the big screen. "I used the dates the doc provided and cross-checked the people working there around the times of the abortions. One name popped up. Thomas Thorn. I called all three clinics and asked for his information. The first two didn't have anything, as all records were destroyed. Apparently, once a doctor leaves, they destroy the records to ensure their privacy. But the last clinic did have something. Mr Thorn no longer works there. He handed in his notice about two weeks ago. Apparently, someone removed his files from their records, but they found one piece of paper with his details on it. No photo, but the name of his spouse, apparently. Larysa Thorn. Born in Romania. 37 years old. Moved here 13 years ago."

Nathan stood up and walked towards the screen. "Now, you can give me the really good fucking news."

Helena smiled. "I contacted central banking and got her details, address, etc. I tracked her bank cards to the exact same locations as the last two victims. Where they went, she followed. I also scanned the CCTV for her." She brought a pic of the woman up. "I found her in dozens of videos and images. Where they went, there she was."

Nathan looked at the woman. She had long black hair, flattened down to a ponytail. Her features were definitely Eastern European. "Got you now, bitch. What about Thomas?"

"All accounts closed and money removed from them. The trail is cold, but hers is still warm. I have tagged her cards, and if she uses them, they will be flagged," she replied.

"We are so close now, people; let's not fuck this up now," Nathan said and smiled at Helena. "Fucking excellent work from the both of you. Excellent. Now, we have something concrete to work on," he said and picked up the phone on his desk. "Hello, it's Nathan. Get Christopher down here right now. I don't care; go in and tell him to get his arse down here." He hung up.

"Right, here is what we do now. Find anything you can on Thomas Thorn. DOB, place of birth, age, what he looks like, anything you can."

He looked at Mary. "You concentrate on Mrs Thorn. Find her for me now." Mary nodded and left the room. "David, I want you to sign out the party poppers for all of us. It might be needed for when we find them."

"It will need his permission. Christopher has to sign off on it," he replied.

"And I will get it. Speak of the devil," Nathan said and turned as Christopher walked in with another man and woman behind him.

"Who was that woman who just left?" Christopher said to Nathan.

"She is with me. OK, Christopher, we may have just cracked this case," Nathan said and showed him the large screen. "Thomas and Larysa Thorn."

Christopher looked at the screen. "What makes you so sure this could be your criminal?"

"Each of our victims had abortions at some point in their lives, and Thomas worked at each clinic around the time it happened. This bitch has been seen following two of our victims all over the place."

"You seem very certain of yourself," said an old man standing behind Christopher.

"Chief Constable Richard Peirce and Deputy Chief Constable Angela Rice," Christopher said, introducing the two behind him.

"Well, chief, this is what I do. I hunt down the bad people and make sure they get their fucking coming justice," Nathan replied to the man. "I don't sit behind a desk with a pen. I actually work for a living."

"Jesus, Nathan," said David with his head in his hands.

The chief constable looked Nathan up and down. "I may sit behind a desk now, but I still remember what it was like to walk a beat. Christopher had warned me about you on the way down. I can see now that he was not exaggerating. This special branch operation doesn't really exist on paper. You have been described as a thug, no better than, how was it put, a rabid animal ready to kill at the slightest whim."

Nathan looked at the captain. "I'm way worse than he described."

"I can see that now," the chief constable said and turned towards his deputy. "What do you think, Angela? What do you think of this man? Is he the thug he was made out to be, or is he something else?"

The woman nodded. "I think he is a man who gets things done no matter what. I think if there is an obstacle in his way, he will break it down. He has a reputation as a man who would take a sledgehammer to break an egg. A reputation that is well deserved, by the looks of it. He doesn't care for rank and talks his mind. Even if it includes swearing. He is friends with some very shady people, criminals of varying degrees. The most powerful criminal organisations fear him. His files are so classified that I doubt there is anyone left alive who has the clearance to read them. He is a danger to himself and everyone around him. I wouldn't have them in my police force. To ruff around the edges and has no care for the law. Too dangerous. But he is what we need, even if it is off the books. I think bringing him on the case again was the best thing we could have done."

"Good. You haven't disappointed me, Nathan. I have examined the work you have done for us before, and I am very impressed with the results you have achieved. I got my rank through hard work and breaking the rules, too. I wasn't born into wealth; no, I was born in an Easter house. I know poverty and the injustices that can happen. I know how bad it can be out there; I remember it very well. To tell the truth, I think we need more people like you on the force. Men and women who will do what is needed to be done, even if that means cracking skulls and pissing people off. Well, Nathan, you have my blessing to go after this lead in any way you see fit. I don't want any paperwork on how you get this done, but get it done. If people complain, then to hell with them. This has gone on long enough, far too long." He looked at Christopher, shaking his head.

Nathan smiled. "I like you."

The chief constable laughed. "Ha, I like you too. What do you need from me since I am here?"

"I don't know what we will be getting into, but I don't want to go in naked and up shite creek without a paddle. I need the party poppers."

The chief constable nodded. "May I use your phone?" Nathan nodded. The chief constable picked up the phone. "Yes, this is Chief Constable Pierce. I want the forms sent to unlock the armoury sent to the incident room in five minutes. What? Yes, all of them. You have five minutes." He hung up.

"I think you have a new best friend," David said behind him.

"About time someone higher up was on our side," Nathan replied and took the flask out of his pocket. "Drink?"

"Don't mind if I do," the chief constable replied. He sat down on the edge of the desk. "How did you find these people?"

"For that, chief, I will let Helena and the doc explain," Nathan said and handed over the flask.

Chapter 8

Nathan, Mary, and Julius pulled up at the house that was on record as the abode of Mrs Thorn. The four-bedroom house was at Ayton Park in East Kilbride. The white building was slightly pale orange because of the street lights.

"Alfonso must be swearing right now," gloated Nathan. "Told him that the house wouldn't be in the city centre."

"You are such a gracious winner," Mary said to him and checked her gun.

"Blah blah blah," Nathan replied and loaded his gun. "No lights are on in the house, but that doesn't mean that he and his whore are not in a bedroom raping each other. Mary, take Julius and scout the back. I will give you the signal to move in. I want it done quietly. No sound. I want them alive and all parts attached. I take the front."

They all nodded, and Mary moved quietly to the back garden. She jumped over the fence with the help of Julius.

Nathan crouched low but moved fast to the front door. He pressed himself against the wall next to the door and peeked through the window. No lights were on at all. He couldn't see any shoes or other footwear near the door. Not a good sign; this was looking more and more like no one was home.

'*Nothing*,' he thought.

Nathan tried the front door. '*You never know*,' he thought to himself as he hoped it was unlocked. No luck. It was locked. He gripped the handle and pulled it down. It resisted. He pulled harder and could feel the internal mechanism begin to give way. Finally, the handle gave in, and the lock fractured inside.

Nathan cupped both hands together and placed them on his lips. He blew hard and it made the sound of an owl. A second later, the same sound came back. Mary was ready.

Nathan counted to three and slowly opened the door.

He crouched inside and swept the area with his weapon. He clicked his tongue and heard a click from the somewhere in front of him. Mary was in.

Nathan moved forward slowly and saw a dining room to his right. He glimpsed inside. Nothing. He moved forward again and saw the living room. There was only one padded chair in the room. Nothing else. No table or TV. He moved forward again and came upon the stairs. He knelt at the bottom of the stairs; gun pointed up.

Mary and Julius moved slowly towards him. Mary shook her head to indicate that she had found nothing.

Nathan nodded and gave the hand signal. *I'm moving, Mary, cover, Julius, follow.*

Mary placed her hand on Julius's shoulder and nodded towards the other side of the stairs. Julius moved and aimed his gun up the stairs.

Nathan moved slowly up, using his foot to test each step. He could feel Mary behind him.

He reached the top landing and saw five doors surrounding him. He clicked his tongue again and moved to what he knew would be the main bedroom. Mary moved in behind him. He saw Julius reach the landing and crouch low, guns pointing at the door.

Breach and cover. No kill shots. Nathan signalled. He saw Mary nod.

He put his hand on the handle and turned it slowly. Thankfully, it never creaked. He slowly opened the door and looked inside. It was indeed the master bedroom, but it was empty. The bed was made.

He nodded to the others, and each went to a door. They slowly opened and looked in the rooms. They were empty. No one was here.

"The house is empty. No one is here," whispered Mary, just in case someone was hiding.

"They must have moved on by now," Julius said quietly.

Nathan looked around the master bedroom and saw a picture of a woman on the bed side table. It was the wife. No pictures of the husband. He opened the wardrobe and saw several skirts and shirts hanging up. No men clothes. There was nothing here to show that a man lived here.

He growled a little and grabbed the picture frame from the table. "Find any evidence you can," he told them. "Mary, you inspect the loft. Julius, this floor, I will take downstairs after I check this room."

He watched them leave the room. He went to the ensuite and turned the light on. Only female toiletries.

He went back to the bedroom and looked around again. He caught something on the carpet next to the window. He knelt down and saw three impressions in the carpet. He touched them. They were circular and deep into the carpet. Something was here long enough to leave an impression onto the carpet as it had set around it. Whatever it was, it was large and heavy. He could feel something else, something that contained power. Whatever was here, it must have been some sort of vessel. Or maybe something else.

He went down the stairs and looked around the kitchen. He opened the fridge and saw a few food items and milk. Nothing much.

"I think that only the female lived here," he said to Mary as she entered the kitchen.

"I believe that also. I have found no pictures of the husband. Nothing," she told him. "The house is very bare. One couch, one table, a TV in one of the rooms upstairs, and one bed." She took a seat at the table in the kitchen.

"This could be a safe house?" he said and opened the cupboards. Again, they were also empty.

"There are signs of someone living here, even if it doesn't look like it," Julius said to them as he walked into the kitchen.

Julius placed a book on the table.

Nathan looked at it and read the title. "History of Glasgow," he said out loud.

"There are dozens of these books upstairs in one of the bedrooms. Some look really old, some new. I brought this one down as it has a label sticking out of one of the pages," he said to them and opened the book to the page. "Glasgow on its history of the occult."

Mary leaned over and leafed through the pages. "This speaks of the witch trials in 1697. The Gorbals Vampire. Edward William Pritchard. The Glasgow ripper."

"Dark crimes," Julius said and sat beside her. "Why would anyone want to read up on this horror?"

"Maybe it wasn't her," Mary said.

"How many books were on this stuff upstairs?" Nathan asked.

"They are all about Glasgow. Six of them are like this. They speak about crimes or criminals linked to Glasgow," he replied. "The occult is in a few of them."

"But who was studying them? Him or her?" Mary asked out loud.

"Doesn't matter. When we find them, we can ask," said Julius. He turned to Nathan. "We could ask the neighbours if they know anything."

"Good idea."

Nathan tapped on the door of one of the neighbours. The others were at other houses. A young woman opened the door. "I am detective Nathan Andrews." He showed his ID. "I want to ask you a few questions about your next-door neighbour. Have you seen them recently?"

"No. Not for a few days at least. There is a woman who lives there. She keeps to herself. Once in a while, a man comes along. Don't know who he is. She keeps to herself," she told him. "Don't know anything else."

"Can you tell me roughly the last time you saw anyone in the house?"

She leaned against the door and thought hard. "Two, maybe three days ago. I saw the woman leave. Think her name is Larysa."

"Eastern European?"

"Yes, I think. She does have an accent."

"Anything you can tell me about the male?"

"Have only seen him from a distance. Maybe 6-feet, black hair. Well-dressed each time. No facial hair."

"Accent?"

"Never heard him talk. I have said hello a few times, but he never replies or even looks at me."

"Thank you very much. You have been helpful," he told her. She nodded and closed the door. He walked back to the street and watched the others approach him.

"Nothing. They all say the same thing. Only seen a man a few times. The description is always the same. Apparently, Mrs Thorn doesn't spend much time here," Mary told him.

"Julius, call this in. Have forensics go over the house. They will find fuck all but we may get lucky," Nathan said. He saw Julius take the phone out of his pocket and speak to someone at the head office. "They took something from the house but fucked if I know what it was. Something big and heavy."

Nathan cursed that no one was at the house. He truly wished that they had been there, but his luck wasn't playing the game.

"We have a ping on her card!" shouted Helena to grab everyone's attention.

"Where?" Nathan asked.

"Buchanan Galleries, Boots."

"Bring me up a live feed of the gallery now." Nathan looked at the big screen and looked for her. "There." He pointed. "Just leaving. Track her. Julius, come with me. David, keep her sighted at all times. Keep me updated with her movements." Nathan grabbed his coat and ran out of the room, followed by Julius. Nathan ran through the building and out into the car park. He opened the boot of his car, put on a bullet-proof vest, and tossed it to his young colleague. "Put it on and take the FN five seven; no that one there." He pointed. "I will take the SIG." He slammed the boot down and jumped into the driver's seat. "Stick with me and do exactly what I tell you. No fucking around, you hear me." Julius nodded beside him. "Good. You hear me, David?" he said into the radio speaker hanging from his collar.

"Yes," David replied. "She is walking down Buchanan Street now. Looks like she is window shopping."

"We will be there in ten minutes. Keep her in sight," Nathan said and raced out of the car park. He turned the car's siren on. The Audi's powerful engine roared as he slammed the accelerator down. "I hope you know people who can take care of a speeding ticket for me, kid."

"The speed you are going, I doubt it," Julius replied as he grabbed the hand hold above his seat. He held tight as Nathan drifted the car around a corner. "Jesus, calm down."

"Ha, young pup. This is the thrill of the hunt. No calming down now," he replied, weaving in and out of traffic.

"She is standing outside Princess Square. Looking at something," David told them over the radio. "Crap, she's going in. Helena, switch the feeds. Do it now before we lose her."

"Keep a fucking eye on her!" Nathan shouted as he slammed down on his horn to warn people to get off the road. "Shite, looks like we need to drive down the bloody street; hold on," Nathan told Julius as he drove down the pavement on Gordon Street. "Fucking move!" he shouted as he kept pumping his horn. He twisted the wheel hard to the right and brought the car back on the road. "Crap." He slammed on the breaks before he crashed into road works. "Fuck it. Get out," he said and jumped out of the car. He slammed the door shut and locked the car. "Follow me." And he ran away for the car.

Julius followed him, struggling to keep up the punishing pace. Nathan seemed to run faster the closer he got to the shopping centre.

"What's her location now?" Nathan said into the mic. He wasn't even out of breath.

"Ground floor. Location at the centre map. OK, she's leaving and heading towards the escalator," David told them.

"Hurry up, Julius!" Nathan shouted over his shoulder as he entered Buchanan Street. He ran down the street towards the shopping centre. "Contact the security personnel and inform them that we are effecting entrance to the building. Lock down the place quietly. I don't want her spooked. Tell them that all exits are to be manned as of now."

"Alfonso is on the phone with them now," David said as he changed the camera view. "She is now on the first floor and entering a clothing store. The right-hand side of the escalator."

Nathan skidded into the entrance of the galley; he turned and waited a few seconds for Julius to catch up. "Right, kid, follow me. Cover me. You know what she looks like. We approach cautiously. If you have to defend yourself, then shoot her leg to bring her down." Julius nodded and they both entered.

"Cover is 10 minutes out. I have armed teams converging on your location now. Don't do anything stupid until they arrive," David said over the radio.

"Sorry, can't hear you; you are breaking up," Nathan told him and made static noises. "There's the escalator." He pointed.

They both went up and saw the clothing store she entered. Nathan nodded and entered. "Stay here, in case she leaves."

Julius stopped and went to the bannister that overlooked the bottom floor. He leaned against it. He kept watch at the entrance.

"Nathan, Nathan, can you read me?" David said over the radio.

"He went into the store," Julius replied.

"Shite. The signal must not be getting through to him. Julius, she is now on the second floor. The store must have had two floors. She is right above you now. You have to move," David told him.

"Hell," the young man said and ran towards the escalator. He ran on and looked around on the second floor. "I have her. She is moving along the walkway."

"I can't get a hold of Nathan. You have to catch up to her."

"I understand," Julius told him and ran off the escalator. He ran across the floor towards the walkway. "Larysa Thorn, drop your bags. Do it now, then lie face down on the ground with your hands behind your head." He approached her slowly.

The woman turned around slowly. "And why should I do what you have asked?" Her voice was sultry and intoxicating. "I have done nothing wrong."

Julius felt strange. "Get down on the ground now." He shook his head, trying to clear his mind. He placed his hand on the grip of his pistol. "Last warning."

"Tut tut, young man. That is no way to talk to a lady." She walked slowly towards him and dropped the bags at his feet. "Where are your manners?"

Julius felt drunk; he was swaying slightly. Her voice was so mesmerising. "I am an officer of the law," he slurred.

"Oh, what a brave one you are. Detaining poor, defenceless woman," she replied and walked around him with her hand on his shoulders. "Are you sure you have the right woman?"

Julius struggled to answer. He felt so strange.

"You should let me go. I'm not who you are looking for," she said with a sugary smile.

"I don't know. You may be right," Julius replied, almost out of energy.

Nathan left the store on its second floor to the screaming of David in his ear.

"Nathan, fucking answer!" David shouted.

"I am here. What's wrong?"

"Julius is with our suspect, but something is very wrong. Look to your left, the walkway."

Nathan turned his head and looked at the scene. "Julius, come in," he said as he ran towards them. "Julius." He saw the woman reach into the young man's pocket and take his gun from his holster. "Julius, fucking answer me!" He pulled his gun out and sighted down the barrel. He pulled the trigger and heard the woman scream as the gun was shot from her hand. "Get your arse on the ground now before I put a bullet in your fucking head," Nathan shouted over the screams of people fleeing. He saw the woman turn and look at him. She ran away, towards the opposite escalator. He skidded to a halt behind the young man, who seemed to be in a trance of some sort. He slapped him hard. "Julius, snap out of it. Come on, she is getting away." He saw Julius begin to come around. "Where is she, David?"

"She is mixed in the crowd; I'm struggling to keep sight of her," he replied.

Nathan leaned over the bannister of the walkway and saw her halfway down the escalator that would take her closed to the exit. "Shite. Julius, get your arse down those escalators now." He looked over the bannister of the walkway and ran through the math in his head, $d=1/2 \ gt^2$. "Around 9 metres, I think, so I will live," Nathan said and jumped over the bannister.

She had to escape and fast. She had been so close to removing that young man until that other one appeared. That other man must be what her master had warned her about. How did he find her? She had been careful. Whoever this man was, he was very dangerous. She felt something from him when she looked at him. She pushed past people, trying to flee the building. She walked down the escalator as fast as she could and looked up to see the other policeman looking down at her. She smiled. He would never catch her. He was too far away, and she would be lost in the crowd. She then watched in shock as he jumped off the walkway.

Nathan dropped down fast. He slammed into the tiled floor, the ground cracking widely below him. He didn't even bend his knees to reduce the force of his landing. He just stood there, with people watching him in amazement and fear.

"Police, get down!" he shouted and ran towards his target.

People fled him or dropped him to the ground as he ran towards the escalator. "Get down on the ground, Thorn!" he shouted as he pointed his gun at the woman. He saw her grab the woman in front of her and push the woman down the escalator. Nathan jumped up and over the lady and wrestled the suspect to the ground. He pushed his gun under the woman's chin. "Don't fucking move," he said as he pushed hard.

"You have…" she began to say.

Nathan head-butted her, her nose exploding with blood. "Shut your fucking mouth. Get up slowly." He kept the gun under her chin as they both got up. He grabbed her coat lapels and dragged her down the escalator. Once at the bottom, he tripped her up, making her fall onto her face. "Oh, I am sorry. You have the right to whatever I fucking allow you to have. You may not say anything, but whatever you do, I don't give a fuck about it. If you cannot afford a lawyer, then you are not getting one," he said and began to put the cuffs on her. He looked behind him as Julius came down the escalator, holding his broken gun. "Glad you could join us."

"What happened?" Julius asked.

"I don't know, but I think we have the right woman. Don't we, Larysa?" he said and grabbed her hair. He pulled her head up. "I'm after your husband. Where is he?" She didn't reply. "The strong quiet type, are we? Well, you will talk." He dragged her up by her hair. Just then, armed policemen entered the building. "About fucking time. Right, I want this place locked down. ID everyone here, especially the men. If you find one Thomas Thorn, then detain him and consider him a fucking killer," he shouted towards the men. "And if you have to shoot to kill, then so be it," he said with relish into the woman's ear. "OK, sweetheart, you're coming with me."

It watched the news. Apparently, there had been an incident in the city centre. An armed response had been called for.

She was out there. She was there.

She had been taken. It knew she had been.

It had felt her pain. Her fear. Her love. Her hate.

It wondered what had happened. Had she gotten careless?

Maybe. But this felt different. It was sure that this man, Nathan, was behind this. Was he a man? It may have been a bad idea to call him. It was sure that in doing so, it had made him angry. Angry people do strange things. Things that cannot be planned for. It had plans, plans that required finishing.

She knew that. She knew that the plan must come first. But she was part of the plan. She was needed.

It was time to act. Time to use the contacts that had been given to it. Yes.

Time to act.

Chapter 9

"You are out of your mind," David said to him. He sat on the other side of Nathan's desk. He watched the man drink from a whisky glass.

"I caught her, didn't I?" Nathan replied, putting his feet up on the desk.

"You threw yourself off a bloody walkway, two goddamn floors up. You could have killed yourself."

"Calm down, Mother. I knew I would be OK. I did the math; remember that I am a genius."

David threw his hands up in the air. "You are serious. I just watched you jump to your death, and you are acting like it was nothing. No broken legs, not even a scratch, but you did turn the tiles you landed on into dust."

"Don't worry about me. I will tell the children in the next room not to do what I did. I will tell them that I am a trained professional. You know, like what they do before the wrestling begins on TV. Don't copy this at home, children; the people you see are trained professionals," Nathan joked.

"Are you fucking serious right now!" David exclaimed.

"You need a drink," Nathan told him and took another glass out of the drawer. He poured a big measure and handed it to his friend. "Drink."

David grabbed the glass and took a big gulp. "You're out of your mind."

"Meh."

"Don't meh me," he replied and took another drink. "You have any idea the shitestorm you caused?"

"I'm paid not to care."

"Well, I am. Jesus, Christopher is livid. He dragged me to the chiefs meeting and pretty much dragged your name through the mud. Driving on pavements. Breaking the speed limit. Assaulting the suspect. You're lucky the chief is backing you up on this. I heard him laughed when he was told what you had done. You shot a gun out of a suspect's hand at 50 metres. No one has ever seen that accuracy before. The chief said, and I quote, 'Fucking hell'."

"Finally, a fan." Nathan saluted.

David shook his head. "At least you caught her. She is getting looked at by medics now. Once they give her the once-over, then she will be taken for an interview."

"And I will be the one doing the questions. Me and Helena."

"Helena?"

"Yes. Julius is too shaken up about what happened to him. I don't know what happened to him. What did the doc say?"

"He couldn't find anything. Seems whatever happened it was fast-acting. Some sort of drug?"

"Unsure. That's why I want Helena. Has she asked for a lawyer yet?"

"Strangely, no. She hasn't said anything. She won't even confirm her name. We know who she is from her driving licence found in her purse. She just sits there staring into nothing."

There was a knock at the door, and Julius walked in with the doc.

"How you holding up, young pup?" Nathan asked.

"I wish to apologise, sir. I don't know what happened. I wish to be removed from the case as I feel that I am a detriment to it," he replied, standing to attention.

Nathan put his feet down and leaned forward onto the desk. He looked at the doc. "Well?"

"Nothing wrong with him. A urine test showed no sign of drugs in his system. Eye response is fine. Balance fine. Blood pressure and heartbeat all normal. I couldn't say what happened to him, but he is fit for duty," the doc said, folding his arms across his chest.

"Julius," Nathan said and watched the young man stand to attention. "Shut the fuck up. Sit down and have a drink." He poured the man a glass of whisky and gave it to him as he sat down. "You did nothing wrong. Don't know what happened to you, but I will sure as hell find out. You have been an asset to this team, and nobody is taking you off it. Let them try. You are my young pup. Take this on the chin and learn from it."

Julius nodded. "Thank you."

"It's nothing. You are young. Shite happens," Nathan said and poured a glass for the doc. "Look at this as a learning experience."

"I really don't know what happened to me. She just started talking, and I couldn't think straight," Julius said to them.

"That's women for you," joked the doc. "I'm old enough to know that."

"No. This was different. She talked, and I listened. I couldn't help but listen. She was bewitching. In truth, I wanted her to talk more. I needed her to talk more," Julius said and drank from the glass. "Her voice, it was demanding obedience. I felt that her voice was needed to breathe. I really don't know how to describe it."

"Ha, sounds like a siren to me," said the doc.

"I killed the last one," Nathan said, taking a drink. The three men looked at him. "What?"

Someone tapped the door, and Alfonso stuck his head in. "She is ready."

"Excellent," Nathan said and left the room. "Helena, you are with me."

Nathan and Helena sat down across from their suspect. The woman had a splint on her nose after a medic performed a closed reduction on her nose to realign it. Under her eyes, bruising was beginning to appear due to the injury.

"Larysa Thorn. You have been detained because we believe you and your husband have been abducting women and then killing them," Nathan told her as he placed a paper pad in front of him. "Where is he?" The woman looked him in the eyes and said nothing. "Ah, the strong, silent type. Very well. We know your husband worked at the clinics in which the women had abortions. We also have tracked his movements during these periods. We know he left the country not long after the last murder in 2003. He went to Russia. No doubt where he met you, there or thereabouts. He returned to Scotland in 2007 with you. He found a job at a second clinic. After the killing in 2008, he then again left. You accompanied him. You lived in Canada for over a decade. From what we can tell, your husband worked in a hospital as a surgeon. You then returned to Scotland in mid-2019. Your husband then got work at another abortion clinic. Again, our victims were treated there." She kept her eyes on him like a snake would. "So, where is your husband? I have some very important questions to ask him."

She smiled. "I want a lawyer." Her voice seemed to sing in the air.

"Nope," Nathan replied and wrote something on the pad. He had an idea but had to make sure of it. It was the voice and how she was acting. He had seen something very similar before. Something very powerful and destructive.

She looked at Nathan questionably. This wasn't right. "Under the law, I am allowed a lawyer when being questioned. Get me a lawyer." Again, her voice sang. Her voice demanded what she had asked for. She watched this man across from her. He just sat there, smiling.

"Nope. No. Fuck no. Nai. Nein. Non. Tidak. Nie. Het. Nej. Take your pick in whatever language you want," Nathan told her and leaned back smiling. Yes, he was sure of it now. It was her.

"You must provide me with a lawyer."

"Ask her," Nathan replied, pointing to Helena. This would finally prove it. The smoking gun.

The woman turned and looked at Helena. "I require a lawyer. Please allow me to call one, or at least provide me one." She smiled sweetly, the voice again pleading, demanding, and wanting.

Helena turned to Nathan and shrugged her shoulders. "Why does she keep refusing a lawyer?"

Nathan laughed loudly. "Buggered if I know. She is a strange one, isn't she?" Nathan wrote again on his pad. He now knew. "It did not work with women the same way it did with men. He was immune, of course. It always pissed them off." He knew now what he was dealing with. He could use this against her. He had dealt with it before and would use the same tactics as before. They got results, and they would again. "Larysa, you really are not gripping the situation you are in. You see, this little operation is classified. Off the books. Doesn't really exist. You are not under arrest in the sense you could understand. I just read you your rights in front of people to give them a show. To make it look as if I arrested you. You are a prisoner. Held under a few different laws that say many, many, many different things using very confusing swords that only very expensive lawyers understand for £1000 an hour. But I will give you the short version. You are fucked. I can hold you here for as long as I like. You have no rights what so fucking ever."

"You can't do this to me. It's inhuman," she snapped back. Her voice now full of venom.

'Got you,' he thought. Now you show your real face. "Ah, but I can. You see, I'm not a police officer. I'm something different. You see, Helena is. She is a police officer. She has to follow the rules. She can't do this, she can't do that, but," Nathan's hands shot forward and grabbed Larysa's cuffed hands. He gripped tight and squeezed gently. "I can do whatever I like." He grabbed her index finger and bent it hard, sideways. The snap filled the room. Larysa whimpered in pain. "I want your husband, Larysa. I want him now. You see, he called me and really pissed me off. And to make it worse, he now has another potential victim. He took great pleasure in rubbing that in my face." He grabbed the index finger on her other hand and held me tight. Larysa looked at Helena. "Don't look at her; she won't help you. Look at me. That's it; look at me. Where. Is. He?" She stared violently back into his eyes.

Nathan snapped her other finger. "You have eight more, Larysa. Tell me what I want to know, and you will receive medical attention. You see, I know what you are. You confirmed it by trying to sweet-talk me. Tut tut. Doesn't work on me, Sybella." He saw her face turn to anger at that.

"Fuck you," she spat through gritted teeth. She then looked at Helena. "Fuck you too."

Nathan punched her on the nose, blood spraying across the desk. "You do not speak to a lady like that. Where are your manners?" He looked across at Helena. "Women these days, eh." His colleague shrugged. "OK, Larysa. I'm done playing." He took out pictures from his pad and placed them in front of her. Each one was the victim of the serial killer. "Six women. Each abducted. Each killed." He pushed the images forward. "These two I can place you with. I have CCTV images, bank statements, etc. that show you were following them for several days prior to their kidnapping. No doubt you were learning their routines and routes. A scout, as it were."

Larysa spat blood across the images. "Sorry." She smirked.

Nathan sighed, grabbed her hair, and smashed her head against the desk. "That wasn't very funny. You did that on purpose." He pushed down and heard her nose crunch. She yelled in pain. He lifted her head slightly and then smashed it down again. He let go, and she slowly brought her head back up. She spat blood onto the floor and smiled through blood-stained lips. "Are you ready to answer?"

She giggled. "He was right about you. You are something different." She smiled, her grin wide. "You are very special. I can see why he took an interest in you. The rage you barely manage to keep under control. I wonder how many people you have killed."

"I stopped counting after 3000," Nathan replied as a matter of fact and leaned back in his chair.

"That is very impressive. If he knew that, then he would like you even more. You have no idea who you are messing with, do you? He is special, too. Very special. Unique. Destined for great things. He is the herald for what is to come."

"Blah, blah, blah. Fucking hell. Just tell me where he is," Nathan told her.

"Ha, why should I tell you? You have killed so many people. Were they all justified? Were they all deserving of it? Something tells me no. You are like him. More like him than you can possibly know."

"I'm nothing like him. He is a dick-less fucking Ken doll who gets his kicks from killing women and then mutilating their bodies. Heh, I bet you take a strap-on to him every night, don't you whore?"

"Mutilation, is that what you think? HAHAHAHAHA. If you only knew. He is blessing them. They were picked for what was needed."

Nathan smirked. "You, sick bitch. You are as crazy as him. Tell me where he is now."

"No. I have no reason to. He is my life, and I am his. He leads, and I follow. His word is the word of a higher power," she said with the conviction of a true believer.

"You are mental. You really believe that shite you just spouted. Cuckoo," he replied to her while spinning his finger around his forehead. "You are a mental hospital's wet fucking dream." He slammed his hand onto the desk, making both women jump. His hand made a large dent in the metal table. "Spune-mi unde este acum." (*Tell me where he is now.*) He spoke to her in her native language.

She looked at him in surprise. Not at the large dent in the table but at how he spoke Romanian so fluently. "Este forate impresionant." (*That is very impressive.*) "What other tricks do you know; I wonder? Do you do back flips?"

"Don't fucking test me," Nathan told her. "This is your last chance."

Someone banged on the mirror behind Larysa. "Maybe not." She smiled.

Nathan slammed his chair back and stormed out of the room. He went into the adjacent room, where David stood with another man. This man wore a suit and looked too smug for his own good.

"I'm in the middle of something," Nathan stated.

"This is Mr Fox. He is with Sis," David introduced the man.

"Secret Intelligence Service. You kidding. What the fuck are they wanting?" Nathan said, looking at Mr Fox.

"You have one Larysa Thorn in your custody. I am here to take her. She is wanted in relation to several high-class murders in London," he told Nathan and handed him several sheets of papers.

"Like hell you are. She is mine. I caught her. You can have her when I'm fucking done," Nathan said and threw the paper on the ground. He turned and opened the door, but an armed serviceman stood, barring his way. "This had better be a joke."

"I'm sorry, Nathan, but they are taking her. It can't be stopped. The paperwork is all there and legal," David said.

Nathan turned slowly and watched as two armed men entered the interrogation room. They began to remove her cuffs from the table and lifted her off the chair. "This total bullshit." He turned to Mr Fox. "Who the fuck got to you? You are nothing but a fucking rent boy. Who is paying you to take one in the arse for the team?"

"Mr Andrews, that language is uncalled for. I have my orders, and I am carrying them out. Unlike you, I actually do what I am told. And now you will do what you are told," Mr Fox replied to him. David put his head in his hands. "In actual fact, we are not even here. This is to be kept under the radar."

Nathan's hand shot out and grabbed the man by the throat. He growled through gritted teeth and lifted the man off the floor with ease. He heard the click of a weapon behind him. "You think you can take me? You stupid mongrel cunt," Nathan said, turning his head slightly round to look at the armed man. "Blink and you will miss it." Nathan spun around quickly and threw Mr Fox through the double mirror. Before the man had even cracked the glass, Nathan grabbed the armed man's gun, yanked it out of his grip and kicked the man into the opposite wall. The man crashed through the breeze-block wall in a cloud of rubble and dust. Mr Fox smashed through the glass and crashed across the interrogation room table. Nathan climbed through the window and lifted the badly cut and dazed Mr Fox. He slammed him against the wall. He turned to the other two arms men who had his prisoner. They pointed their weapons at him. "Give her back!" he roared. Both men took a step back.

David ran into the room, pushed past the two armed men, and grabbed Nathan around his chest. "Nathan, stop it. They can take her. You are making things worse."

Nathan slammed Mr Fox into the wall again, making the man scream in pain. "That is my prisoner, and she stays here." Nathan could hear more people running down the hall. He could hear the clink of metal. More armed people.

"Nathan, please, before they come in shooting. Put him down and let them take her," David pleaded.

Nathan looked at the two armed men. "I could kill you all. I could kill you all before you even got a fucking round-off. You stupid fucking little things. Get your friends, all of them. I will skin you all and mount your bodies from the walls as trophies." Nathan watched as the two men began to tremble. His voice screamed the truth.

The men knew deep in their souls, the primitive part that caveman used to hide from predators, that this man before them could do what he threatened to do and there was nothing they could do to stop him.

David stood between him and Mr Fox. "Nathan, stop it. More armed men are about to enter, and it is going to get bad quickly." David was scared. Nathan seemed to have some sort of black haze around his body; you had to look hard to see it, but it was there.

Nathan grunted and could hear the others begin to slow down, no doubt what he had said had made its impact. He threw his head back and roared, the room visibly shaking with his rage. The armed men almost dropped their weapons. "TAKE HER," he shouted. He turned his head quickly and looked at Larysa, his eyes boring into her soul. The woman was shaking in fear, trying to back out of the room. His eyes were terrifying to behold. "I have your scent now. There is nowhere you can hide from me." The woman wet herself. Nathan turned his attention back to Mr Fox and grabbed the man's limp arm. He snapped it with a simple twist. He then pushed the arm up, so the broken and splintered bones tore the inside of his arm apart. Mr Fox screamed. "That's something to remember me by. But then again, you aren't even here, are you!" He threw the man out of the interrogation room door. The man crashed to the floor and lost consciousness.

David looked at the two-armed me. "Get the fuck out of here, or I will let my friend here do what he said he would. Go now."

The two men pushed the woman through the door and dragged the screaming Mr Fox away.

Nathan turned and kicked the bolted-down table hard, sending it flying into the next room.

"Shite," he said quietly.

"I have been informed from London that one-armed serviceman has four crushed ribs, spinal bruising, and a severe concussion," David said, sitting next to Nathan at his desk. "He is currently in a critical but stable condition. And to top that off, Mr Fox has several deep cuts across his back, one of which splintered a vertebra. He also has a severely broken arm which may need to be amputated if they cannot fix it during the operation which he is currently in. He also has a concussion and a bruised throat."

"It could be worse," Nathan said as he drank whisky straight from the bottle.

"Pray to tell," David said in disarray.

"I could have killed them all."

"I have no doubt you would have. Christ, Nathan, what is going on with you?" David said, standing up and walking around the room. "The captain is going nuts. He has had several high-ranking calls from the service, and they are calling for your head."

"They can try."

"They bloody well tried; I can guarantee you that. They were all lining up to take a shot. Then guess what? They all stopped calling. I have a friend in the spy business, and he called me to say that it never happened. Apparently, the ones calling for your head were told that if they didn't stop, it would be their heads. Jesus, Nathan, who do you have protecting you?"

"Meh, many people. I have lots of people who owe me big time."

"Well, I don't know how many favours you used up, but don't do it again," David said and flopped onto the couch. He turned his head and looked at Mary. "Do you want to add anything to this discussion?"

Mary shrugged. "The Nathan I knew wouldn't have even given them a warning. He would have just killed them and been done with it. He is getting soft in his old age."

"You're just as crazy as him," David said, throwing his hands up in the air. "Both of you are insane."

"And drunk," said Nathan, raising the bottle.

David shook his head. "Nathan, I am saying this as your oldest friend. You have to calm down. If this investigation is getting to you, then walk away. We have enough to go on now."

"Like fuck, I will. I am going to catch this son of a bitch and kill him with my bare hands."

"Nathan, you can't. He needs to be caught and brought to justice."

"It will be my justice."

David nudged Mary. "A bit of help here, please."

"Don't look at me. If I knew how his mind worked, then I would be able to control him. As it is, I am surprised he hasn't lost control more often. He really has changed. If he is going to kill this man, then who am I to stop him? Who are you to do either? No. Let Nathan proceed with how he feels. I think it will be better for all if he does," she replied. "Plus, I'm not in charge of him. No one is and hasn't been for a very long time." She stood up and smoothed out her long coat. "I will leave you now and see what I can find out. I will return when I can."

David watched her leave the room. "Seriously, who is that bitch?"

"Someone I have known longer than you," Nathan said as he tipped the contents of the bottle down his throat.

David sighed and rubbed his eyes. "I'm knackered. Been a long day. I'm going home to get a wash and a few hours of sleep. Maybe my wife will remember who I am and open the door for me," he said and walked to the door. "You should go home also. Get some rest. The team will call if anything happens."

"I will crash here. I'm comfortable just where I am." He finished the bottle and took another from his desk.

David shook his head and left.

Nathan knew he was losing his temper. His rage was just there, over the horizon.

"Yes."

"Hmmm?" Nathan asked as he opened the oven. "What did you say?"

She sighed. "I said yes. I would like a drink." She turned and looked at Alessia. "Does he ever not hear you?"

Alessia giggled. "Sometimes. I think he does it to annoy me."

"I do not," Nathan replied to them as he took the piping hot steak pie out of the oven. "I'm just a bit preoccupied here." He placed the dish on the counter and took the oven mitts off. "Plus, I remember everything you both say."

"Yeah, yeah." She laughed. "That smells good."

"Nathan is the best cook I have ever seen," Alessia said, drinking her wine. "He taught me."

"Well, that is very interesting," she said in a quizzical tone. "Where did you learn this special skill?"

"Here and there," Nathan replied, draining the water from the potatoes. "You pick it up."

"Here and there, he says. Where exactly?" she asked.

"India. France. South Africa. Australia. Brazil. Russia. New Zealand. Balkans. Blah, blah, blah, etc, etc, etc." Nathan told her as he started to put the food onto the plates. "Just something I learned throughout my life."

"Trust me, he is an extremely good cook," Alessia told her. "He cooked a proper Italian meal for my family here in Scotland and relatives from the home country. It was the best meal I ever had."

"Until now," Nathan told her while still dealing with the food.

"We will see. My gran is old Italian. She cried when she tasted it. Reminded her of the old days. And my gran was renowned for her cooking back home. Don't you remember? She asked if you would go back to Italy with her."

"I remember. She slapped my arse and gave me a wink when she said it," he replied and glanced at her sniggering. Her red hair jiggling as she tried not to laugh. "Not funny."

"It is," She replied, wiping a tear from her eye.

"Well, just you wait and see." He turned around with two large plates and presented his food. "My special steak pie."

"It looks amazing," Alessia said as Nathan put the plate in front of her. She leaned forward and smelled deeply. "My mouth is watering already."

He looked at her and smiled. "Well, take a taste."

She took her fork and took a bite. She chewed and leaned back in her chair. "My god, that is amazing." He leaned forward and kissed her. Her green eyes glinted in the light. She pushed her long red hair to the side and took another fork full. "This is so good, Nathan."

"I told you it would be," he replied and took a seat beside her.

Alessia patted his hand. "You have outdone yourself. If I sold this at the restaurant, then I could retire."

"I will give you the recipe, Mother Bear," Nathan told her and began to eat his meal.

"Honestly, Nathan, this is amazing. I really didn't know you were this good a cook," she told him. She had almost finished having the plate already.

"I am glad you like it. Just wait until dessert."

"You made dessert also?"

"Yip. Lemon sorbet with a chocolate fudge cake. Freshly made this morning."

"All by yourself?"

"Yip."

"And who says men can't multi-task?" She laughed. She leaned forward and kissed him. "I love you."

Nathan smiled. "I love you too."

He put the plates into the sink and brought out the desserts. "Hopefully, this will top off the meal."

He watched as she took a bite of the cake and watched as her face beamed. "Oh, my god. That is delicious. So moist. Nathan, how did you do this?"

He shrugged his shoulders. "It just comes naturally to me." He looked at Alessia. "So what do you think, Mother Bear? Does it meet your approval?"

She nodded and took another bite of the cake. "I am hating and loving you at the same time right now. I was on a diet, you know."

"Well, you are going to hate me even more as I have champagne to go with it," he told them and went to the fridge. "That can't be right. Seems something is stuck in the cork." He took the bottle out and looked at it quizzically. "How did that get there?" He turned around and looked at the woman he loved. "Can you explain?"

She turned and saw what was stuck in the cork. It was a diamond ring. A large diamond ring surrounded by green emeralds. "What the…"

"I take it; this must be yours then." He knelt down in front of her. "You can't go losing things like this. Too important. So, I guess I will have to put it on your finger, marry you, and make sure you don't lose it again." He took her hand, which trembled. "Will you marry me?"

She was crying. "Yes," she whispered. "Yes, I will."

He slipped the ring on and kissed her hand. "Thank you."

Alessia watched through teary eyes as they both stood up and kissed. "I am so happy for you both." She got up and hugged them both. She looked at the ring. "It's so beautiful."

"Beauty for a beautiful lady," Nathan said to her. He held her hand and looked into her eyes. Her green eyes glowed with love. "Are you sure?"

"Yes," She replied.

"Yes."

Chapter 10

He woke up. He kept his eyes closed. He dreamed of her again. His dreams were getting more real. Was he dreaming or reliving the moments? He could live with dreams but not reliving the moments. It would be too painful. He loved her. She loved him. He knew that. Was he being punished for that love? When she died, he died also. A part of him, at least, did anyway. He had taken his revenge for that. But she would never have wanted that. She was the very best of him. She understood him like no one had for a very long time. She calmed him. She was his anchor. His northern light. But what was he to her? He knew what he was. Who he would always be. He didn't want to be that for her. She didn't deserve that. But she loved him. She. Loved. Him. He knew he didn't deserve her. She deserved better than him. He had told her that once, and all she did was Smile and tell him not to be silly. Not to be silly. He smiled a little at that. This woman loved him, and he couldn't figure out why. He missed her. He actually felt pain in that. Maybe that's why he drank. No. He couldn't do that to her. That wasn't her fault. It was his choice. It wasn't a disease; it was a choice. He chose to drink. He wasn't forced to. It was his choice and had nothing to do with her.

He heard the door open quietly. Someone tried, at least. He felt the movement of the air. He kept his eyes closed.

"It's about time you showed up," he said, still pretending to be asleep.

"I made no sound whatsoever," the voice replied. It was a man's voice, and it was old. "You are the only person I have never managed to catch out. Pisses me off."

Nathan raised his head up but kept his eyes closed. "I have my gifts, and you have yours."

"Bull. Remember, I know you."

Nathan turned his head and opened one eye. "Good to see you, Frank." He saw his old friend. He had long white hair and a thick white beard covering most of his face. "You look old."

"You look like shite," Frank told him and took a seat. "My condolences, by the way."

"Thanks," Nathan replied and closed his eye again. "How was your trip?"

"Fine. I was on a job, by the way. I had to rush it. Bit messy," Frank told him. He put his feet up on the desk. "But when you sent me the message, then I knew I had to come here." He saw Nathan nod. "Alessia picked me up. I take it that was your idea?" Again, the nod. "She slapped me. Well, I did deserve that. She got me everything I asked for. Don't know how she managed to do it in such a short time. She always knew how to work the system."

"That she does," Nathan said to him. "I know what you want to ask, so ask."

"Are you sure? I mean, you did tell them. I was there," Frank asked.

"95% sure now." He opened his eyes and took a file out from his desk. He leaned over and gave it to Frank. "She confirmed it." Frank read the file. He grunted. "It was her; I am sure. When I said it, she knew I knew."

"Well, that's great. Been ages since we came up against something like this. Will be good to shake off the rust," Frank said and kept reading. "You should have killed her."

"Politics."

"Never stopped you before."

Nathan shrugged. "I have been told I am changing."

"By who?"

"By me," Mary said as she entered the room.

"You forgot to mention her, Nathan," Frank said, not turning around to look at Mary.

"I was getting to that," he said to Frank. "Play nice. You know, like you used to."

"Fine. So, queen bitch, what have you been up to since we last worked together?" Frank asked her, and he finally turned around to look at her.

"Better than you, by the looks of it. I would say it is good to see you, but that would be lying. Are you sure we need him, Nathan?"

"I said play nice, and that goes for you too," Nathan replied to her. "I need the two of you to get along until this is over with. You have before, so do it again."

"That was a necessity," Frank said to him.

"Well, it is again. So, Mary, what do you have for me?"

She sighed and flopped onto the couch. "She's gone."

"Gone?"

"Yes. I lost her on the outskirts of the city. East side. Towards Baillieston. Took a while, but I tracked the van she was transported in. It was firebombed. Found the flaming wreckage on a B road in Cambuslang."

"You lost the target?" Frank mocked. "You."

"Even I have my limits. I must follow the same rules as you do, both of you," she replied sadly. "I'm limited in what I can do here."

"I hear that," said Frank.

"Well, I expected as much," Nathan told them both. "Just tell me that our target knows what strings to pull. Means we have people in government in on this also." Nathan sighed. "Which means this is big." He looked at Frank. "Now you know why I called you."

Frank threw the file onto the desk. "Seems you were right to do so. But you could handle this very easily yourself."

"Yes, but I know how pissed off you would be if I left you out of this. Plus, with her here, I need you to annoy her so she doesn't annoy me."

"You are all heart," joked Frank. "Well, let's get this show on the road again."

Nathan stood up and took both of them to the other room. He looked at his team as they entered. "Good news. Bad news. Fucking awful news. Who's going to start?"

"Our suspect, Mrs Thorn, has disappeared," said Mary.

"That's the fucking awful news," Nathan replied, holding up one of his fingers.

"She hasn't used any of her bank cards or tried to access any of her accounts," said Helena.

"That's the bad news," Nathan said, holding up a second finger. "Is someone going to give me good news?" The room went silent. "Anyone?"

His team was silent.

"We have nothing," said David. "I questioned the sister of the person we think our killer has, and she couldn't add anything. She is only seven years old. She is staying with a neighbour where she lives. Her parents died of cancer a few years back. Her big sister has been bringing her up."

"I am sure it is her he has," Nathan said and pointed towards the whiteboards. Frank walked to them and looked at what they contained. "It fits into the sequence better than the other two."

Frank nodded. "I agree. She is the one."

"This is Frank Power, and before anyone asks, that is not his real name. He is a specialist and requires some secrecy. So, don't bother asking. He is here to help at my request, just like Mary was."

"So, from what I can tell in the five minutes I have been in this room is that we are back to square one," Frank said to the room but still looking at the whiteboards. "You really are making this difficult."

"Our one and only lead is now gone," Nathan said to him. "What can I say? You like a challenge anyway."

Frank laughed.

"I may have something," said Julius.

"Spill it," Nathan told him.

"I spoke to an art supplier about the Plaster of Paris. They are the only ones in the past few months who have delivered a large quantity of the stuff," he told the room and brought the information up on the canvas screen. "It was bought by a company called 'Royal Sculptures'. They bought half a tonne of the required materials. Paid cash. The buyer was a woman. I sent the image over, and the owner recognised Mrs Thorn as the purchaser. I looked into the company, and it was wound up the day after the delivery."

"Where was it delivered to?" Nathan asked.

"That's the strange part. It was delivered to a cargo container on an old bit of grass strip. The container was situated on Barrack Street, across from the Tennets Factory," Julius told them. "They were told that it was being used for storage while their factory was being updated. The building the company was registered to was an old factory on the same street. But it has been knocked down since then."

"Is the container still there?" Mary asked.

"Yes," he replied. "Em, Here. The container was bought from a shipping company. Again cash."

"OK. So, we have a weenie tiny bit of good news then," Nathan told the room. "Frank, Mary, and Julius, you will come with me. We will check out this container. Everyone else, I want you to trace the route the van went, which took my suspect. Find out where she disappeared. Use your sources."

Nathan drove them in his car. They pulled up beside the container.

"Been here a while by the looks of it," Nathan said as he closed the car door. "Lots of graffiti."

"Locked," Frank told them, jiggling a lock.

"You open that up, and I will take a walk around the container," Nathan told him and began to walk around. "No other entrance. No sounds from inside."

"Open!" shouted Frank. He twisted the lock open, and the door creaked open.

Nathan came around and looked inside. He saw a mound of dry plaster powder at the far end. Nothing else. "That's still a lot of plaster." Nathan wondered why it was all piled up and not in boxes or a sugar bag. It looked abandoned.

"You would need, what, 10 pounds of plaster for a body?" Mary asked.

Nathan nodded. "Roughly a tiny bit more, depending on body shape and size." He walked inside and scanned the interior. "Julius, call the boys back at the station and get a team out here to look at this more closely."

"What are you thinking?" Frank asked.

"Don't know. He didn't need this much. He has been doing this for a long time. He would know what he needed to make a mould of a body after the first victim," Nathan told him. He squatted and took some of the powder in his hand. He rubbed it in his palm. "Did he buy this for something else?"

"Possible," Mary said from the door. "This is a very good spot. No one here. One business behind me but surrounded by high walls. All their cameras are pointing directly at the ground. They wouldn't have seen a thing. No other buildings here. No CCTV cameras anywhere else. It's perfect to do stuff without anyone near you."

"He knew this area. He knew how isolated it was," Nathan agreed. He left the container and looked around. He turned left and looked down the street. He walked to the end of the pavement. Armour Street. He looked down the street. Nothing. He walked down the street. He came to a junction. One way led to the main road and the other to a business car park. He walked on to the end of the other pavement. Melbourne Street. He looked to his right. Flats. Left. An old building. He could see plants and other shrubs growing from several areas on the building. It was definitely abandoned. An abandoned building so close to the container, surely he couldn't be that lucky? Could he? He walked to the building. It was all boarded up, with plants growing from its gutters. An old gate to his left and an old fence to his right. He inspected the metal door to the building. The lock was old and rusty.

"You see anything?" Frank asked him as he walked towards him. He was closely followed by Mary and Julius.

"This was part of the old slaughter house here. Behind it," Nathan told them.

"A place of death?" Mary asked.

"Yes. For a long time," Nathan answered.

"Doesn't look like anyone can get in. The place is secure. Old locks. The boards on the windows show no signs of damage. Can't speak for the other side of this building, though," Frank told them.

"Julius, go to my car. There are bolt cutters in the boot," Nathan said to the young man, throwing his keys at him. "Get them." Once Julius was out of earshot, he said, "Look at the door."

The other two looked. "It looks as old as the rest."

"Yes, but look at the top right corner, just below the door frame," Nathan told them as he walked slowly to the gate on his right.

They both look at what he pointed out. A mark. "A symbol older than recorded history. A pentagon with a diamond in its centre, lines branching out from its centre as if reaching for you."

"Shite!" Frank swore.

"That's a very powerful symbol," Mary said and touched it. "It still has power." She pulled her hand away as if stung. "This should not be possible. The power died with them!"

"You know the last time I saw that symbol, it wasn't a good day for me," Frank said and followed Nathan to the gate. "I can't believe it's happening again."

"Tell me the fuck about it. Mary, care to add anything to this?" he asked her.

She stood beside him. "No. I know what that symbol means. It would seem I have been lied to. With something like that symbol being here, they surely knew."

"I told you, didn't I? Cant fucking trust them," Nathan said and saw Julius drive the car up the street. "This is getting worse by the fucking day."

"And what shall we tell him?" Frank asked, flicking his head in the direction of the car.

"Nothing. Not yet anyway. And if he finds out, you will do nothing, Frank. That goes for you, Mary. I'm warning both of you now. He is not to be touched." Nathan warned them.

"Very well," Mary replied.

"If you say so," replied Frank.

Nathan nodded and grabbed the bolt cutters from Julius as he re-joined them. "OK. I take it we all remembered to bring our weapons?"

Frank pulled out a large pistol from his jacket. Mary pulled out a type of 9mm pistol.

"I didn't!" exclaimed Julius.

Frank sighed and pulled another gun from his inside his jacket. He handed it to Julius. "This is my favourite gun. I used it in battle once. Modified desert eagle. It kicks like a comet."

Julius looked at the large gun. "Why do we need this for searching this abandoned building?"

"Fucking hell, Julius, you never heard of protection." Laughed Nathan. "Think of it as that one-night stand you thought about not wearing a condom. Protection or no protection for that is the question." He cut open the padlock on the gates. He kicked them open. "You really need to get out more."

"I have a girlfriend, you know," Julius grunted at him. He checked the gun and pulled back the breach to make sure it was loaded. "We fuck every night thank you very much."

Frank laughed. "You are turning out like Nathan, Julius."

"He couldn't take after a better bastard," joked Nathan and pulled out his gun. He checked his breach. "Right. We check the area. We make entries and search in twos. Julius, you're with me. That leaves you two to play nice and work together." They all nodded.

All four entered the via the open gate and walked slowly to the back of the building. It was overgrown with vegetation; the tarmac is nothing but grass now. Nature had taken it all back. Nathan looked around; gun ready to act. He was the team leader and checked to make sure there were no nasty surprises. He turned the corner slowly and saw the back door. It was old. Like the front, but the lock was new. He took the bolt cutters from Julius and cut the lock open. He looked at Frank. *On three.* He mouthed it to him. Frank nodded and aimed his gun at the door. Nathan counted to three and kicked the metal door open. It snapped its hinges and smashed into the ground. The other three turned and looked at him. "Oops."

"Christ, Nathan," grunted Frank.

"Wasn't my fault; the hinges are rusted to fuck," Nathan swore as he entered the building. "Next time, you can kick the door open."

"Oh, I will; don't you worry," Frank said behind him.

"You two be quiet," Mary scolded them. "Let's check the building."

"Right, you two upstairs. Julius, with me. We clear room by room." Nathan said and proceeded forward. Julius walked behind him. Nathan could hear the other two climb up the creaky stairs. They came to the first room, its door open. Nathan stuck his head in quickly and saw that no one was there. He entered the room and cleared the room. They did this for another three rooms.

"Last room, I think," Julius said to Nathan.

"I think so," he replied. He slowly opened the door and went inside. It was a small room with a hatch on the floor. He walked over and saw that it wasn't padlocked. "You open, and I will cover you."

Julius nodded and grabbed the handle. He began to lift slowly. Nathan heard the click. Without thinking, he surged towards Julius and pushed him out of the way. Julius flew across the floor and heard a large explosion a fraction of a second later.

His ears were ringing because of the explosion, and he held his hands over them. He fought to stand up and, with wobbly legs, stumbled over to the hatch. It was gone. He fell to his knees and shook his head, trying to get the ringing to stop. He looked to his right and saw Nathan pinned to the wall by three large metal spikes.

"NATHAN!" he shouted. He picked himself up and zig-zagged towards the man. All three spikes impaled themselves through the right side of his chest. Blood flowed freely from them. Wood splinters covered his entire body. His right arm was a bloody ruin. He aimed his gun at the door when he saw something through the dust and smoke.

"It's me, Julius; stand down!" shouted Frank. "Oh, fuck," he said when he saw Nathan. He ran over and checked for a pulse. "He's still alive."

Mary ran into the room and saw the situation. "This is very bad."

Nathan opened an eye and groaned. "This stings," he whispered.

Frank smiled. "I can't get you off. One of the bars is bent, and I can't cut it before…"

Nathan roared in pain, and he placed both feet onto the wall. Julius fell to the ground, his head swimming. Even though the blast had deafened him, he could still hear Nathan roaring. This was a primal roar, a roar that struck at the very heart of your soul. A roar of a predator, an apex predator. He managed to gather enough energy to lift his head off the floor and watch in horror as Nathan used his legs to push himself forward on the metal spikes. When he reached the bent one, he grabbed it and pulled it out with his left hand. The sound of his roaring got louder, and dust fell from the ceiling. As he reached the end of the spikes, Frank grabbed him and pulled him off completely. Nathan crashed to the floor. Julius went to sleep.

He woke up. He was being carried by Mary out of the building, her arm under his.

"I am calling Alessia," she shouted.

"He won't stop bleeding. Something is really wrong with him!" shouted Frank.

Julius couldn't turn his head. Surely, Nathan must be dead.

"Alessia, there's been an accident. Yes, it's Nathan. I need you to get to his house now. Bring whatever you can. No time to explain; just grab it all," Mary said into the phone as she dragged Julius to the car. "Julius is hurt also. Not bad. Nathan saved his life. Probably a head injury. Yes. Yes. Yes. We will be…How long, Frank?"

"Fuck me. Err, 20 minutes if we don't care about the red lights," Frank replied and grunted as if carrying something heavy.

"We don't care. Did you hear that, Alessia? Good. Get there before us and make sure you are ready," Mary said and hung up. She placed Julius against the car and frisked him for the car key. She pressed the fob and tossed him into the passenger seat. She opened the back door and jumped in. "Give him to me. You drive."

Julius turned his head around and saw Nathan getting passed across the back seat. He looked dead, but blood still flowed from his wounds. He looked at Frank as he jumped into the driver's seat.

"You look like shite, Julius," the man said and slammed the car into drive.

Julius went back to sleep.

He regained awareness and saw that he was lying down on a couch. He turned his head and saw Alessia. She was kneeling beside Nathan. Nathan's body was covered in blood, but through it, he could see dozens of tattoos and scars. Alessia turned Nathan over to look at his back. Blood ran out of the three wounds. Julius saw more tattoos but also saw large vertical scars on the man's back. One at each shoulder, and the other two were lower but closer to the spine.

"What in the hell happened to him?" she demanded as she put Nathan back onto his back. She started taking stuff out of a large brown leather bag.

"Some sort of explosion. He took the full brunt of it," Frank told her.

"And where were you two when this happened?" she said. She took something out of a jar and put it in her mouth. She began to chew. "This is bad." She took a syringe out of the bag, and Julius could see a greenish liquid in it. She plunged it into Nathan's heart and depressed the plunger.

"I know," Mary said, kneeling beside Nathan. She took something out of a jar from the bag, looked like some sort of vial and shook the liquid inside it. "He saved Julius. You know Nathan. Always the martyr."

Alessia took the stuff she was chewing out of her mouth and placed it over one of the holes left by the spikes. "I'm struggling to keep him here. He is fading," she said and rummaged through the bag again. "Frank, go to the shed out back and get the blood of Ixas. And if he complains, you have my permission to shoot him."

Julius heard Frank run out of the room.

"Nathan, you stay with us now," Alessia pleaded.

"I want to go," Julius heard Nathan whisper. "I can see her." He coughed blood onto his chest. He tried to lift his left arm up as if reaching for something. It crashed to the floor with a loud thud.

"No, Nathan. It isn't her," Mary replied and poured the liquid from the vial into his mouth. "He doesn't want to stay. Do you see what she did to him?"

"He loved her," raged Alessia to the woman. "A thing like you would never understand. Pass me the root bane." Alessia chewed a piece of stick. "Nathan, my boy, it isn't her. Listen to me now. You have to stay. You know what happens if you don't. We can't lose you."

Julius coughed and said, "How is he still alive?"

Alessia turned to him and shuffled over. She opened his eyelid and looked at his eye. "No brain damage. Pupils reacting normally. You have a concussion, Julius. Don't fall asleep; you hear me. I need you to stay awake."

"I have it," Frank said as he ran into the room.

Julius turned his head and say Frank holding a bottle of red liquid. "Is that blood?" Julius said it drowsily.

"What? No, it's not blood. Its…"

Julius passed out again.

He woke up, and it was night. He could see that one small lamp was on in the room. He was lying on the same couch as before. He saw Nathan still on the floor. Alessia sat behind Nathan, asleep. His head was pounding. He saw Mary approach him. She placed her hand on his forehead. He felt sleepy again.

"You don't want to be awake for this, Julius," she said and stroked his head. "I think it is better you sleep again."

Before he could ask, he heard a noise from the direction of Nathan. He looked over and saw his right arm smoulder. He could hear bones move, break, and snap. The arm seemed to be repairing itself. He then saw the three wounds left by the spike burst into flames. The skin regrew over them. Julius wanted to speak but couldn't. He didn't know what he was seeing. A black haze then began to cover Nathan's body. He witnessed movement above Nathan and saw something hovering. It was smoke but had form and shape. It showed glimpses of many faces.

"Don't fucking think about it," Frank said, appearing at the head of Nathan. "Just do what you have been asked to do and fuck off."

Whatever it was hovering above, Nathan flew towards Frank.

We are not to be threatened. It said in many voices. *We have been summoned only, but do not need to do anything. Remember to whom you speak. I know you. I know her. I am powerful.*

"Don't push me, underling. I have spoken, and you will do what you are told. Remember what I did to your predecessor?" Frank pointed to Nathan. "I owe him. Aid him, or I will make you answer. My pets need feeding anyway."

Julius heard something begin growling in the room. It didn't sound like a canine growl. He hadn't seen any animals in the room before.

This is beyond our power. He is healing himself. He will live without our help. You are wasting our time. It spat out. *We know what he is.*

"I know. You are here to help him. He is dying," Frank said, pointing to Julius.

Julius's mind raced. He wasn't dying. He felt fine, other than the absolute killer headache he had.

The figure shot over and hovered above him. *You want this saved? It is nothing. You really want this thing saved?*

"Yes," Mary told it. "He is to live. It is not his time."

The figure extended arms of smoke and touched the head of Julius. The touch felt like burning ice. He tried to move, but his body was locked, and his muscles not responding.

He is bleeding into his skull. It is crushing his brain. He will die in the morning. Why should we save him? It said and moved Julius's head from side to side. *I have better things to do.*

"I am not asking for filth. You want to complain, take it up with my friends," Frank told it, followed by the sounds of more animals growling. "I have the target for this. Take what you need from him and fix Julius." Frank showed the floating smoke a picture. It looked like an old man.

The figure grunted. *Ah, I can see clearly now. I think this man deserves what is about to happen to him. It will be painful for both. You know the laws. You know the rules. Once I begin, it cannot be stopped, or both will die. Are you sure?*

"Yes. He has had it coming for a while now. Time to collect," Frank told the figure and tossed the picture into its smoky body.

Very well. This will hurt BOY. It said and plunged its hands into his head.

"What…?" Julius said, as the headache came back with a vengeance.

"This will seem like a very bad dream in the morning," Mary told him and stood up. It will be painful, but only for a moment. I am sorry, but this must be done.

Julius began to writhe in agony on the couch. He felt his head get warmer and his body began to spasm. He felt as if his entire body wanted to crawl into itself. He could see images of a street and a man walking with a few other people. He felt his hands plunge into the man's chest. The man screamed. He felt the man's beating heart in his hand. He could see the man's friends trying to catch him as he fell to the wet ground. The man's heart was racing, the beats like a drum against his hands.

Julius screamed in agony, and his back arched back until it nearly snapped. He threw up goblets of blood. The pain was overwhelming. He saw the figure in the smoke smile and then it poured it into his eyes. Julius felt the man die. He could feel the life leave the man's body. He felt his head crack and the bones splintering under pressure. Then suddenly, he felt his body come back under his control.

This will sting a little, he heard a voice in his head tell him.

He then exploded.

Chapter 11

Julius sat bolt upright. He was breathing heavily, gulping in the air. He felt his head; it was still there. He looked around and squinted as the sunlight streaming through the blinds stung his eyes. He saw Alessia still sleeping on the chair, and that is when he saw that Nathan was kneeling beside her. He was holding her hand and just looking at her while she slept. He stroked her hand.

"Nathan?" Julius croaked.

Nathan lifted a finger to his lips and whispered, "Shhhh."

Julius swung his legs off the couch and tried to stand up. His legs were still too wobbly. "Where am I?" he asked Nathan.

"My home," he whispered back, not taking his eyes off the woman. "How are you feeling?"

"I don't know. I don't know if I was dreaming or if it was real, but I saw you dying, and something flew into my body," Julius said and rubbed his eyes.

"Oh, I think that was a dream. Things like that don't happen," Nathan said, smiling, still stroking her hand. "You had us all worried. I pushed you out of the way of the booby trap. You hit your head against the wall pretty hard. That was my fault. I am sorry."

"I saw you impaled on the wall," Julius replied, remembering the scene.

"It never happened. Do I look like I have been impaled? No, of course not," Nathan said to him and then stroked her cheek. "Mother Bear, time to wake up."

Alessia woke up slowly and saw Nathan in front of her. She smiled and grabbed him. "My boy. You had me so worried," she cried.

"You were worried about that small scratch I had. You're getting soft on me again," he said as she hugged tightly. "Ouch."

She let go and slapped him hard against the face. "That's for scaring me."

Nathan rubbed his cheek. "I get a slap for a splinter."

"And everything else you put me through," she said and hugged him again.

"Bloody hell. You were right," Frank said from the door. "She hugged him before she slapped him."

Mary walked into the room with cups of coffee. "Yes, I was. There is no whisky in this one, Nathan," she said, passing him the cup.

Julius looked at them all. "Hold on. Does someone want to explain to me what is happening? I know what I saw wasn't a fucking dream. I saw him impaled. Arm shredded to ribbons. I then saw him on fire, and then something made of smoke flew into my body after Frank said I was dying," he said to them quickly. "That wasn't a dream."

"I said you were dying," Frank said as he sipped the coffee. "This is fucking awful. What beans did you use?"

"I wasn't dreaming!" shouted Julius. "It really happened. I heard animal growls. I could smell the fire. I felt its heat."

"That's a very powerful dream you had, Julius," Alessia said as she took the cup of coffee. "You hit your head pretty hard. I have been looking after you."

"You? What medical qualification do you have? There was a hospital, not five minutes from where we were," he said, getting angry.

"If I had taken you to the hospital, then there would have been too many questions," Frank told him. "Plus, Alessia is better than any doctor."

"Frank did the right thing, young pup. Alessia has lots of experience on her side. She knows the human body inside and out. She has helped more people than I can count. Trust me when I say that you were better in her hands than anyone else's," he told Julius. "I have already called the station, and there is a team at the building now. They are removing the rubble from the hatch and checking for any more booby traps," Nathan told him and drank the coffee. He pulled a face. "It really is awful."

"Shut up," Mary replied and took a drink. "Tastes fine to me."

"Not surprised," Frank said, putting the coffee on a table like it would explode if put down too heavily.

"You can shut up also," Mary replied.

Julius leaned back onto the couch and sighed. "I can't believe it was a dream. It felt so real."

Alessia walked over and flicked his nose. "You feel that. That means you are awake. I watched you all night. Nothing happened." She stroked his face. "I wouldn't let anything happen to you."

"I believe you," Julius replied, but didn't know why he believed her. In that instance, he knew she would die for him. She leaned forward and kissed his forehead. "What was that for?"

"Motherly love, you could say," she said to him and smiled. "You look OK now. Just take it easy for a while. No point rushing off into danger quite so soon," she said and went to the kitchen. "I hope you are hungry. I'm going to make breakfast. You all need to eat something."

Julius looked at Nathan. "Don't look at me. It was your dream, not mine."

Julius stood up and asked, "Where is the bathroom?"

"Out to the left, second door down," Nathan told him and drank the coffee. "Shite, forgot about that. You really should have put whisky in it." Once Julius left the room and he heard the click of the lock, he looked at Mary. "You should have taken that memory from him."

"There wasn't time. He was dying," she replied.

"Well, I just hope he believes us," Nathan replied and put the coffee on the table. "We have enough to deal with." He looked at Frank. "How did you manage to pull it off?"

Frank just shrugged. "I can be a scary bastard when I need to be."

"I owe you."

"No, you don't. I owe you, remember? I can never repay that debt. Plus, I enjoyed scaring the little bastards."

Mary coughed. "How are you feeling?"

"Meh. Bit stiff, nothing else," Nathan told her.

"We almost lost you. You know you cannot leave. They are not ready."

"I wasn't going anywhere. It's just been a while since I have had to do that. Bit rusty that's all."

"It was more than that," Frank said to him. "You wanted to go."

"I wouldn't. Never crossed my mind," he told them, but he didn't believe himself.

"It was a close thing, Nathan. You are too important to them. If they lose you, then they lose everything. There would be no coming back from it," Mary told him and stretched her legs. "It would be carnage. We couldn't even hold it together."

"I know. Look, it's done now, so let's move on from it. No point dwelling on it," he told them and smiled as he could smell the food being cooked in the kitchen.

He heard the bathroom door open and Julius shout, "Can someone explain to me why my urine is bright green?"

Julius stood outside Nathan's house and looked at the brand-new BMW M8 sitting in the driveway.

"What happened to the Audi?" he asked Nathan.

"Frank dinged the side bringing you here," Nathan replied to him as he walked around the car. "Bought this a few hours ago until the Audi is fixed."

"Yeah, sure, that makes sense. Buy a new car because the slightly older car has a ding in it," Julius joked. "This car is over seventy thousand pounds, and you just bought it."

"Yes. Well, one hundred and five thousand. It has almost every optional extra."

"How much money do you have? I mean, seriously, who does something like this?"

"Me."

"Oh, that answers it. Why didn't you just buy a Bugatti? I mean, if you are crazy enough to do this, then why not."

"That's coming in two weeks," Nathan replied to him.

"You are winding me up now."

"Nope. I am having a special edition Chiron built for me."

"You're not kidding, are you? Fucking hell. How much money do you have?"

"Don't know. My account deals with that. Probably a lot of money. I stopped caring about that a long time ago." He closed his eyes in thought and ran through the numbers. "All in all, a lot." He pulled out a small writing pad, wrote down a number, and handed the pad to the young man.

Julius's jaw dropped open. He knew that Nathan wasn't lying to him. "Why the fuck are you a police officer? Why the fuck?"

"A man has to have a hobby," Nathan told him.

"What, catching serial killers?"

"That does help during the boring times." Frank and Mary walked towards them. "Ah, thanks for picking up the car, Frank."

"Well, it's the least I owe you," he replied.

He saw Julius. "What's wrong with him?"

"Told him how much I have."

"Hell, Julius, it's only money." Frank laughed.

Nathan stood in the ruined room of the building.

Explosive teams moved through the building, making sure that there were no more nasty surprises in store.

"Bit of a mess," he said to the excavation team. He saw three men removing rubble for the staircase the trap door was covering. "How much longer?"

The furthest down shouted, "I can see the door now. Give us another five minutes, and we will let the explosive team sweep the door."

"Good," Nathan told them and turned to see Julius look at the far wall. He knew what he was looking for, but it had gone now. Had never been there. "What are you looking for?"

Julius looked up and down the wall. "This is where I saw you impaled after the trap had activated. There are no marks on the wall. No holes. No blood."

"See, it was all in your head," said Frank, winking at Nathan.

"Don't worry about it. I'm fighting a fucking fit," Nathan told Julius and patted him on the shoulder. "How is your head?"

"Fine. I feel nothing. I feel really good, actually," he replied. "I had concussions before and felt terrible for days, but I feel absolutely fine. Can't explain it."

"That's Alessia for you. She knows how to fix anyone up. She brought up three burly boys, so she is used to a few scrapes and bruises," Nathan told him and turned to see the explosive team go down the staircase. "I know he isn't down there, nor is our abductee, but we may find clues. Be careful once we enter."

"All clear!" someone shouted.

Nathan walked down the staircase and entered the dark room. He flipped on his torch and scanned the room. Three other beams illuminated the room.

He saw six body statues laid out on six different plinths. Each was lying as if laid to rest. Nathan walked over to one. No eyes. The statue was perfect. Someone had spent a lot of time refining the statue, it looked extremely life-like.

"Plaster of Paris," Nathan told them. "This is Youna Kim." He scanned the statue and saw a mark in the uterus area. He examined it. "Found the mark of the son on this statue. Uterus area."

"Same here. Mark of Christ," confirmed Mary.

"Here also," Frank said.

"And here," Julius told them.

Nathan looked around the room and came to the centre, where a large table stood. It has chains and restraints. There were scratch marks that may have been made by fingernails. Suddenly, lights turned on above him.

"Found a light switch," Frank said as the room lit up.

"That could have been a trap and blown us all up," Mary told him as she turned her torch off.

"50/50," replied Frank.

"Well, we are still alive, so keep looking," Nathan told them. He could see the room more clearly now. The six plinths, three on either side, perfectly in line with each other. The six statues were all in the same positions. On each plinth were the six symbols, drawn on with some sort of black paint. It was crude. Not like the statues. He saw shelves on the walls surrounding them. They had jars of liquids, nails, screws, modelling equipment, tools, electrical equipment, and medical equipment. Nathan walked over and looked at the medical equipment. "Looks clean," he said to the room. He sniffed the blade. "Can smell blood." He saw a bed in the far corner. Frank was standing at it. "They weren't killed here, were they?"

"No. They were brought here to be made into moulds," Frank said to him as he examined the bed. "There is no blood residue anywhere in this room. I would smell it, plus no smells of cleaning agents. None of those jars contain any. No. They weren't killed here."

"The marks on the central table?" Nathan asked him.

"Not from the girls. Nothing but dirt was found under their nails. No wood or metal. I don't know who or what was on the table, but it wasn't the woman he killed," Frank told him and looked under the bed.

Nathan nodded. "Keep looking," he told Frank. He walked to the central table. He lifted one of the restraints and pulled hard. The chain snapped tight and held firm. "Titanium. Expensive." He could have snapped the chain easily, but not with Julius in the room. "Have forensics look over this room," he said to Julius. "We found his monument to these women. Maybe they will find something, but I really doubt it." He looked up at the ceiling and saw the same symbols carved into the statues. They seemed to be surrounded by other symbols. "Mary, what do you think?" he said, pointing up to her.

Mary looked. "Now, those are old symbols. Haven't seen them in a very long time."

Frank looked up also. "Well, isn't that just fucking fantastic? I think we all know what those mean."

Julius looked up. "I don't."

"What do they teach you in school today?" Nathan smirked. "That is a language before the first recorded civilisation. Oh, everyone thinks it was the Sumerians, but it wasn't, not even close. The oldest pyramid in the world is what, the Pyramid of Djoser. Built around 2,630 BCE, if I remember correctly. The Sumerians were around 6,000 BCE. Jericho was in 9,000 BCE. And the people who created this language were around 10,000 BCE."

"And even then, they still were not the first," Mary told him. "There have been humans in Scotland since 13,000 BCE. The standing stones in Scotland are…"

"5,000 BCE," Finished Frank. "But there are older ones, around 17,000 BCE. Who knows who built them."

"We are looking at a language created by people over 9,000 years ago. They were called 'Vingtors'," Nathan said. "Nasty people, well, if you could call them people. They were civilised up to a point but were crazy."

"Crazy how?" Julius asked.

"Oh, you know the sort, blood sacrifices. Cannibalism. Trying to rule the world. Wearing the skin of their defeated foes. You know, crazy shite," Frank replied.

"They were worse than that. A lot worse," Mary said and wrote down the symbols onto a paper pad.

"Yes, they were. Once their civilisation collapsed, all evidence of them was erased from history. They were located in northern Persia. There are only two pieces of information that still exist today that name them," Nathan said as he scanned the ceiling. "Legend has it that warriors from a northern land marched to face them in battle. These warriors were supposed to have come from Eden."

"Seriously?" Julius questioned.

"Like I said, only a myth. The legend goes that the warriors met the Vingtors near modern-day Azerbaijan. From what has been gathered from the two remaining sources of information on this civilisation, the Vingtors were slaughtered. From the rising sun to the setting sun, the battle raged. From the numbers mentioned, which may be a bit exaggerated, over 100,000 Vingtors were slain. From dawn to dusk. It was said that the ground turned red because so much blood soaked into the soil. The myth goes that is why the world has red dirt, soaked in the blood of a civilisation. Their army scattered at nightfall and fell back to their capital. The warriors followed them and fought their way in. By sunset the next day, every man, woman, and child was dead. Maybe close to a million people."

"Seriously. You make it sound so bloody. Surely, it must be wrong," Julius said. "I'm no genius, but I know that no city that far back had so many people in it."

"Like I told you, myths and legends," Nathan said to him. "Head back up and wait for the forensic team. Bring them down when they get here."

Frank watched Julius head up the stairs. "I knew those bastards would come back and bite us in the arse."

"Shite. If it is them, then how much time do we have?" Nathan said, looking at Mary.

She studied what she wrote down and closed her eyes. A bright light shone from behind her eyelids. "Well, I could lie if it makes you feel better," she smiled. "Oh, that's bad."

"Well, don't leave us in suspense, woman; tell us," Frank said to her.

She opened her eyes. "Two days. No more."

"Fuck my life," Nathan said and kicked the middle table. "You sure you're not wrong?"

She pointed to the ceiling. "It's all up there. You know it can't lie."

"This is all you and your friend's fault; you know that. You were fucking told to keep an eye on this type of shite," Frank shouted at her. "As if I don't have enough to deal with, you had to go and drop the ball."

"I know, and they know. The ball has been dropped, as you say," she replied and crossed her arms. "But we were blindsided, and now we must deal with it."

"Again. Fucking again," Nathan said and tilted his head back in disbelief. "Well, both sides fucked this one up in truth. You were supposed to be looking at each other and not letting shite like this happen again. Why do you think we wiped the Vingtors out? I still remember, don't you?"

"Yes, I remember; I was there beside you," Mary told him. "I stood beside both of you."

"It was so long ago, surely no one remembers. We left no survivors. That was the plan. We go in, remove the problem, and that would stop them. Bing, bang, boom. Job done," Frank said and scratched his beard.

Nathan took the flask out of his jacket and took a deep drink. "And here we are, once again cleaning up the mess left to us. I swear, if we manage to pull this off, then both fucking sides are getting a kick in the balls." He looked at both Frank and Mary. "I told both sides the last time to get a fucking grip. I told them both that this shite has to stop happening. Don't you remember 1960? Tens of thousands died. Worldwide. It even set off a volcano, for fuck sake. I fucking killed them. It happened because I had to push myself to stop it the last time. Last time, it wasn't the fucking Vingtors, it was the survivors of the South American cleansing."

"We know. It should have been sorted out then, but remember it happened again in the highlands. Somehow, they keep managing to stumble across something, and it all starts over again," Frank told him and held his hand out for the flask. Nathan handed it over. "How the fuck do they keep bloody getting into this shite?"

"Genetic memory. Apparently, they all have it. It was part of the deal, you know. Both sides have an equal share, equal stake in all of this," Mary said and put the pad back into her coat.

"Well, they can both expect an equal share of my foot up their arse," Nathan told her. "Anyone has a fucking clue where to even start?" Both people shrugged their shoulders. "Fan fucking tastic." Nathan let out a big sigh and closed his eyes in thought. "Two days to figure this out. Great."

Julius came back down with a team of people. "I want this room examined inside and out. I expect a preliminary report by the end of the day," he told them. "Armed guards will be stationed outside at all times; no one, and I mean no one, is to leave the area without an armed escort."

Nathan patted Julius on the back. "Good work, young pup. Let's head back to the station and see if we can figure out where our prey is."

The figure stood and looked at the barriers at the door. It stood taller than him by metres. It was covered in symbols and writings. It knew what each one meant. It knew what each one could do. It knew this door. It extended its hand out and touched one of the symbols. It burned its hand.

They were clever. The only side of the door it could open was covered in symbols it couldn't touch. They were very clever.

It turned and saw her approach. It saw her face broken. Bloody. Bruised.

"He did this to me," she said in the voice it relished. "He beat me. Tortured me. Threatened me. I never broke."

It stroked her face and nodded.

She loved the feeling she got when she was touched by her mentor. Her skin felt alive and real. "He is strong. I am terrified of him," she said, and it stopped stroking her face. "I felt fear beyond reckoning. He let some of his anger out, and it tore into my soul. He could have killed me on a whim, and nothing would have stopped him. Nothing. Not even you."

It pondered on this. It now knew that making the call was the wrong choice. It thought it would be funny to tease him to find out what kind of man this Nathan was. It was now realising that this Nathan was no ordinary man. It walked away from her and back to the barrier. It pondered.

"He will not stop hunting us," she said as she hobbled towards the barrier. "He is something powerful. He knew my name, my true name. He knew what I am. He could speak Romanian like he was born there. This man instilled fear in armed men. Into me." She spat blood onto the dusty ground. "What will you do? He must be dealt with."

It shrugged. What could it do now? If what it was being told was correct, then what could it really do? No. It was too close now. It knew Nathan had been lucky the last time to find out so much before. No, it wouldn't do anything just yet.

"Ah, I understand," Larysa said. "The time is almost here. I will prepare. It will take time, but I will make sure all is ready for you."

It watched her leave.

This Nathan was a problem. A problem that required lancing. It would not deviate from the plan. Not now.

It touched the barrier again and flinched in pain.

Chapter 12

Nathan sat at his desk, with Frank and Mary opposite him. "We need to move fast. We need to find him and stop this."

"We know. But the leads have dried up," Mary told him.

Frank played with his white beard. "She is right. There is nothing left to go on."

Nathan sighed. "Shite."

"I have asked around if there has been any movement, but I have been told there is nothing," Frank told him.

"I have heard the same. Both are blaming the other. Both are saying the same thing; it isn't them," Mary added.

"Well, someone must be lying," Nathan told them. "Something like this doesn't happen without someone knowing."

"They are adamant that they don't. I am inclined to believe them," Mary said.

"That's a first," Frank said to her. "I don't believe any of the fuckers. Doesn't matter what side they are on; they both know how to lie."

Nathan drummed his fingers on the desk. He was thinking. '*What would he do if he was the killer?*' Well, for a start, I wouldn't call the cunt who is trying to catch me. He should have pushed that bitch, Larysa, harder. He cursed himself for that error. He reached down into his drawer and brought out a bottle of whisky.

"Really. I don't think this is the time," said Mary as he poured out two glasses.

"I do. This may be the last drink we have. Fucked if I know what we are going to do to find out where this cunt is hiding," Nathan told her.

Frank took the glass and downed it in one gulp. "Good year."

"King James special. 200 years in the barrel. A gift," Nathan said and poured another glass for Frank.

"Must have cost a few bucks."

"1.1 million of them, actually."

Frank smiled. "Well, here's to me drinking a few hundred thousand pounds of it, then." And raised his glass.

"You two are idiots," Mary told them.

"Idiots with expensive tastes," Nathan replied to her. "Plus, I have six bottles of this. No point letting it go to waste." There was a tap at the door. Helena walked in. "Helena, you want a drink?"

"No, thank you, Sir, I mean, Nathan," she replied. She handed over a file. "Forensics went all over the place. Found a few fingerprints which are not in any system. No blood residue from any of the victims. They can't make heads or tails of the writing on the ceiling. The statues were hand-carved. They are exact replicas of the victims, down to the millimetre. Someone took a lot of time over each one."

Nathan read the report. Nothing contained within it surprised him. He caught something in a picture. "What is this?" he asked her.

Helena looked over. "A broken toe."

"None of the statues had anything broken off them," Nathan told her.

"Yes, sir. If you turn to the next page, you will see that a broken finger was found outside the building."

"Why would broken pieces of unbroken statues be found outside?" Mary asked.

"There were no signs of broken statues anywhere near the building, no piles of powder to say anything had been smashed down," Helena told the room.

Julius walked into the room. "Latest report from about our missing suspect. Whoever took her drove all over Glasgow once they left here. They stopped at multiple locations. People got out and went to the building, but the same number got back in not long after. I have sent teams to the buildings, but I'm not expecting much."

"What do you make of this?" Nathan asked Julius and handed him the file.

"Broken pieces of statues?"

"Don't know," he replied. "Practice maybe."

"Show me the room again, where the status was," he said and took the picture. He looked at it. What was he missing? He flipped through several pictures. The statues were all intact. Nothing was missing or broken. "I wonder if it is symbolic."

"What do you mean?" Frank asked.

"Broken status for broken women," he replied.

"It would fit the scenario," Helena said. "He broke them before killing them." She looked at the file again and leafed through the pages.

"The young lady is right," Mary said. She took one of the pics. "The symbols over the womb have significance. We know who used to do things like this."

"Wait, wait, wait. It's the soul. The broken soul. The soul of a killer," Frank said leaning forward.

"They had abortions. They spilled the blood of their own," Nathan said, coming to a realisation. "They marked their souls. Poisoned them. They took the lives of their own children."

"Their souls would be considered lifeless," Mary added.

"He made two copies of each victim. One pure and unblemished, and the other broken and impure," Nathan replied.

"He wouldn't break them in that room. He wouldn't have to be gentle with them either. He had to symbolise the journey. If they got damaged on the way, it wouldn't have mattered. He would have to go somewhere special," Frank told Nathan.

"But he would have to make sure they got there. They would be fragile. It would require special transportation," Nathan told the room. "That requires someone with knowledge."

"Son of a bitch," Frank said in triumph. "He would do it."

"He would, wouldn't he?" Mary said.

Nathan slammed his hand on the desk in anger. "He would. Bastard. I know where he will be."

"Then we better go and ask him," Frank said, getting up. He pulled out his guns and gave them a check over. "This is going to be fun."

Julius looked at Nathan. "What's going on?"

Nathan put his guns into his shoulder holsters. "We are going to see someone we know about special transportation. He is a collector of rare treasures." He grabbed his car keys and drained his whisky glass. "Grab your stuff, Julius. You're going to see a devil."

Nathan pulled up outside a warehouse on Govan Road.

"How do you want to do this?" Frank asked, smiling. "You know he won't be happy to see you."

"I don't care how happy he is," Nathan told him. "Let's get in, get out, and hopefully, with the information we need." He stepped out of the car. "I fucking hate speaking to him."

"I seem to remember he hates speaking to you," Mary told him and walked around the car to get to the pavement. "It did not end well the last time. He had a few scars after that chat."

"Yeah, I think your kill count that day was high." Frank laughed and pulled out his weapons.

"Who are we going to see, and why does it require weapons in our hands?" Julius asked.

"We are going to see Mr Mai Chin Hok. He is North Korean," Mary told him.

"He is a cunt," Nathan told him. "You're about to meet a really sick piece of shite."

"He couldn't be worse than Hanz," Julius said and took out his gun.

"You want to bet?" Nathan said, looking at him. "Stick close to Frank. Mary, cover us. Frank, do not kill that cock sucker until I get my answers."

"Cross my heart," Frank told him.

"You don't have one," said Mary, and Frank flipped her off.

Nathan opened the door and walked inside.

The building was cold, but most warehouses are. The lights were on, and it seemed to sell antiques. Julius saw dozens of shelves containing vases, rugs, candle sticks, jewellery, and other items. He walked towards one shelf that held several strange knives. The blades were in the shapes of dragons.

"Chinese. 3rd Dynasty, Zhou. That dynasty ruled China, from 800 years between 1,046 to 256 BC. Those blades are over 2,500 years old. They will be as sharp as the day they were made," Mary said as she looked at them also. "Very very rare. Very expensive also. I wonder how he got them."

Nathan walked between the shelves and saw various rare items on them. Mai Chin was not allowed to sell these items; they were forbidden in Glasgow. Ceremonial blades, death masks, tiger bones, and other illicit items. He stopped at one shelf and picked up a small mirror. He saw something flicker in his reflection and swore. "He has hook mirrors."

"You're kidding," Frank said and walked over. "Shite."

"That bastard," Nathan said and smashed the mirror. He heard a small cry and then nothing.

"Someone made that and recently," Mary shouted over. "None have been made in three thousand years."

Nathan had seen enough. His temper was fraying. "Mai Chin, I want to speak to you!" roared Nathan. He pushed over a shelf full of antiques, and they scattered over the floor. "MAI CHIN."

Seven burly Asian men ran out of a back room and ran towards them. Nathan saw that they carried swords and axes. He shot the first one right between the eyes. The man crashed into a small table, which exploded under his weight. The other six closed the gap quickly and jumped at the group. Nathan ducked the swing of a sword and grabbed the man by the testicles. He pulled down hard and brought his head up, smashing into the attacker's chin. Teeth and blood rained onto his head. Nathan grabbed the sword from his attacker's hand and plunged it into his thigh. The man screamed from a ruined mouth. Nathan thrust the barrel of his gun into the man's mouth and pulled the trigger. He saw Julius struggle with an axe-wielding attacker. He pulled the sword from the dead man's thigh and tossed it into the throat of the young man's attacker. The man sprayed blood all over Julius. Julius used the arm of his jumper to wipe the blood away from his eyes. He watched as the man before him stood swaying, his eyes wide open in fear. The man's hand came up and felt the sword sticking out of his neck. He tried to speak, but blood dribbled out of his mouth instead. Julius watched as the man collapsed to the floor soundlessly.

Mary dodged the sword sweeps and punched her attacker in the chest; the sound of his ribs breaking causing the man to collapse to the ground. Mary stood on his chest and pushed down hard, blood erupting between the man's clenched teeth. She lowered her gun and cocked it slowly. She saw the pain and hate in the man's eyes and smiled slowly at him.

"Tut tut, that's no way to treat a lady," she said and shot him through the nose.

Frank fought two at once and laughed in glee. He shot one on the foot and grabbed him before he fell. He pulled the man in front of him and watched as the other attacker's sword plunged into his back. Frank brought his gun up and shot the man in the left eye. He dropped the man and heard him cry as he fell onto the sword, the blade piercing through his stomach. Frank kicked the blade slightly and laughed as the man cried in agony. He walked away to leave the man to his slow and painful death.

146

The sixth man jumped over his dead friend towards Nathan. He shot the man in both knee caps. Nathan held out his arm and the man's throat rammed into it, flipping him over and crashing into the ground, screaming. He crawled over to his back and watched as Mary stood above him. She took a knife from her coat and sliced the man's throat open. The man scratched at his throat as he bled to death.

Julius stood and watched this happen in less than 40 seconds. He had taken his gun out and aimed at one of the attackers but watched in horror as his companions tore the men apart with such ease.

"Mai Chin. You are fucking pissing me off. Get your fat arse out here now," Nathan shouted and made his way to the back room. He kicked the door open and raced inside. He saw an oldish Asian man scramble around a desk. "Where the fuck is your boss?" The man shrugged his shoulders, so Nathan shot him in the arm. The man fell back into a chair. "I won't ask again." He pushed the gun into the side of his head. The man's eyes darted to a large filing cabinet. "Thank you." He pulled the trigger.

Frank walked over to the cabinet and tore it from the wall, tossing it across the room. There was a door on the other side.

Nathan walked calmly to it and tapped politely. "Knock. Knock," he said.

"He won't answer, you know," Frank told him.

"I'm giving him the choice." Nathan sighed. "He won't open, will he?" He looked at Mary. The woman shook her head. "Mai Chin, you know why I am here. Open this fucking door now before I lose my temper." Still nothing. "You would think by now they would know to listen to me," Nathan said and began kicking the door in. "He has it protected. Well, won't fucking work with me," Nathan said, ramming the door with his foot.

Julius saw the man kick large dents into the metal door. It buckled and bent with the force of the kicks.

The door smashed open, and Nathan walked calmly in.

Julius followed and couldn't believe what he was seeing. There were dozens of people all chained up against the walls. They were all girls. "What the fuck?" Julius swore.

There in the large room were what looked like six operating tables. Two ladies lay on tables with people around them. They were doctors and nurses if you could call them that now. They were operating on the ladies. Blood pooled on the floor and trickled into a drain.

"What the fuck are you doing?" Nathan shouted in Korean.

"Who are you?" a masked figure replied. It was a man.

"Your fucking death," Nathan replied and shot the man in the eye. The others tried to run, but Frank and Mary were upon them in a flash.

Mary's knife flashed like quicksilver and red as she cut her way through the fleeing figures.

Frank laughed as he shot out the knees of the rest. Frank watched them crash to the floor, screaming in agony and trying to crawl away. Frank still laughed as he brought his foot down hard on their heads, their brains exploding over the blood-stained floor.

Julius stood rooted to the spot as what he had seen stunned him. He watched as Nathan walked purposefully towards a doctor, swinging a scalpel at him in defence.

Nathan's hand shot forward and grabbed the scalpel from the man's hand. *"You fucking waste of skin,"* Nathan roared in Korean. *"How many?"*

"What?" the man replied in terror. Nathan flashed the scalpel, and three of the man's fingers fell to the floor. The man screamed in agony and grabbed the stumps of the missing fingers. *"Seventeen."*

"Seventeen, it is then," Nathan shouted and moved so quickly that Julius could barely see what he had done. Nathan had stabbed the man 17 times in the vital organs. The man crashed to his knees, blood spurting from his lips. Nathan grabbed his head and pulled it back so he could look into his dying eyes. *"When you get there, tell them that Nathan sends his regards."* He plunged the scalpel into the man's Adam's apple.

Nathan turned to see how the others were doing.

Mary had slit the throat of the last nurse, and Frank was stamping down on another. He looked at Julius. "Breathe, Julius."

"What the fuck is this?" Julius croaked.

"It fucking looks exactly what it is," replied Frank to the young man. He looked at Nathan. "I'm pretty sure this isn't allowed here."

"I told him not to do this again. I warned him," Nathan said and lifted the head of one of the girls very gently. He spoke Korean to the girl, asking, *"Are you OK?"* She shook her head and fainted. "I'm going to kill him."

"What is this?" Julius demanded.

"The man we are looking for is an organ harvester," Mary told him. "He takes orders."

"For fucking organs!" shouted Julius.

"It's a billion-pound business," Frank said and pushed past him. "He would only start this up again if he knew something like you wouldn't be around to stop him."

"MAI CHIN, you sick mother fucker!" shouted Nathan. He saw some girls had scars on their bodies, their organs having been removed. He looked over to Julius. "I swear; I did not know this was here."

Julius looked on in terror at the scene before him. "What did you think he was doing?"

"That he started up his old illegal trade in antiques. Not this." Nathan moved along the wall. Some of the girls were dead. Some had scars. Some did not. "Frank, Julius, other side."

They passed more girls, and Nathan checked each one. Some were close to death; others looked like they had just been taken. He saw movement under one of the operating tables and grabbed out a female nurse. He lifted her off her feet and held her in the air.

"*Where is he?*" he roared at her in Korean.

The woman was crying hard but managed to lift a shaky hand towards a far door.

"*Tell me why? Why now?*"

"*He said he could. He got orders!*" she screamed in terror.

"*From who?*"

"*From everyone.*"

Nathan began to close his fist and heard the woman struggle to breathe. He turned his head slightly to look at Mary. "If she is telling the truth, then I want to speak to your chaperon."

"It would seem that both of them need to answer, I would say," she replied and looked over at Frank. He nodded.

"*As for you,*" he told the nurse, "*stick around,*" he said and smashed her head against the wall, knocking her out. "You will answer questions later."

He walked towards another door and kicked it open. He was very angry now. The door flew off its hinges and embedded itself in the wall above a sitting figure.

Nathan walked in and stood in front of the man sitting at the desk. "Mai Chin. Oh, how I have missed you."

The man stood up and leaned closer to Nathan. His face was covered in scars. He had patches of differently coloured skin all over his face. He was getting fat, maybe 25 stone. Probably more. He sneered at Nathan, "I have protection now. You are not welcome here."

Nathan punched the man and sent him crashing into the wall. The wall cracked as Mai Chin hit. "Not from me; you fucking don't." He grabbed the table and threw it against the wall on the right; it hit and disintegrated into broken pieces of oak. He walked over and picked the man up by the throat. "I know you transported something special. You would have done it very recently. Six statues. All of them women." The man spat blood into his face. Nathan slammed the man into the wall three times, the brickwork crumbling under the assault.

Mai Chin laughed with each strike. "That tickles." He punched Nathan.

Nathan's head didn't even move with the strike. He grabbed the man's hand and squeezed. The man's fist snapped and broke, with blood spurting out between Nathan's fingers.

Mai Chin grunted. "Ouch," he mocked.

Nathan pulled down hard and ripped the man's hand off the arm. He threw the stump into the waste bin over his shoulder. "Mai Chin. I will get my answers one way or another. Where did you make the delivery?"

"You think I am scared of you? Do you know who are you dealing with? Who you are looking for?" He laughed as blood poured from the stump of his wrist. "Do what you want with me. I will not talk."

"Listen to me, fucker. I want that address," Nathan told him. He clicked his finger, and Mary gave him a long knife. Nathan placed the blade on the man's forehead. "You know me, Mai; I can make it quick or I can make it painful."

"Oh, I'm scared," the man chuckled.

Nathan dug the knife into the skin and began to cut around the man's face. He didn't care about the screaming. He was now so angry that it didn't matter. He dug the knife in above the man's lips and began to cut around them. He did the exact same thing around each eye. Once finished, he plunged the knife into the man's shoulder.

"Last time, Mai, tell me," Nathan said and grabbed the side of the man's face.

"He will kill me if I tell you," Mai screamed.

"Wrong fucking answer!" Nathan shouted and pulled the man's face off. He threw the skin to the ground and looked at the man's ruined, wet, bloody face. Only around his lips and eyes had skin. He had to speak after all. "Frank, find what I know is here." Frank nodded and started to rummage through the table's drawers.

"He will do worse to me," Mai spat out. "Just kill me!"

Nathan shook his head. "No, Mai. Do you think, after what I have seen out there, I will make it that easy? No. You told me that all you would do was sell very rare antiques. You lied to me. And you have something I want. Information. Tell me where he is?"

"I can't!" the man screamed. Whatever was blocking it, the pain was starting to wear off. He squirmed in Nathan's iron-tight grip.

"Like I fucking care," Nathan shouted and lifted the man higher. He pulled the knife out from the shoulder and plunged it into the man's chest. "You know I will. You know I will, Mai."

"Clyde Street. That's where I delivered what you are looking for. Near the suspension bridge. Old building, next to the new flats that were opened last week. That's all in now," Mai told him as blood spurted from his mouth. "Let me go now."

Nathan looked at Frank. The man grabbed the file from a few days ago. He flipped through quickly and then nodded. Nathan grabbed the knife and pulled it down on the man's body. Blood sprayed all over him, and the contents of the man's abdomen poured out. Nathan dropped the man to the floor. "Now, I am finished with you." He looked at Frank. "You have the address?"

"Yes. I have it," Frank confirmed.

Julius stood rooted to the spot. He couldn't believe what he had just witnessed. This was brutality he had never seen before. "I will call an ambulance," he said and grabbed his mobile with shaky hands.

"For the girls out there, but not for this piece of shite," Nathan told him and kicked Mai in the stomach, quite literally.

Mary looked down and inspected Mai. "A fitting punishment," she said, then turned to walk out of the room. She grabbed Julius and guided him out.

"Frank, you know what to do."

Frank smirked. "Oh, that I do," he replied and snapped his finger. "Well, Mai, it wasn't a fucking pleasure to meet you again. See you again, hopefully never." And spat in the man's face and left the room.

Nathan knelt down and grabbed the man by the hair. "Stop playing dead, you piece of shite."

Mai's eyes snapped open. "I will be back, Nathan, and I will kill you."

"No, you won't. Can you not hear that?" Nathan cupped his hand around his ear. "Frank's friends are coming."

Mai could hear howling in the air. "They wouldn't."

"They would. Frank has made sure of it," Nathan said and stood up. "Enjoy the little time you have left, Mai. Now, you play nice with your new friends." He left the room.

Mai scanned the room but couldn't move. He heard them. He could smell them. He knew they were all around him. He could feel the breadth on his scar-covered skin. How was this possible? They didn't work for Nathan. He didn't have that kind of pull. They would never be given to him. It was a trick, one final insult to him. Then he heard Nathan shout, "Sick 'em." Mai was torn to pieces.

Nathan walked back into the operating area and smiled as he heard Mai getting what he deserved. He saw his companions helping the women from behind the walls and making them comfortable.

"When are they arriving?" he asked Julius.

"I made a serious incident call. Police and ambulance should be here within minutes," he replied as he helped a young woman to the ground. "Jesus, how does this happen?"

"Humans allow this to happen. They are greedy and selfish," Mary said to him, carrying an unconscious woman to a table.

"Evil like this happens because no one fucking cares," Frank replied to them all. "You honestly think humans care? Of course not. This stuff happens worldwide. Bastards all of them."

Nathan walked over and looked at a dead woman hanging from the wall. He wondered what pain and terror she felt before the end. No doubt she prayed for help, but no one was listening. No one was ever listening, not now. He snapped the chains holding her against the wall and let her body fall onto his shoulder. He walked over to a table and laid her naked body down. He saw the scars covering her body. "She died for what exactly? Greed? Stupidity? Rage? Wealth? These women suffered because humans are fucking animals." He sighed and whispered something under his breath.

Julius caught what he said, "*I should have killed them all when I had the chance.*" He walked over to the man. "What did you mean by that?"

152

Nathan looked up at him as if this was the first time seeing him. He shook his head. "Nothing. Just thinking out loud." He heard sirens outside the warehouse.

"There are good people out there. Not everyone is scum. There are people out there trying to make the world a better place. I like to think that I am one of them," Julius said to him with honesty.

Nathan smiled and put his hand on the young man's shoulder. "One man can't change the world. I will give you an A plus for trying though." He looked at the door as Mary led paramedics and police through the room. "OK, I want the paramedics on these seven ladies first. They are in critical condition. You, officers over there, you help these women as long as they can walk. Take them to the waiting ambulances outside, one at a time. Once more police arrive, I want this warehouse locked down and a cordon around the entire building. No one gets in or out once the ladies have been dealt with. You," he said and pointed to a sergeant, "get more men down here now. Call in for armed police right this fucking moment."

"What happened in the previous room?" the sergeant demanded, his face a cover of terror.

"They fucking asked questions when they should be doing what they were told," said Frank as he helped a paramedic treat one of the women.

Nathan laughed. "My friend is right. Do what I say and do it now." He took his mobile out of his pocket and called David. "David, I have an address. Have armed police ready to go to Clyde Street. I am heading over there now. I will leave the sergeant here in charge of this crime scene. What? No. Tell our dear captain to stay out of this. Yes. Yes. OK. Look, I don't have time; I'm going with the team now. I don't care; I'm not waiting. Fucking hell, David. No, you're not coming. Stay there, coordinate what's happening here, and make sure the police get to Clyde Street soon." He hung up. "OK, we are going, sergeant. Make sure each of these woman is treated or you will personally answer to me."

A woman ran out of the room where Mai Chin was. She vomited onto the ground. "What happened in there?" She vomited again.

The sergeant walked over to the room and looked inside. Blood covered every wall, and in the centre of the room was just a pile of torn body pieces. He turned and almost walked into Nathan, who was standing right behind him. "What…"

"He is not your concern. Now, sergeant, I want to make myself absolutely clear. You didn't see anything in that room at all. What room? Never existed. Do I make myself clear?" The man nodded. "Good. Now make sure your officer here, who is throwing up because she is distraught at the sight of these women, also understands." Nathan told him. The sergeant just nodded, sweat breaking out on his brow. "Good. Now, sergeant, you have a scene to secure. Get to it."

Julius saw the sergeant move quickly away from the room. He helped and the paramedic put one of the ladies onto a trolley. He felt a hand on his shoulder.

It was Mary. "Time to go."

Julius followed her outside, and he saw several ambulances and police vehicles blocked the street. His head hurt in the dying light of the day. He turned and saw the sun sink behind the motorway bridge. Soon it would be gone. The street lights flickered on, and he slumped against the BMW. He closed his eyes, trying to come to an understanding of what he had just witnessed. He could smell the whisky. He opened his eyes and saw a flask in front of his face.

Nathan held the flask out. "Drink. Trust me."

Julius grabbed the flask and took a large gulp of the burning liquid. "Fuck."

"The day isn't over yet," Nathan said to him and nodded for him to take another drink. Julius did so gratefully. "Do you know why I have been so tough on you? The world you thought you knew doesn't exist. Never has and never will. What you saw was the tip of the iceberg. I see potential in you, but first, you need to see the world for what it is really like."

"I can't believe that," the young man replied.

"I am sorry to be the bearer of bad news, but it is. I told you to toughen up, and you have, but you need to toughen up more. You think what you saw in there was bad; trust me, there is worse out there. Much worse. I have seen it."

"How do you cope?"

"Who says I do? You learn to detach yourself from life. Being crazy helps." And he smiled.

Julius smiled also. "Oh, I know you are crazy."

"I will take that as a compliment. Look. I don't know what we are heading into. My gut tells me that this is going to be bad, very bad. If you want to stay and lead the team here, I won't think anything less of you. It may be better that you do."

Julius looked at the paramedics and the police helping the women out of the warehouse. He had no idea that such a thing could happen, let alone in the city he lived in. He knew that Nathan was right and that there would be worse out there. What kind of monster would do this to innocent women? Mai Chin was evil, and the person who allowed him to do this was worse. In the short time he had worked under Nathan, he had seen things that could never be unseen. He allowed a man to burn to death. No, change that. He had allowed a paedophile drug-making prick to burn to death. He had seen Nathan be a complete monster at times but also seen him be kind and gentle. He had listened to the phone call made by the killer and knew that if there was a chance to save the girl then he would. If he didn't, then he would not be able to live with himself. "No. I will go with you. I want to see this through to the end."

Nathan slapped Julius on the back. "I will make a bastard out of you yet, young pup. Good. Go and tell that fat sergeant that we are leaving, and make sure he locks this area down." He watched as Julius walked away and started yelling at the startled sergeant.

"He is brave. Stupid but brave," Mary said as she appeared beside Nathan.

"He has balls, I tell you that." Frank chuckled as he walked towards them. "Didn't think he would come with us. Just shows you that after all this time, I can still be surprised by them."

"I must be rubbing off on him," Nathan replied and saw several police officers hold back news reporters. Nathan saw that Robert was among them. "That arsehole." He watched as Robert was shouting questions towards Julius.

The young man walked over and gave a short statement to all of them. But Robert kept interrupting and asking more questions. Nathan stood in glee as Julius punched the man with an uppercut that would make Ali proud. Robert crashed to the ground, and the other reporters just stood in shock.

"I take it that this is the end of questions for the time being. Yes! Good. Then please allow the emergency services to do their work," Julius told the stunned reporters.

Julius walked back, rubbing his fist. "Don't hate me, but that felt good. He asked a very rude question that deserved a very direct answer."

Nathan laughed hard. "Julius, my boy, you just graduated in my eyes."

Mary sighed as Nathan patted the young man on the back. "Great, now there are two of them."

Chapter 13

Nathan pulled up outside the abandoned building on Clyde Street. The old building was four stories tall and decaying badly.

"You feel that?" Frank asked.

"No," replied Julius as he stepped out of the car.

"Yes," said Mary. "This is not good."

"What are you on about?" Julius demanded.

"Can you not feel it? The rumbling," Frank said to him.

"No."

"It takes practice," Nathan said as he passed the young man. "This is us up the shite creek without a paddle time."

"Not the words I would use, but I do agree." Mary nodded.

Nathan walked around to the side of the building and tore one of the doors off its hinges. He threw it to the ground with a large metallic clang. He took out his gun. "We stop this now." He went inside the dark building.

Nathan slowly went inside. It was pitch black, but that didn't matter to him. He could see just as well. He had entered the main hall area. He saw an old reception desk, badly degraded. Puddles of water were everywhere. He saw stairs leading up, but it was the stairs leading down that interested him. A beam of light shone behind him as Julius turned on his torch. Didn't matter. He proceeded to the staircase and looked down. He could see a very faint light.

"They dug down deep. Below the building," he said to the others. He saw various excavation equipment scattered throughout the reception area. He looked at the stairs and started to go down. After a while, he reached a set of makeshift stairs; they were poorly built and wouldn't last long, but long enough for whatever was happening further down.

The group kept going down until they reached the bottom. Nathan saw a tunnel lit by dull light bulbs crudely attached to the walls. The walls were stone and looked very old.

"This takes us below the river Clyde," he said to them. "This tunnel was built long ago. Possibly, a coal tunnel or something, but the stones look older than that. I don't know of any tunnel network like this here in Glasgow this old."

"I don't hear any pumps. How are they keeping the water from flooding this area?" Julius asked. He stopped. He could feel the rumble now. "What is that?"

"Nothing good," Frank told him.

"Mary, do you know what's going on?" Nathan asked her.

"Sadly no. This feels different from last time. Something has changed," she told him. "I am beginning to think I may have been wrong."

"Oh, great fucking time to admit that," Frank growled to her.

"Frank!" chided Nathan. "Mary, what do you mean?"

"This is different. The energy is all wrong. It feels reversed. It feels all wrong," she replied and sighed. "I think whatever is happening here is something I have never come across before."

Nathan cursed. "Great. OK, we go forward. We end this now. We find our two killers, stop what they are doing, and save the girl. You know, typical Hollywood bullshit."

"You don't ask for much, do you?" Frank giggled.

"Shut the fuck up." Nathan smiled. "I lead. Julius, cover our 6." He entered the tunnel. He walked slowly and could feel pressure against his skin. Whatever power was being used further along the tunnel was old and powerful. This type of power was reserved for very old and powerful beings. He flinched as he felt something painful in his head.

"I fucking felt that," Nathan grunted.

"That shouldn't be here," Mary said as she rubbed her brow in discomfort.

"Fucking hell!" swore Nathan. "It's here. Why the fuck is it here?" He looked at Frank.

"Don't look at me," he replied in discomfort. "Last I checked, there wasn't any here. Oh, wait. There was one, wasn't there? You know, when he built them."

"What's here?" Julius asked.

"Fucking trouble," Nathan said. He held his head again. "Fuck, that was two." Nathan held out his hand and steadied himself against the wall. "What the fuck is he doing?"

"We have no time," Mary said and sagged.

Nathan nodded and ran down the tunnel. He and the team exited the tunnel after 40 metres and found themselves running out onto a large balcony inside a large cavern. Nathan looked around and saw dozens of petrified trees in the cavern, standing around 20 metres tall. He could hear sounds from below the balcony and saw three figures below. The missing girl was lying on a large stone slab in front of some sort of archway. The archway glowed with a green light which flickered. Standing in front of the archway were two figures. Nathan could make out Larysa, but the other figure seemed to be surrounded by some sort of darkness. They were looking not at the archway but at crumbling plaster statues of their victims. Nathan could see that the archway contained a large twin door, almost 10 metres tall. Nathan could make out the writing and symbols of the doors and cursed.

"You two, tell me right now how that door is here?" he demanded of Frank and Mary.

"How did they find that?" Mary replied.

"Oh, shite," Frank swore.

"We are out of time. We stop this now. You three take the stairs over there. I will take the more direct route," Nathan said and looked over the balcony, and then shouted. "You two stupid cunts down there heads up."

It could feel the barrier begin to break. The symbols flared brilliantly as they fought against what it was doing, but already they were beginning to fracture. It smiled in glee. It turned to its newest treasure. She lay on the slab, asleep, the morphine slowly dripping into her body. Soon she would complete her task, and then they would come.

It saw her walk towards him, her face awash with awe and pleasure.

"I never thought I would see this. This is exhilarating," she squealed in please. "Soon your work will be complete, and we will have our reward."

It nodded and felt one of the symbols shatter. He turned and saw one of the plaster statues of his other treasures crumble to fine dust. It was working.

Another symbol shattered, and another statue disappeared.

The barrier was breaking and collapsing before his very eyes. Soon, very soon, it would get its reward.

"You two stupid cunts, down there, heads up."

It looked up and saw Nathan looking down at them. It took a step back as Nathan jumped over the balcony and fell towards them.

It watched as the man smashed into the ground before him, the ground cracking under his weight. It watched as Nathan stood before it, smiling.

Larysa ran at the man, and it watched as Nathan roundhouse kicked her across the chamber, smashing her into the cavern wall and screaming in agony at the impact.

"It's so nice to put a face to the voice," Nathan said to it. "So, this is what a psychotic prick looks like. Not much. So, 'ya bastard, you ready to die?"

It laughed.

Nathan heard the laugh. He lifted his gun and aimed it at the head of his foe. The darkness surrounding it seemed to hide its features.

"*Well, well, well.*" The figure laughed. "*So this is the much-feared Nathan. I see your reputation is much earned.*"

Nathan heard several voices come from it. The shroud of darkness moving to some unknown force. "Oh, I'm much fucking worse," he replied, his gun still pointing at what he hoped was the head. "Stop what you are doing, and I may let you live. One chance. Who am I kidding? I won't let you fucking live."

It laughed harder. "*May let me live. Tut tut. Not very good at bargaining, are you now?*"

"Who's bargaining? I'm telling you what you will fucking do. Stop this now."

"*Oh, I don't think I will. You see, I have planned this for a very long time, and it would be such a shame to let all that effort go to waste. No, I think I will keep going.*" It chuckled as another symbol shattered.

Nathan caught a glimpse of another statue crumbling to dust. "Well, don't say I didn't warn you." He pulled the trigger. The figure just stood there, and nothing happened. The bullet stopped as soon as it touched the shrouding darkness. It just hovered there, rotating quickly. It then fell to the ground with a clink. "Nice trick."

"*I am protected. I have the protection of higher powers,*" it told him. It raised a hand out of the darkness and pointed to Nathan. "*Who will protect you from me?*"

Nathan saw the misshapen hand appear from the darkness and growled. "I do not require protection from the likes of you. It makes sense now. I know what you are."

"*And, pray tell, what is that?*"

"Fallen," Nathan said.

The darkness fell away from the figure. Nathan watched as a tall man appeared. His body was very muscular but uneven in places. His hands were long and crooked. His face was gaunt, and his eyes were a dark blood red. Burned and damaged wings sprouted from its back.

"*And so, the veil is lifted,*" It said to him. "*How did you know?*"

"This isn't my first time fighting you fuckers."

"*Really, now that is very interesting,*" it spoke and began to slowly walk around Nathan. "*What else do you know about me, then I wonder?*"

"I bet I can guess your name," Nathan told it and put the gun back into its holster.

"*Oh, really. Now this will be very interesting. I'm all ears.*" It leaned its head forward and where an ear should be, there was just a misshapen lump.

"You are working with that whore over there, Sybella. I knew what she was the second I spoke to her. Been a very long time since I came across one of her kind. She was shocked when I said her name. But I know her other name, 'Citadel'. The teller of false truths, the mother of abominations. The actual whore of Babylon," Nathan told it and watched its grisly smile widen in pleasure. "So, I had to think, what piece of shite would work with such a creature. And then it hit me just now when I finally got to see you in all your fucked-up glory. I do not know what happened to the real Thomas Thorn, but I know you are not him. No, you are not him; are you Orobas?"

The fallen had stopped walking and narrowed its eyes. "*Well, that's unfortunate. You know me. But that does not matter, does it? I will complete my given task. They will not allow you to stop this.*"

"That you are trying to break the six seals. You know I will not allow that to happen," Nathan told it as he turned to keep his foe in eye sight.

"*Very good. You have knowledge. Well, how do you plan to stop me?*" it giggled.

Nathan laughed. "Ask my name."

"*What!*"

"Well, if you ask my name, you will find out how I will stop you."

"*So be it, what is your name?*"

"Alasdair Raum."

The chamber shook with the roar of anger from the fallen.

Chapter 14

Julius ran down the stairs behind Mary and Frank. He watched as Nathan jumped off the balcony and fell in front of the two people. He couldn't make out who was standing beside Mrs Thorn, as it was covered in something that made it hard to make out. He watched as Nathan kicked the woman across the massive cavern with such ease. He saw her crash into the wall and scream in agony.

"Julius, you get the girl. Get her off that slab and get her to safety," Frank told him as they reached the bottom of the stairs. Frank saw Julius look over at Nathan. "He doesn't need our help. We will just get in his way. Fucking get the girl, Julius. We will get that bitch over there. Go, now."

Julius nodded and ran over to the young girl on the slab. She was asleep and had a drip going into her arm. She wasn't tied down, so he pulled the needle out and tried to lift her. She wouldn't move. He checked again to see if she was tied down, but there was nothing there.

"I can't move her!" he shouted over to Frank. He turned and saw that Frank and Mary were fighting with Larysa. How the woman could fight after being smashed into the cavern wall was something that truly surprised him. Both Mary and Frank punched and kicked out at the woman, but she deflected the blows quickly and attacked. He looked down at the woman on the slab and grabbed her around the waist. He pulled, but couldn't move her off the slab.

"*Wait,*" a female voice whispered into his ear. He turned around, startled, and saw no one around him.

The cavern shook with the sound of roaring.

"*Seraphim,*" Orobas roared.

"Bingo, mother fucker!" Nathan shouted and punched the fallen in the face. He watched as it crashed to the ground. Nathan ran and grabbed its leg and blocking the other leg and kicking him away. Nathan backed off and grappled with the fallen as it shot towards him.

"I will kill you for what you did."

"Many arseholes better and more powerful than you have tried and fucking failed," Nathan shouted into its face as they fell to the ground, still grappling.

The fallen head-butted Nathan and his head smashed into the ground. Nathan grunted in pain and twisted his hips to get a better purchase. Nathan shifted his body weight and turned the fallen on its back. He managed to get an arm free and punched the fallen three times in the face. Black blood splattered over Nathan and onto the ground.

The fallen wings opened up and flapped, forcing them out of Nathan's grasp. It hovered above Nathan and took out a sword from somewhere in its tattered clothes. *"How could you do it? To them?"*

"Easily," Nathan replied and stood up. He held out his hand in front of him and saw a crack of light appear before him. He plunged both hands into the light and tore it open bigger. He reached inside and brought something out.

The fallen watched in horror as his foe tore open the veil. It knew what he was getting, fear and terror flooding in its cursed blood.

Nathan held his double-headed axe and smiled. It had been so long since he had held it. The two axe heads sparkled in the weak light of the cavern. Each head had a wing engraved on it, one inlaid with red rubies and the other with black diamonds. The handle was made from a tree from the old world and was stronger than steel. The handle had leather made from a sacred beast wrapped around it. Titanium strips covered the handle to hold it all together. At the very top of the axe smouldered a brazier. Nathan blew softly onto the brazier and watched as flames ignited. It had a name. A name that no one remembered but him. It was ancient. He had built it. Created it. Moulded it. Baptised it in the flames of war. "I used this. They fucking deserved it. I used *Morrigan.*" He smiled. "Your turn to feel it touch, cunt."

Julius watched on in terror as the figure appeared out of the darkness. He couldn't believe what he was seeing. It looked like some sort of angel but was all disfigured. He watched as Nathan and the figure were talking and then attacked each other. He had no idea what was happening but knew it was very bad. He grabbed the girl again, but still, she would not move.

He watched the thing fly into the air. He struggled to comprehend what he was seeing. He then saw Nathan tear open the air in front of him and pull out a large double-headed axe.

"What the fuck!" Julius swore.

He pulled with everything he had to get the girl off the slab, but she was rooted to it by some unseen force.

The fallen dived towards Nathan as fast as light, its sword aimed at his heart. It crashed into the ground as Nathan easily sidestepped his foe. In one hand, he held a black wing, its end dripping black blood onto the dirt floor. The fallen cried out in agony as it registered that its wing had been torn from its body. It stood up quickly and charged at Nathan.

Nathan blocked the blow of the sword with his axe and held it in place. He pushed hard against his foe and looked into its dead eyes. He could feel the two weapons begin to heat up because of the force the two of them were applying to them by friction pressure.

"*You cannot stop me. They both want this. When the barrier falls, then they will come.*" It spat into Nathan's face.

"I will not allow that to happen. I told them long ago that I would no longer tolerate this shite." He spat back. He pushed harder and managed to push his foe back a few inches. "I am fucking sick and tired of all sides. The sooner you all fuck off, the better."

"*They would be nothing without us. We give them purpose. After you killed your betters, that is when it all began to fall apart. This is on you,*" It screamed and jumped back.

"Blah, blah, fucking blah. Don't blame me for doing what was right. They were out of control. I should have done it earlier."

It pointed the sword accusingly at Nathan. "*How many did you kill to get to them? Thousands? Tens of thousands? More? I fought against you; this is why I look like this. I stood against you, and I failed. But this will make it right. I will bring forth the new age. The new era. This is because of you.*"

"Do not blame me for your failures. Do not blame me for theirs either. I did what was right. I did what needed to be done. They were mad. Insane. Yes, I killed them, millions, to get to them, and I have zero fucking regrets in doing so. I would have slaughtered millions more if it was required. I alone had the courage to do what was needed. No one else can say the same. While I acted, the others stood back and watched. They watched on in terror as I walked through entire seas of blood and came out changed on the other side. They fear me. They are terrified at what I became in order to do what they could not." He then stopped and looked at the barrier. "Bastards. That's what you are doing. That is why you needed the seventh victim. You needed an anchor for the power. You are using her to control the energies."

The fallen laughed. "*And finally, the curtain has fallen from your eyes. Yes. And soon those whom you cursed will come here, and finally, the plan can be completed.*"

"You are fucking insane, like them," Nathan shouted and readied his axe. "You know what they want. Are you that fucking mad to allow that to happen?"

"*Not insane, for those who know the truth are blessed,*" it raged and stepped purposefully towards Nathan. The last symbols fractured, and the doors began to open. The fallen smiled. "*Soon, you can explain yourself to them.*"

The two struck at each other so fast that their movements couldn't be seen. Flakes of dust were bisected into pieces because of the ferocity of their attacks. Each strike hit with the force of breaking continents. Each strike was made to kill.

They pushed each other away and circled one another, thinking about their next moves. The fallen moved first.

From Nathan's left hand, he flipped the axe up and dodged the attack easily. The axe spun and dropped onto the back of his left hand, the handle rolling down his arm, past his shoulders, and down the right arm. He grabbed the handle with his right hand and blocked another strike. He was showing off, and the fallen knew it.

This made the fallen angry and forced him into its mistake.

Nathan ducked under the swing and smashed his axe into fallen's chest. The shock wave of the hit rushed out across the cavern. He pushed hard, and blood splattered over his shirt. He heard the sword clatter to the ground. He pushed the fallen back and saw the massive hole in its chest. He watched as it fell to its knees. "You know, you arseholes are always the same. Think you are so fucking invincible. What you all keep fucking forgetting is that once here, on this plane, you are all fucking mortal when hit with this," he told it, tapping his axe. He brought the axe up high above its head. "Oh, by the way, there is no coming back now. Morrigan consumes and only oblivion awaits you. But not to worry, it will hurt like a bitch." He then brought the axe straight down. He watched, and the fallen screamed in pure agony and slowly split in two. The two parts fell away from each other and splattered onto the ground.

Julius saw the twin doors in front of him begin to open. A bright white light began to flood into the cavern. He couldn't stare into the light and covered his eyes, but even that wasn't enough. He put his body over the girl's head to try and protect her. That's when he noticed she wasn't breathing.

"*Take her and go back up the stairs,*" the female voice said again.

Julius couldn't see anything as the light was so strong. He shut his eyes as much as he could and grabbed the girl. Finally, he could move her. He lifted her off the slab and threw her over his shoulder. The light dimmed. He opened his eyes and saw Nathan run towards the twin doors.

"All of you out of here now," Nathan shouted as he charged towards the door.

Julius turned and saw Mary and Frank manhandle the battered and bloodied Mrs Thorn towards the stairs.

"Come with us, Nathan. You can't stop this," Mary shouted back.

"I have to try," Nathan screamed back. "Get your fucking arses out of here now."

"Julius, fucking move," Frank said and grabbed the young man. "This is way out of our league."

Julius felt himself being dragged and turned to run up the stairs.

Nathan watched as his colleagues ran up the stairs towards the balcony.

"So, how do I close this?" he said to himself.

He reached out, grabbed a door in each hand, and pushed. They wouldn't budge.

"Give me a fucking break," he pleaded. He pushed harder, yet they wouldn't budge. "I've had the fuck enough of this shite," he shouted into the light. He could make out distant shapes and cursed them. "You had your chance. You fucked it up. I made the choice, and it was just," he roared and pushed again. He was breathing large gulps of air as he fought against the doors. He knew the weight of the universe held each door open. Once opened, they were never meant to be closed again. That was the deal. That was the law. "Well, fuck that," he roared and closed his eyes. He didn't want it to come to this, but he knew now that he had no choice.

Time slowed to a crawl.

"What's wrong?" he heard a female ask.

"I am tired of this. If I do this, it could go sideways. Remember what happened in Chile in the 60s. I caused that earthquake," he replied, his eyes still closed. He knew the voice but had not heard it in such a long time.

"That happened because the excess power had to go somewhere. It will take everything you have to do this. You have the mass of several universes in each hand to move. Are you willing to try?"

"What would she think of me now, I wonder?"

"Hmmm. I think she would ask you to try at least," the voice said. *"I must admit that it is strange that the young man could hear me. What did you do?"*

"Wasn't me. Blame Frank and Mary. That one is on them." He smiled.

"Oh. Well, I didn't know that. I must be slipping."

"You are getting stronger. It has been such a long time since you have spoken to me, let alone anyone else. Especially from that plane."

"I felt you calling me. I felt your heart."

"You knew I would need you?"

"Yes. You did put me into your weapon after all."

"And then I breathed life into you." He smiled.

"Yes. Well, I did help create everything, you know. What do they call it? The big bang. Hmmm. Well, wasn't as much as a bang, more an eruption of wonder and understanding. Well, it did take me a while to recover from that exertion. I do need my rest. So, what are you going to do now?"

He sighed. "You know that I am going to try. I promised her that I would never do this. I was not that man anymore."

"You're not a man, though, are you? No. Your special. The first. The tree. The executioner," the voice said. *"You were created before all others. Before*

even them. You have stood since the first second of this universe. You stood and watched it all being born. You saw the first elements come into being. You have seen so much but learned so little."

"I know everything; you know that. I know the rules. If I do this, If I change the path, then it will begin all over again. Both sides will demand it."

"You could say no."

Nathan thought about this and smiled. "It will piss them off if I change the rules and mess up their game. Oh, it will really piss them off. Ha. Well, it seems I have something to live for now."

"I am so happy that I could help," the voice said. *"Oh, I can see them coming. They do not sound happy to see you."*

"Fuck them!" Nathan smirked. "You may want to go back now. This is going to get rough."

He opened his eyes and roared. He pushed harder and harder and could feel the doors creak under his strength. He focused, and he could feel his shirt torn at the back. He felt his skin split open along the scars and felt the heat emanate from them. Four massive wings erupted from his back, a white flame exploding out behind him. He focused all his energy on closing the doors. Slowly, the doors, which weighed as much as several universes each, began to close. He saw the figures in the light begin to run towards him. He could hear them cursing him. He could feel their rage aimed at him. He laughed. He focused once more, and an explosion of light surrounded him.

Julius ran out of the building. It was late at night, and the sky was thick with clouds. There was a slight drizzle. He skidded to a halt when he saw several semi-automatic weapons aimed at him.

"Freeze!" some shouted at him.

"It's me, Julius," he shouted back.

"Stand down!" someone shouted.

Julius squinted at the group and said, "David?"

"Yes, it's me. Jesus, someone gets me paramedics. Julius, come over here!" David shouted and pushed past the armed officers. "Is she alive?"

"I don't know," he said and ran over to the police line. He saw two paramedics run over with a trolley. He gently placed the girl on and watched them work on here.

"Faint pulse. No breathing. Beginning CPR," one of the paramedics said.

Frank and Mary ran out of the building, dragging their prisoner with them.

"Oh, now you fucking turn up!" shouted Frank towards the police. "And where, pray fucking tell, have you been?"

"Frank. Jesus, is that Mrs Thorn?" David asked as he walked over.

"Yes," Mary said and tossed the woman onto the road. "I apologise for how she looks. She resisted us."

Larysa looked up at David and spat blood onto his shoes.

David snapped his fingers, and two armed policemen aimed at her. "If she moves or speaks, then make sure she has an accident." He smiled at her. He walked past her, stepped on her hand, and smirked as she cried in pain. "Where is Nathan?"

"Still in there with our killer," Frank told him. "What was that?"

Everyone felt the rumble. The ground shifted below them and felt like an earthquake. They all looked at the building and jumped back as the roof exploded in light.

On the international space station, one of its scientists was looking out down on Earth.

It made her smile every time. The world was beautiful, especially at night. You could see all the lights of the cities and towns across the countries. She was looking over western Europe when she saw the light. It looked like it was Scotland. She watched in awe as the clouds melted away for almost two thousand miles around Scotland. The light got brighter and brighter; she couldn't even look at it. The light seemed to reach into space and beyond her vision. She switched on the camera and started to record what was happening.

"What's going on?" she asked the empty science station.

As suddenly as it appeared, the light vanished. Out into the Atlantic Ocean, to the middle of Europe, there were no clouds, all destroyed by the light.

She flicked a communication panel. "Em, Paris, please come in."

"This is the ESA; what's wrong?" a woman's voice came.

"Does someone know what happened over Scotland?"

David picked himself up off the ground and saw the others do the same. He heard someone crying and looked down to see Mrs Thorn in tears. She looked broken and defeated.

"What the fuck was that?" Julius said and stood up.

Frank and Mary looked at each other. They had both felt it.

"He did it," Mary told Frank.

"And we are still alive. Fuck, there will be hell to pay for this," Frank told her and burst out laughing. "But he closed it."

Nathan staggered out of the door and fell to his knees. He was coughing badly, and people could see him covered in a black liquid. He smouldered as if someone had set him on fire before. He held something in his left hand.

He looked up. "Well, don't everyone fucking run to help me all at once," he said and coughed again. He fell to his knees.

Frank walked over and helped Nathan to his feet. "Didn't think you would make it?"

"Well, you know me. Always surprising people."

Nathan limped over to David with Frank's help.

"What the hell just happened?" David demanded. "What was that light we just saw erupt out of that building, destroying the roof in the process?"

"Gas leak, big explosion. Lucky to be alive. Blah blah blah," Nathan joked. He looked down at Larysa. "Present for you." He then tossed the severed head of Mr Thorn into her lap. He smiled as the woman screamed in despair. He then chuckled as Mary walked over and knocked out the woman with a kick to the face.

Julius walked over and took Nathan's other arm. "You look like shite."

"Feel like it." Smiled Nathan. "So, young pup, how have you found it working with me then? Interesting? Scary? Exciting?"

"All of the above."

"Good answer. Well, I suspect you will want some answers from me, but not just yet. Seems I will have a shiteload of paperwork about this little jaunt down there." He limped over to a waiting medical trolley. "Fuck me," he said as he sat down, wincing in pain. "I'm getting old." Nathan looked over to the building and watched as it began to collapse in on itself. He spat on the ground. "Good fucking riddance."

David walked over and picked up the head that was thrown at Mrs Thorn. He walked over to Nathan and held the head up before him. "Dare I ask?"

"That's you, serial killer. Sorry, I couldn't bring the body up, but you know, gas leak, and explosions. So just grabbed the head," Nathan told him as the medics began to check him over. "You like a little head anyway," he joked.

"Not funny, Nathan," David told him and saw trouble coming. "Oh, shite."

Christopher marched through the police line towards them. "What in the hell happened here? I am getting reports of gunfire, explosions, strange lights, and earthquakes." That is when he saw the severed head. "WHAT IS THAT?" he shouted.

"Christopher, serial killer. Serial killer, Christopher," Nathan said to him.

Christopher's jaw dropped open. Once he had regained his composure, he said, "Where is the rest of the body, or dare I ask?" Nathan pointed over to the collapsed building. "Why?"

"David, you want to explain," Nathan said looking at the man holding the head.

"Em, gas explosion. This is the only thing that Nathan could recover," David said putting the head down beside Nathan who then patted it.

"So, you see there, Christopher, job done. Serial killer taken care of. So, this is the point where you congratulate me and my team on doing such a great job."

Christopher's face went red, "Are you fucking kidding me! How am I supposed to explain this to the press? To anyone?"

"Not my worry," Nathan told him and handed him the head. "Any questions, then ask him," he said, pointing to the head. "Isn't that right, cunt?" he asked the head and shook it so it looked as if it was nodding.

"You are fucking insane," Christopher said in disgust. He waved over an officer and placed the head into an evidence bag. "I will make sure you face charges for this."

Nathan sighed and leaned forward. He waved Christopher to come closer. Nathan's hand shot out and grabbed Christopher's attention tightly. He heard the man squeal in agony. "You asked me to catch the serial killer. I did. You asked me to catch his accomplice, and guess what? There she is lying over there. What charge are you going to bring against me? Doing my job? Don't fucking think so, you stupid bastard." He squeezed harder and could feel that the man was close to passing out. "Well? Sorry, can't hear you." He cupped his free hand around his ear. He heard Christopher squeal some inaudible words. "You are welcome. On behalf of my team, I thank you for those kind words. I am sure they will appreciate it. You appreciate them, don't you, Julius?" He turned and saw the young man trying to hold the laughter back while wincing in compassionate pain with Christopher. "You see, kind words go a long way. Oh, wait, you don't look well. Looks like you are about to faint." And with that, he gave his hand a quick twist and smiled as Christopher passed out. He looked down. "Poor man, he got too excited."

"Nathan, even for you, that was evil," David said, looking down at the captain. He watched his friend shrug his shoulders. "I guess we need another medical team here."

Chapter 15

Nathan sat at the booth in the bar, the same bar in which he met her all those years ago. He hadn't been here since she died. Too many memories. He drank whisky and savoured the taste. He had earned it; of that, he was sure.

"Yes, it was a team effort," he heard from the TV. He looked up and saw the chief constable giving a statement on TV. "Our team finally caught the serial killer called Keeper of Eyes three nights ago. The killer was one Thomas Thorn. Through extensive record checks and tracing his history, we have linked him to the six murders and one attempted murder."

"How was he tracked?" a male reporter asked.

"He was tracked using CCTV, bank statements, and good old-fashioned detective work. My crack team cornered Mr Thorn in a building. Sadly, he could not be arrested as the man took his own life."

"Chief constable, sources say that he was the cause of the building collapse on Clyde Street," a woman shouted over the others.

"Yes, he caused a gas leak and ignited the gas, leading not only to his death but the collapse of the building," the chief replied to her. "No one else was injured or killed in the explosion, only the serial killer."

"Chief constable, what do you say to the reports that at the time of the explosion, the international space station registered a strange light over Glasgow?" another woman asked.

"I have no knowledge of that. Maybe you should ask the ESA or NASA." He smiled.

Nathan smiled; the old man was giving as good as he got. He poured more whisky into his glass.

He looked at his watch. "5,4,3,2,1, and," he said and looked at the door. Four people walked into the bar and looked around. One was Frank, and the other was Mary. The other two were female. One had long black hair and, worse, dark glasses. The other had long brown hair, and you could tell she looked very similar to the other woman. You could mistake them as twins. He waved them over. "Right on time," he said to them. He looked at Frank and Mary. "Glad to see you found them."

"Well, you didn't give them much choice," Mary said and sat beside Nathan.

"I think they wanted to speak to you also," Frank said and sat on the opposite of Nathan.

The two women sat in front of Nathan. They did not look happy. "I don't give a fuck about what you have called yourselves. You won't be here long enough for me to care."

"You broke the law. You broke the rules. You know you are not to interfere in the way things are done," the dark-haired woman said.

"I see you two woke up on the wrong side of the fucking bed. Well, you don't sleep, do you?" he said and took a drink. "Did you really think I would allow them to escape? Are you lot that stupid? I put them there for a reason. They are mental. Cockuu. I may have broken the rule, but I don't care. I know I am not to interfere in the plan laid down by both sides and that the apocalypse should have maybe happened, but guess what? I DON'T CARE. Remember that it was me who laid down the law for both sides after what I did. Humanity may be worthless, a waste of energy and matter for the universe, but it is more than likely they will wipe themselves out before you two get a chance. I broke the plan because what Orobas did was vile. He used forbidden powers, and that's why I stopped it. Plus, pissing you both off gives me a warm glow inside that makes me feel happy."

The brown-haired woman said, "You are wrong. The plan was laid out by them at the very beginning. It was to be followed, no matter what. We all agreed to that."

"Well, I changed my fucking mind, so sue me," Nathan replied and stared both women down. Once they looked chastised enough. "So, what one cares to explain how this cluster fuck happened? And one word of warning: no lies."

"We do not know," the dark-haired woman said to him.

"Nor do we," said the other.

Nathan sighed. "So, let me get this straight. With the power both sides have, it sort of just slipped under the radar. Is that what you are telling me?" Both women nodded. "You're kidding, right? I mean, shite like this doesn't just happen. It takes time to plan. It takes people from both fucking sides to get it working. And right here, right now, you are telling me what, neither side fucking knew anything. That's what you're telling me?" Again, both women nodded. He looked at both Mary and Frank, who both shrugged their shoulders. "Well, I think both of you should go back and find out, don't you? That bastard managed to open the fucking cells upstairs."

The dark-haired woman looked guilty. "Yes. We don't know how he managed that. The power required for that is something he should never have been able to hold."

"We do not know how he managed it. My side has checked and from what we have gathered, he has not been with us for centuries. Much seems to have been lost regarding him," the other woman told Nathan.

"Fantastic. Both of you have given me nothing. Once again, I clean up your mess, and it is starting to piss me off," Nathan told them both and emptied the glass. "Tell your friends that if this shite happens again, I will finish them. I will travel to both of their houses and bring it all down." Both women looked shocked and angry but nodded. He looked at the black-haired woman; she was not telling him something. He could tell. "Spit it the fuck out."

She looked at him with fierce determination but then sighed. "Four escaped."

Nathan leaned back into the couch. "Fuck me. How?"

"It seems they used the opening as a distraction. When you were dealing with the fallen and you were distracted."

"Dare I ask?"

"The Echoes of Ruin," the other woman said.

Nathan closed his eyes and took a deep breath. "So, from the unbreakable cells, four escaped. From upstairs."

"It would seem so. We believe they had help from some in our camp."

"No shite, Sherlock," Frank said to her.

Nathan leaned forward and opened his eyes. "Let me guess, you do not know where they are?" Both women nodded. "This keeps getting better and fucking better."

"I am ordered to ask for your assistance in this matter," the brown-haired woman said to him.

"As am I," the other said.

"Lucky me," he told them as he filled his glass. "You fuck up, and it's me left to clean up the apocalypse." He looked at both women. "Fuck."

"What say you?" the brown-haired woman asked.

"I don't have a fucking choice in the matter. If they escaped, then they must be caught and put back. You two are really starting to piss me off. I'm no fan of humanity, but even they don't deserve what the four of them could do unchecked," he told them. He felt them back away from him in fear. "Both of you go back and tell everybody to be on the lookout for them. I'm pretty fucking sure they won't leave Glasgow for a while. They will need to get their bearings, money, food, etc. This has been planned, so they came here for a reason. Find out who helped them. Find out and bring them to me. I will make sure they answer my questions."

Both women nodded. They stood up.

"Frank, you are to return upstairs," the black-haired woman said.

"Fuck that," Frank replied and folded his arms and leaned back to relax.

"Mary, you are wanted downstairs," the brown-haired woman said.

"No, I think I will stay here," she replied calmly.

"They stay right here with me. I know that once you get them back, you will make their lives a misery. No, they stay with me. These two I can trust, so I'm keeping them. Consider it a fucking goodwill gesture," Nathan told the two women.

"He must return. They will not like this," the black-haired woman said to him.

"Fucking tough. And that goes for your side also. They stay here. They ask questions and you fucking answer. They want something, and you fucking give it. Consider them now unfucking touchable. They work for me, not you. I promoted them to badasses." Both women looked as if they would argue but then stopped. They seemed to be listening to something in the distance. Nathan could hear but pretended not to. "Ah, good, you agree. Then you two better be going then."

They turned to leave but then stopped.

"What about Sybella?" the brown-haired woman asked.

Nathan grinned. "Who?"

He watched as both women walked calmly out of the bar.

"Well, there goes my retirement plan," Frank said and poured whisky into a glass.

"It would appear that mine has also gone," Mary said and sighed.

"They will get over it. Fuck them," Nathan told them. "So, you two are stuck with me now. You, poor bastards."

"Well, it seemed the best option," Mary said and took a glass of whisky. She sipped the liquid and made a face. "Doesn't taste very nice."

"It is an acquired taste," replied Frank and lifted his glass to her.

"Why do you keep sticking up for humanity? After everything you have seen, everything you have witnessed them do. We three know that at the end, they will wipe themselves out, either through war or by killing the one world they live in," she asked Nathan.

He smiled at her. "She showed me a small glimpse of light at the end of a very long tunnel. She asked me that question once before, and I will tell you what I told her. Who am I to judge? After everything I have done, am I any better than them? No. There is a small, extremely small, microscopic chance they may actually come good, so I think I will help when and where I can."

Mary nodded. She could understand his reasoning. "What about the woman?" Mary asked.

"Her mind is broken. The effect of losing her master has rid her of any sanity she had left. I barely got anything sensible from her. She says that both sides agreed to this, but I can't prove it," Nathan told her. "I gave her over to David. She is rambling about angels and other strange things she swears are true. She is very mad."

Mary smiled. "Those things don't exist."

Julius walked down the path at the side of Nathan's house and could hear beautiful music. He didn't know the tune, but it was wonderful. He opened the gate and saw Frank playing some sort of strange musical instrument. It looked like some sort of violin with piano keys on the neck but was played by turning a handle at the bottom of the instrument. Julius stood there, listening to the heavenly tune.

Once it had finished, "What is that instrument?" Julius asked.

Frank turned around. "It is called a Zanfona. It is an old instrument from eastern Europe."

"That music was so soothing," he said to Frank.

"A very old song. Forgotten by the world now. Only I remember it." Frank looked at Nathan. "I played it before the battle, remember? The sound even calmed the skies." Nathan nodded.

Julius sat down in the empty seat next to Nathan.

"So, I guess this is where you give me some answers?" Julius said.

Frank, Mary, Julius, and Nathan all sat in Nathan's back garden. They all sat on his decking, looking out to a large garden surrounded by trees and flowers.

"Yes. You saw much and I think that deserves answers," Nathan said to him. "So, what do you want to know?"

"Who are you really?"

Nathan smiled a little. "The first. When the universe came into being, I was the first heavenly host created. I am what you would call a seraphim. Oh, everybody thinks arch angels are the best of the best, the most powerful, but they are pussies compared to me. I am the strongest of my kind there ever was and ever will be. There are only three seraphim left: me and two sisters. The others died in various battles and wars."

Julius looked and asked, "You're not winding me up, are you?"

"Nope," Nathan replied. "I was the very first. I am in the Bible also. They call me the tree of knowledge. I have the collected knowledge of the universe. Everything past, present, and future. You know the saying, 'knowledge is power', well, imagine how powerful I am and multiply that by a few hundred billion." He poured tea into a cup and passed it to Mary. Julius looked at him quizzically. "Mary says I should try to be more sophisticated, so hence the tea. I was commanded by what you would call God to wait for his creation to come into fruition. So, I waited for billions of years until humanity evolved into what you are today. I saw life born on this planet, from single-cell organisms to you."

"So, you're an angel. I mean a fully-fledged honest angel?" Julius asked, and Nathan nodded. "You don't speak or act like one. I thought angels would be nice and holy, but you're not. You're an arsehole."

"Hahahahaha. That I am. When angels are upstairs, then they are all nice like you say, but once down here, we have free will. We can do what we like, and that's always part of the fucking problem. Once here, both sides lose control at some point and always let it go to their heads. And trust me, after everything we have witnessed in this world, we like to let loose and be ourselves. I'm the biggest bastard of them all. Isn't that right, Frank?"

"The biggest," the man replied.

"This isn't a movie or a book. This is real life, people swear. Your PG-13 world doesn't exist and never has. Admit it, when you watch a movie and see the good guy trying to solve a crime or fight, in your mind, you are screaming at him to swear and fight dirty. Everyone does. No shame in that. If movies and books actually portrayed what happened on the streets, do you think people behind their rose-tinted glasses would like that? Of course not. Humanity has gotten to such a point that actually seeing the real world and how it works would drive them to fucking depression. That's the state humanity is at now, and it's fucking pathetic."

Julius sat silent for a moment and digested what he was told. Then he asked, "So, what I saw in your home that night, you on flames, that was real?"

"Yes. I can heal myself from any wound; I am immortal, after all. It just took me a bit of time, as I haven't had to do it in such a long time. Seems I was out of practice."

"But I heard Mary and Alessia say that you were dying."

"I can choose to die. All immortals can. It is something we have, an ability to just die. Don't get me wrong; throughout history, I have been killed, blown up, incinerated, etc., etc., but I haven't died. What you saw that night was me deciding if I wanted to stay or not."

"But you were told you couldn't go as someone still needed you. Who?"

Nathan looked at him. "Humanity. They need me. I am the tree of knowledge, the fountain of all knowledge. If I die, then knowledge dies."

"You make it sound as if you die then humanity becomes stupid."

"Ha, humanity is already stupid. Look. The progress humanity has made in the past 50 years is because of me. Microprocessors. Quantum mechanics. AI technology. All of it is from me. Let's just say I have sped up the process of getting there. If I die, then knowledge doesn't really die, but instead of taking 50 years to get to where humanity is now then it would take a few thousand. I sort of supercharge the process of beings getting the knowledge."

"So, you are like a library?"

"Yes. Have you ever heard of the Kardashev scale? No. OK. It is a scale on which civilisations are along a technological curve. Type 1, 2, and 3. Humanity isn't even really at type one yet. Barely able to control nuclear fusion and hasn't even started harnessing anti-matter yet. Let's call humanity type 0.25. Type 2 would be able to travel to other star systems, etc. Type 3 are able to harness the energy from an entire galaxy, from black holes to quasars. If you put me on that scale, I would be type 6. That's how much knowledge and power I have."

Julius let out a long whistle. "Well, that makes me feel really stupid. And that thing I saw, the thing that told me that I was dying, that was real."

Frank took this one. "Yes. You can call it a doctor of sort. They work for, death you could say, but can give as well as take. It owed me. It takes life from something to give it to something else."

"What! You mean someone has to die? Wait, I remember seeing an old man. I could feel his heart in my hands. I felt him die."

"Yes. Trust me. He deserved it. He was a very bad man," Mary told him. "He sold his soul long ago, and it was time to collect."

"So, a man died so I could live. I feel sick," Julius said, shutting his eyes in despair.

"Not different from organ transplants," Nathan said to him and then drank his tea. "Look at it this way: a total bastard died so you, not a total bastard, could live."

Julius shook his head. A man had been killed so he could live. His mind was terrified by this news. Was his life worth the killing of another? He sighed. "I don't know how to react to this. You tell me that a man was killed in order for me to live. I don't know what to say or do. I mean, does that make me a killer?"

"No. It makes you nothing more than you are now," Mary told him. "That man made a deal. He knew the terms of the deal. He knew that at some point, the debt would be collected. He was not forced to make the deal. He chose to do it willingly. You have nothing to fear."

"Look, young man, you were dying. If we had taken you to the hospital, there would have been a very good chance you could have died. This way you would live. Guaranteed. Nathan told us to make sure you lived. I made the call. I do not regret it," Frank told him, putting his hand on the young man's shoulder. "Nathan saved you from that explosion for a reason. I believe I did the right thing. Look, the man who signed the deal was scum. He was a robber, a killer, and worse. You are young and have a great future ahead of you. Nathan saw that and told me. We are a team, and I look out for my team."

Julius nodded his head. "Thank you," he said to them all.

"No need," Nathan told him.

Julius drank his tea. "So, who were Mr and Mrs Thorn really?"

"Well, Mr Thorn was a fallen angel. His real name was Orobas. A real nasty piece of shite. He wanted to open a way for some very bad, what would I call them, absolute cunts to come to earth and create merry havoc. He was one of the first fallen. Followed that arsehole Lucifer like a lost fucking puppy. He would have killed the original Mr Thorn a long time ago, and well, took his body. You know, like a costume. As for Mrs Thorn, she is what you would call the whore of Babylon. She is a sort of demon called Citadel. She speaks lies and helps others of her kind in any way she can."

"Why didn't Frank and Mary kill her? I saw them fight her, but she held her own for some time," Julius asked.

"I wanted her alive for answers. I need to know names and who was involved in this action," Nathan replied. "She is very powerful, that's why you went all strange when you confronted her the first time. She speaks to men and warps their minds. They eventually do whatever she says and do it with total love and devotion. What they were doing would have led to the death of every man and woman on this planet. You would know it as Armageddon. In reality, it would have more than likely led to the end of the universe. The forces they would unleash on each other would have consumed everything. They know no other way. Total destruction of their enemies. The hate they feel for each other would have been let loose, and nothing would have been able to stop it."

"When I tried to get the girl off the slab, I heard a voice whisper in my ear. No one was there. Who was it?"

Nathan coughed, "My axe."

"Your axe?"

"Yes. Short version or long?"

"Short."

"It's alive."

"Oh, that explains it. Let's go for long then."

"Well, there were once three gods, not one. Your gods, Saptrum and Baneila. Each one fought against Lucifer at the beginning. Saptrum was God's equal in pretty much everything. She was one evil cunt, though. Hated the light of the universe. Baneila was Lucifer's equal. She was the first reaper and gave birth to death. She revelled in the death of entire star systems as the universe grew. Both of them were complete arseholes. A few million years after Lucifer was thrown out of the heavens, Saptrum and Baneila had had enough of your god's plans for the universe. They got pissed and tried to take over. So I stopped them. I told them that they would not be allowed to challenge their god. I was still wet behind the ears back then and didn't know better. They refused my request to lay down their arms and leave. So I attacked first. There is an area in the observable universe called Boötes Void. It is 300 million light-years in diameter. That is where I fought them. There are a few planets and systems in that void because of the battle. We laid waste to millions of worlds in our battle." He sighed in regret.

"It took a long time to win, a few hours for us, but 189,000 years had passed for the universe in general. I laid both low. In my rage, I tore the wings from their backs. Then, one by one, I broke their backs against my knee. I cast their broken bodies into the void, outside the universe. There they will remain until the very end times, broken, paralysed, and extremely pissed off with me. Once I calmed down, I took one wing from each and cast them into axe heads. I made them from the strongest material in the known universe, as of yet unknown to humans. The wings are extremely powerful in their own right, but together they are extremely dangerous. They can kill immortals with ease, but only here on Earth. In heaven or hell, it just banishes the essence from the body. Leaves it in a kind of limbo. When something dies, it leaves an essence behind; you would call it a soul. The axe consumes that and leaves nothing. Only oblivion."

"But the voice you heard comes from the brazier on top of the axe. It's the fire of creation, a portion of the big bang. It found its way to me during the battle, and I used it to fight the two gods. So, I forged it onto my axe as an extra weapon. What I didn't know at the time was that it was sentient. For millennia, it wouldn't shut up. I was the only one who could hear it, it was bound to me by war. So, you had the most powerful being ever to live, wielding the most powerful weapon ever created. I called it Morrigan, and even she doesn't know why you could hear her."

Julius leaned back in his chair and tried to understand everything he had just been told. "Huh, so angels and demons are real. Both sides hate each other but want to work together to go back to the old ways, which you tell me could lead to the destruction of everything. Fantastic." Smirked Julius. "But wait. I have always been told that all angels and demons, or the fallen, are immortal. They cannot die. According to the Bible and other religious texts, nothing can kill them."

Mary took this one. "In a sense, that is true. Angels cannot die, as your god decreed it. Nothing created by immortal or mortal hands can kill angels. As for the fallen, they can technically die. Your god removed their grace, as it was that that made them immortal." She stirred her tea with a spoon and took a sip. "But Nathan's axe is different. It contains the spark of creation, and not even an immortal can survive that power."

"Look at it this way, young lad," Frank said, leaning forward. "Angels and the fallen could take a direct hit by every nuclear weapon on earth and just walk away from it like nothing had happened. Nathan's axe contains a power that existed before your god popped into existence. So, it isn't really a weapon forged by mortal or immortal hands. It's a loophole, but it is one that works."

"But only on earth?"

"Yes," Nathan told him.

"Why?"

"I have never really understood why. I did ask once before, and the only answer I got was, 'Don't ask me'," Nathan told him.

"What? Your axe told you it didn't know why it could only truly kill on Earth. The actual thing that created everything says it doesn't know."

"I know right? Go figure," Nathan giggled.

Julius just shook his head. Maybe they were telling him the truth, or maybe not. More than likely, he would never find out. So he moved on to his next question. "What was the door that was opening?"

"Even heaven has its prison," Mary told him.

"Prison? Who in heaven would need a prison?" Julius asked.

"Very bad angels. Heaven and hell are pretty much the same. Both are very depressing places. Upstairs, you have to be nice, and downstairs, you get tortured non-stop. Both are prisons if you actually look at them in depth." He leaned back in his chair and remembered the past. "When the war was happening, some angels turned traitors. Those angels are the ones in prison. Like I said before, in heaven and hell, my axe only banishes the essence of the being from the body. The prison holds not only very naughty angels but also the essence of those angels and the fallen that were captured. They are strong beings, fuelled by their hate for everything. They were caught by me and thrown into the most secure place you can imagine. But somehow, someone figured out how to crack it open. Don't know how they managed that, but the killing of the six women was part of the process. A very very old ritual. Your god created the prison to hold them for eternity, but as you witnessed, it failed. If they had managed to leave the prison, then they would take human form, like Orobas did with Mr Thorn. Millions upon millions of pissed-off angels here on earth taking out their anger on anything and everything." Nathan didn't mention that some escaped. He didn't want to answer those questions just yet.

"Shite. I can't imagine heaven having a prison. You imagine heaven as being pure and unblemished, but the way you describe it, it is no better than hell." Then a thought hit him. "Wait, so God is real? I mean, he is real, and up there, what, just looking down and watching the world go to shite? And, Lucifer, he must be really also?"

"They were," Nathan replied and smirked.

"What do you mean they were?"

"Frank and Mary belonged to both sides of the divide, you could say. Frank works for the cunts upstairs, and Mary works for the cunts downstairs. Well, worked. They recently quit." He sighed. "Both sides would not stop fighting. I watched as the world was ruined dozens of times by their actions. I refused to take a side; I was too smart for their petty wars. Mary and Frank at the time had enough also and joined me on the side-lines. Then the battle of Gora happened. Both sides unleashed such destruction on each other that the solar system broke. A planet the size of Mars smashed into Earth and boom, the Moon was born from the destruction. I had had enough of them. So, I told both sides that there would be no more fighting. They were to stop at once. As you can imagine, both sides didn't like that. So, they sent their armies against me."

"That's when I really lost my temper. I slaughtered tens of millions on both sides. I was the first, the most powerful, the tree of knowledge. That power made me unstoppable. After decades of fighting, I finally stood before your god and Lucifer. I didn't give them the option to stand down, to make peace. I cut both their heads off and unleashed my rage onto their remains, erasing them from existence. Both sides collapsed into anarchy at my actions. Leaderless and aimless, their actions threatened to destroy the universe. So, I gathered their last generals and formed a truce. Both sides would follow the peace, or I would wipe them out. If one side broke the peace, I would erase both. Mutual destruction, you could say. They would play nice, and I would be watching. From time to time, factions on both sides try their luck at bringing back the old ways, but so far I have stopped them."

"You killed God? You killed Lucifer?" Julius gawked.

"Yes. It was very easy. You know, bop, bop, heads off," Nathan told him.

"So, if I get this right, you're in charge of everything." Julius leaned forward with a worried grin on his face. "Are you god now?"

"Fuck no. Why would I want that? Fucking awful job. No, let things run as they are. Let humanity fuck itself over. Truly, I don't care."

"So, if you hate us and humanity so much, then why do you stop both sides from destroying us?"

"Ah, that's easy. I enjoy pissing off both sides a hell of a lot more than you bastards."

Chapter 16

In the dark room, four figures sat around a table with a single beam of weak light at its centre.

"Our agent failed," said a female.

"Yes. Only we four managed to escape in the confusion," replied a male voice. His voice sounded strange as if it was not used to speaking a human language.

"We should have known that the seraphim would have gotten involved," said the female again. "We must find another and complete the task. There is still time."

"No," said another male voice. His voice was heavy, like lead. "It is too late. He sealed the doors again, and the barriers have been reinforced by his power. He used the unbreakable code he created. It has so many variables that unless you have the key, you could never understand the code. It is now truly unbreakable."

"I curse him a thousand times over," the woman raged.

"This time though, we are free," said the man with the heavy voice. "We can act and not through agents. We can direct the course now."

"Yes, we can," said the first man.

A woman leaned into the light. Her face was pale and looked new. Fresh. Smooth. "Yes, and this time we infiltrate. We make the cattle do the task for us. I lead, and you follow. Politics, military, services, everything. With these bodies we have taken, we will move ourselves into positions of power. This body is in politics and is led by the ruling party in the country bordering this one. I will use that. We will use it. And when the time is right, we will move. It will take years, but we will make it work."

"And what of the seraphim?" the first man asked.

"Let him think he has won for the moment. In time, we will move against him once our power base is solid. Then we remove him from the game."

Nathan sat at the bar, where he had talked to the female owner before. He wanted to buy her a drink for helping him out on the case. He had sent Frank and Mary out to find out anything they could about the four that escaped but didn't have much hope they would find anything.

He had spent hours speaking to Julius about who he was and what was going on. He asked so many questions that, in the end, he told the young man to relax before he had a brain bleed. He could understand the questions; there was a time when he needed answers also.

The young woman who had been kidnapped for the final ceremony had recovered from her ordeal. Mary had worked her magic on her, and the young woman wouldn't remember what she saw. Nathan had watched as the young woman's little sister had run and hugged her tightly when he dropped her at her home. She had told Nathan that her parents had both died of cancer and that she was bringing her little sister up alone while working two jobs and attending college. The girl had been through so much lately that he decided to do something. So Nathan had arranged for the young lady to come into some money. She was handed an envelope by one of his accountants, informing her that her parents had taken out a life policy and somehow it had been forgotten about. She was given a cheque for over half a million pounds. Nathan had given the money, but the accountant knew how to spin a good yarn. He had told Alessia what he had done, and she had told him that he was a saint. He was no saint, but he knew that his wife would do the same as he did. He knew for sure she would be proud of him, and that was enough for him. He wasn't getting soft; just once in a while, he would do something for her memory.

He turned as the door to the pub opened, hoping it was the woman. It wasn't. He saw a young man come through the door and bump into a young woman who was leaving.

"Sorry."

Nathan looked up and saw her face for the first time. She was gorgeous. Her smile was beauty personified. He was holding four pint glasses and four packets of crisps in his teeth. "It's OK," he mumbled through clenched teeth.

She smiled and walked past him to the bar.

Nathan walked to the table, spat out the crisps, and put the pints onto the table. "I will be back," he said to his friends.

"What? Where are you going now?" David said to him as he snatched a packet of crisps from the table.

"Oh, he's going back to the bar. I wonder why?" Matteo said.

"Well, since you're going back, get me peanuts!" shouted Alberto.

Nathan walked over to the bar and saw that she was still there. He saw her fiery red hair and tapped her on the shoulder. "Hello."

"Hello," she replied.

"Look, I'm sorry I mumbled those words. The mouth was a bit preoccupied at the time." She smiled, and he felt warmth from that.

"That's quite alright. You didn't have to come back for that."

"I did. It was my fault really. I turned too quickly. Didn't look to see what was in front of me. I am sorry for that."

"Then we are both sorry," she joked.

"Would you let me buy you a drink? Please. My way of apologising to you."

She folded her arms and grinned a little. "Are you hitting on me?"

"I don't know." Nathan smiled back. "Are you hitting on me?"

She laughed. "Maybe."

They both took their drinks and went to sit at a free table. They talked for what seemed like hours. They talked about their work, their hobbies, and their lives in general.

"Well, this is where we find you," said a woman behind Nathan.

She looked over Nathan's shoulder. "I'm sorry, lost track of time."

Nathan saw a woman appear over his shoulder; she was a bit drunk. "Well, he is handsome. Isn't he?" she said.

"This is Nathan. He is nice." She smiled at him. "You be nice. Why don't you go back to the others? I will join you shortly."

The woman shrugged her shoulders and went away. "Sorry about that."

"It's all good," he replied. "I think my friends are still here, or they left me. But I won't complain. Spending time with you has been great."

"Oh, you are good. I will give you that." She smiled. She stood up. "Here is my number." She took out a pen from her bag and wrote it on his hand. "I hope you call me." She began to walk away.

"Wait, what's your name?" he asked.

"Bloody hell, Tamara, hurry up!" shouted the woman.

"Well, as you can guess, I am Tamar," she said, shooting darts at her friend with her eyes. "Sorry."

"Sorry."

He smiled at the memory. He could remember every detail of that first time with her. The way she smiled, her perfume, and the way she brushed her hair away from her face. Even the music that was playing.

He loved her. He loved her in a way that he had never loved for such a long time. She made him happy. She had made him better. She brought him peace.

"Well, hello stranger," a woman said behind him.

He turned around and looked at the female owner of the pub. "Hello." She had had a haircut and dyed her hair. She now had short blonde hair cropped into a ponytail.

"So, what brings you here to my humble establishment once again? Hunting more dangerous criminals?" she asked him. She went behind the bar and stood in front of him.

"Nope. Caught them."

"Well, congratulations."

"I came here to buy you a drink. Thought it was the least I could do. You helped crack the case."

"Did I? Oh, well, then by all means, buy me a drink then," she grinned.

"Ladies' choice. I bet I can guess her vintage."

She laughed and brought over the expensive bottle of whisky. "Does sir agree?"

He smiled. "I believe I do."

She poured the liquid into two glasses. She raised her glass, and Nathan clicked him against it. She drank it in one go. "So, can you now tell me what was going on?"

Nathan downed his glass. "Two bad people doing very bad things."

"And you caught them?" She poured another two drinks out.

"Yes. Well, one and a half. The bad guy lost his head in all the excitement," he told her.

"You mean he actually lost his head, or just metaphorically?"

"Actually."

She whistled and drank her drink. "Well, good riddance to them."

"We even managed to save another woman from their evil claws."

"That is good. So, I take it that is what I saw on the news the other day?"

"Yes," he said and downed the glass. "Can't go into too much details because of the upcoming court case, but suffice to say you did help."

"I am very happy that I could. So, that woman you were looking for, was she involved?"

"Can't tell you, sorry," Nathan said to her a bit loudly but nodded.

"Well, fuck me. Can't believe I had someone like that in my establishment. Just goes to show you how bad the world is getting."

"Yes. But without your help, I would never have linked her as quickly as we did."

Nathan placed £200 on the bar. "That is for the drinks and the company." He stood up to leave.

"You know, you never asked my name," the owner said to him.

"I didn't, did I?" He smiled. "So, what's your name?"

"Mara."

He sat back down for another drink.